“This fast-paced adventur
antitotalitarians. Highly re

“It’s always seemed to me
vehicle for showing a new world. *Murder in the*
is an exceptionally good illustration of the point. Besides being an excellent mystery, it is a convincing look at the near future of nanotechnology.”

—Vernor Vinge

“Nanotechnology, cyberspace, and glitzy weapons technology spice up McCarthy’s third novel but take a backseat to fast and frequently graphic action and exciting plot twists. Well-written, escapist futurism.”

—Booklist

“McCarthy does an exceptional job developing both the SF and mystery elements, and the fact that he has a fine cast of characters doesn’t hurt any.”

—Science Fiction Chronicle

“McCarthy’s story weaves politics and science so deftly that the mystery shines.”

—Midwest Book Review

Also by Wil McCarthy

Aggressor Six
Flies from the Amber
The Fall of Sirius
Bloom

MURDER IN THE SOLID STATE

WIL McCARTHY

A TOM DOHERTY ASSOCIATES BOOK
NEW YORK

MURDER IN THE SOLID STATE

A Tor Book
Published by Tom Doherty Associates, Inc.
175 Fifth Avenue
New York, NY 10010

Tor Books on the World Wide Web:
http://www.tor.com

ISBN: 0-812-55392-6
Library of Congress Card Catalog Number: 95-52863

First edition: August 1996
First mass market edition: November 1998

Printed in the United States of America

0 9 8 7 6 5 4 3 2 1

This book is dedicated to the memory of artist and teacher Evelyn B. Higginbottom, who remains a lady even now.

ACKNOWLEDGMENTS

I would like to thank Shawna McCarthy, Amy Stout, Walter Jon Williams, and especially David Hartwell for suffering through early drafts and helping to shape this novel into its current form. For technical assistance, I am deeply indebted to the following people: In the field of nanotechnology, K. Eric Drexler, J. Storrs Hall, and all the regulars on sci.nanotech. In the area of law enforcement and courtroom procedure, J. Michael Schell and Donald Polk. In the martial arts, Gaku Homma Sensei and Michael Fuhriman of Aikido Nippon Kan and Sherry Woodruff of the Cheyenne Fencing Society.

A number of other people are also very much in need of thanks. For character inspiration and notes on academia: Richard M. Powers and Gary Snyder. For clearing the path for me in large ways and small: Charles C. Ryan, Dorothy Taylor, Ed Bryant, Rose Beetem, Doug and Tomi Lewis, Karen Haber, Robert Silverberg,

Richard Gilliam, Al and Penny Tegen, and Bruce Holland Rogers, all of whom believed in me on the very flimsiest of evidence. For musical inspiration: Enya, Phil Collins, David Crosby, Lemon Interrupt, and Antonio Vivaldi. Literary influences are too numerous to mention, but I would like to extend special thanks to Vernor Vinge, John Stith, and Walter Jon Williams for showing how it ought to be done. For moral and logistical support: my parents, Michael and Evalyn McCarthy, and especially my wife, Cathy, who puts up with an awful lot.

When tyrants tremble in their fear
and hear their death-knell ringing,
when friends rejoice both far and near
how can I keep from singing?

In prison cell and dungeon vile
our thoughts to them are winging,
when friends by shame are undefiled
how can I keep from singing?

—Anne Warner, 1864

CHAPTER ONE

It was the sort of night in which careers were built or broken, in which connections were made that, with the ponderous inexorability of scientific advancement, would alter the course of human affairs. It was the sort of night David Sanger would kill for. The hum of the elevator seemed to echo his own nervous energy, his anticipation of the reception that waited below.

A bunch of old farts puffing and posturing at each other, Marian had warned when he'd tried to invite her along. *My theory is better than your theory, blah, blah, blah.* She'd spoken in the deep mock-masculine tone she reserved for satirizing academics in general and, when she felt he needed it, David himself in particular. *Molecular fabrication is important,* he'd countered somewhat irately. *You could cover it for the* Bulletin. *Your readers should know more about what we're doing.* But she'd just laughed at that, and launched into a dry narration of what she thought such an article might sound like.

Annoyed at the memory, David glared across the elevator car at his own face, reflected back at him through the ripply burnished brass of the doors. Dummy. He knew the excitement of his work, felt it fresh every morning as he pedaled to the U of Phil campus, his mind snapping and buzzing with solutions to the problems of the previous day. But he could not express this feeling to Marian, and after two years of staccato romance he should know better than to try.

Have a nice time, she'd said by way of mollification. *And stay away from Vandegroot, hey?*

Easy for her to say. Big Otto's grudge was like a force of nature, everywhere at once and impossible to quell. Henry Chong, David's faculty sponsor, would of course shield him as best he could, but David did not like the dependence that implied.

The floor indicator, counting slowly but steadily downward, floated above the reflection of his face—green holographic numerals that stood out from the wall, hovering above the door with an inch or two of air between them and the gloss-black projector plate. Something was not quite right with the numbers; solid-looking and yet less substantial than mist, they jarred the eye, like the view through someone else's glasses. Immature technology, David thought, rushed to production for the luxury markets. He shrugged. Costume jewelry for buildings, a tiny and irrelevant victory of glitz over substance. David thought of himself as a substance man, willing to let the little victories go.

Presently, the floor indicator clicked down to *04,* and then to *03.* His stomach began to feel a little heavier as the car slowed. His eyes studied the green, misfocused letters for a moment, at once drawn and repelled by their strangeness. He considered himself well informed even outside the narrow discipline of molecular fabrication, and yet he had not known that synthetic holography had progressed so far, that real-world applications like this existed.

So much news every day, so much crime and unemployment, so many protests and plane crashes and little countries going to war, so much damn *stuff* going on, you *had* to filter it if you ever wanted to leave the house. But how to pick and choose? In what ways might the world be changing, behind his back? The question troubled him for half a moment, but then the floor indicator went to *LOBBY* and a chime rang out, quietly startling in this close and quiet chamber.

The brass doors slid open with lazy grandeur, and, like Dorothy stepping from her dichromatic Kansas porch to the Technicolor vistas of Oz, David left the elevator and strode out into the cavernous spaces of the lobby. White ceilings high above him, skylights alternating with haute couture fixtures that cast warm rays all around. Marble pillars held it up, brass-shod at their bases. The black-and-red carpet sank beneath his feet like a paving layer of marshmallow.

Dodging potted ferns and knots of well-dressed strangers, David made his way to the entrance of the grand ballroom, some fifty paces distant. He walked for once without hurry, taking in the view he had earlier ignored. This was a far cry from his normal accommodations, and he didn't mind taking a moment or two just to appreciate it. He reached the ballroom.

The line at the security detectors was not long; David had come down a little early, both to beat the rush and to quell his own restlessness. He'd been to AMFRI conferences before, but this time around he had patents to brag about, papers to present, colleagues and contacts with whom to rub elbows. This time around he was no mere observer. He also had Vandegroot, the Sniffer King, to worry about, yes, but this did little to dampen his enthusiasm.

Half a dozen people were cycled efficiently through the security system ahead of him, each taking no more than a few seconds. Then his turn came, and he stepped through the doorwaylike frame and into the short false-wood tunnel of the detector itself. Feeling, as always, the prickly and entirely hallucinatory sensation of "being scanned." In fact, in the soft fluorescent light the detector was harmlessly and invisibly flashing his body with radio waves, imaging it magnetically and positronically, sniffing it for traces of suspicious chemicals. Using a Vandegroot Molecular Sniffer for this task, of course, and all the more humiliating for that.

Like Big Otto himself, the machine seemed more interested in impugning your background than protecting your safety; it sniffed not only for explosives and tear gas and gunpowder residue, but for a broad range of other chemicals, from drugs to machine oils to smuggled perfumes, and what in God's name did *that* have to do with the security of an AMFRI reception?

His eye caught something in the dim light, and he turned to see a graffito scribbled low on one wall, in bright orange ink. A drawing, a deadly accurate caricature of Otto Vandegroot, roly-poly and with grossly enlarged nostrils and a caption beneath: YOU ARE BEING SNIFFED. PLEASE BEND OVER.

A wave of snickering swept David's discomfort aside. Whoever had done this had chutzpah for sure, and judging by the freshness of the ink, he or she was an AMFRI scientist, and not long gone. Still snickering, and wishing he could have done the deed himself, David shook his head and stepped out of the detector.

He was greeted, almost immediately, by giants.

CHAPTER **TWO**

Above the crowd, a huge banner announced: BALTIMORE WELCOMES THE ASSOCIATION FOR MOLECULAR FABRICATION RESEARCH, INTERNATIONAL. Crepe paper hung along the walls and spread out like telecom wires from the chandeliers, and a solid layer of helium balloons covered the ceiling, long strings of shiny Mylar dangling just out of reach of the crowd beneath.

The display was obviously intended to be festive, but the color scheme, beige and peach and subtle maroon, simply made it look expensive. Or perhaps that was the intent after all. The buffet, which by itself must have cost tens of thousands of dollars, sprawled across a dozen tables, filling nearly half the cavernous ballroom. Anything David might possibly want to eat, be it sashimi or spaghetti or *Schwarzwaldekirschtorte,* could be found somewhere nearby.

Indeed, the very *world* seemed similarly laid out for

him, or at least that portion of the world he'd worked so hard to become a part of. Had you asked him to name the five most significant inventions of recent decades, he might well have answered: the Chong precision epitaxy assembly, the Yeagle, the Quick sorter, the Busey trap, and the Henders/Shatraw ion gate. And here, within arm's reach, stood Adam Yeagle, Denzl Quick, Elaine Busey, and *the* Robert G. Shatraw! And Henry Chong, of course, but after eight years at the U of Phil, three of them under Chong's direct supervision, David thought of the man more as an aging and slightly bumbling relative than a Serious Heavy Hitter in the molecule biz. His genius seemed deeply mired beneath layers of bureaucratic malaise. The cost of living in academia, David supposed.

"I'm afraid classical nanotech is in a state of full retreat," Professor Shatraw was saying mournfully. "You hardly see even the *word* in the journals anymore."

David nodded respectfully. Only twenty minutes into the reception, and he thought he was doing quite well, thank you kindly. *Vandegroot v. Sanger* was a much hotter topic du jour than he would have guessed; it proved quite easy to trade on, so long as he kept his voice down. Speaking of which . . . He looked around again, trying to spot the shine of grease-slicked hair or, failing that, the knot of Germans and Swedes that seemed so often to surround it. Inexplicably, David thought, since Big Otto was about as Ugly American as they came.

The Japanese and Koreans tended to cluster together as well, despite the official tensions between them, as if they realized after all that they had more in common with each other than with the wider world. The Chinese, of course, kept their own company, except for Hyeon "Henry" Chong, who flitted between them and the masses of English speakers like a kind of pollinating insect. And David . . . Well, it seemed he could go where he liked. He knew enough people this year that he could leap from conversation to conversation, finding welcoming handshakes the way a rhesus monkey finds new branches to swing from. It was a new sensation for him, and quite welcome.

"I couldn't agree more," Elaine Busey said to Shatraw. "The mol-bio crowd soured the whole concept for us. Ten years ago they were honest-to-god calling the *aspirin molecule* a prototypical nanomachine. Hemoglobin I could forgive, since it does have moving parts, but aspirin? Come on; that kind of statement just makes us all look goofy, never mind who's doing the actual work."

She glanced several times at David as she spoke. While hardly youthful in appearance, Busey was the youngest of the Serious Heavy Hitters, and visibly sympathetic toward him for some reason he hadn't figured out yet. Maybe he reminded her of someone. Maybe she had a son or a daughter his age. Or maybe she was just a nice lady who wanted to put him at ease. In any case, he sensed his moment, and leaped.

"That's what nobody understands anymore," he said. "Most everyone here is a brilliant scientist, but it's ass-in-chair that gets the job done. Trying to let protein folding do all the work for you is a cheat, and it's a dead end. You'd do better building a car engine out of pasta shells."

He paused. Had he said too much? He suddenly felt socially off-balance, for perhaps the first time that evening. Would they frown, raise eyebrows, raise accusing fingers at him? But to his relief the Heavy Hitters simply chuckled and nodded appreciatively, as if he'd voiced their thoughts, but in words they would not themselves have chosen.

"Your pupil has a sense of humor," Professor Yeagle said to Henry Chong. "Wherever did he get it? Not from you, I'd guess."

"I've tried to discourage the boy," said Chong, with a not-half-bad attempt at good cheer.

"Well," David admitted, "I was only partly joking.

Everyone wants to be a gene-sequence programmer these days, when what we really need is ship-in-a-bottle types."

"Have you ever built a ship in a bottle?" Elaine Busey asked with a smile.

David nodded. "Yeah."

At age twelve he'd put the *Niña, Pinta,* and *Santa Maria* in an eyedropper. The following year he'd copied the Eiffel Tower in spidersilk, the whole structure less than a millimeter wide at the base, kept safe inside a tiny magnifier box of clear plastic. When he dropped the box and its lid popped off and the model vanished forever into his bedroom carpet, he had cried hysterically for two days, until the family doctor knocked him out with an adult-strength sedative cocktail.

Weeks of depression had followed and, deeply worried for him, David's father had finally offered to buy him a new tool for his hobby, any kind he wanted. Taking Dad at his word, David had asked for—and received!—a precision dual-probe scanning/tunneling microscope that cost as much as a car, and which was capable not only of imaging individual atoms, but of *picking them up and moving them.* From that day forward, the SPM had been the center of David's world.

When he'd finally gotten to college and linked up with others who shared his interest in very small things, he'd been shocked and disappointed to learn that their attitudes, for the most part, differed sharply from his own. "Why mess around with scanning probe microscopes when God gave us the ribosome? Why build up from individual atoms when you can design proteins that fold up into any shape you need?"

He remained shocked to this day. Had you asked the throngs of people in this room about the five most important inventions, most would certainly name the free-culture ribosome and the RNA sequencer/multiplier, and possibly the PanProteia VR modeling system. And that, by itself, said damn near everything that needed to be said about the current state of molecular fabrication research.

Fact was, proteins would fold up into messy squiggles that might or might not approximate some crude machine parts. OK for medicinal applications when you just needed something like a molecular cage or sieve or catcher's mitt, but for serious manipulation, for gears and levers and gripping appendages, they were useless. Fragile and floppy, they waited for even a mild fluctuation in temperature or contaminant levels to cross-link them into useless goop.

Real, classical machinery was commonplace these days on the micrometer scale, though in David's opinion it wasn't good for much. Cooling systems for computer chips, yes, and a few lumbering "microbots" that were little more than windup toys, too small to move a dust speck and far too large and clumsy to move an atom. Even David's childhood SPM had better motor control.

The microbots were also both too large and too small for most medical applications, sized just right, in fact, to provoke a massive immune response: tens of millions of antibodies, the body's own nanomechanical soldiers, swarming them, gluing and trapping them until the kidneys could flush them away with the rest of the garbage.

Building machinery on the nanoscale, a thousand times smaller than this ungainly microtech, was perhaps the most important thing the human race had ever attempted, and certainly by far the most difficult. Accommodation was necessary not only with the Newtonian laws, but with the voodoo of quantum mechanics and the plain orneriness of atomic chemistry as well. You couldn't image a work in progress, either, except by methods so indirect and so imprecise that you felt like a blind, groping mechanic with boxing gloves on.

Mere brilliance was not enough for a task like that. Not nearly enough. And yet brilliance seemed the most you could ask from most of the AMFRI membership, who were content to spend their lives playing origami with pond slime.

"You seem a little down, suddenly," Denzl Quick opined. "Nothing we've said, I hope." He chuckled a little.

David shook his head and forced a grin. "No, sir. Just thinking how badly the world needs saving."

"Ah," said Quick, "then you are Henry's student after all. Now, you've been talking to us for five minutes, and not a word about your court case. I'm sure we're all dying to hear about it, so come across."

David shuffled. "Well, sir, it wasn't a court case at all, fortunately for me. Vandegroot could have bankrupted me if he hadn't been so sure he was going to win. He's tightfisted, that man."

"Please forgive my pupil," Henry Chong said, putting a hand on David's shoulder and looking around at the Heavy Hitters in mock sorrow. His accent was terrible, as usual, but the words were spaced and clearly enunciated. "His education has crowded out his manners. Very unfortunate, considering his education."

Surprisingly, Henry chuckled. "Let me be fair: I think he remembers some original substance of our discipline, even if he has forgotten the details. Molecular fabrication is that way, for some students. For others it's the push and pull of a thousand tiny influences. Like warfare, eh? If you're so smart, David Sanger, we'll let you work out the *ju* of numerical techniques for yourself."

He made a light fist and mimed with it as if knocking on David's forehead. "The boy's head is like a rock. I warned him, repeatedly, not to get in Vandegroot's way. So many bodies on that field, I didn't want to be responsible for another. But does David Sanger listen to me? No, he does not."

"It was a binding arbitration, wasn't it?" Elaine Busey asked with a laugh.

"Yeah," David said. "ECS express, no appeal. Even *I* can afford that one. What I can't figure out is why everyone thought I was going to lose. I mean, Big Otto never actually invented anything."

And once again, David went silent, fearing he'd spoken too boldly. But again, the Heavy Hitters laughed.

And a good thing; had you asked David to name off the biggest obstacles to human progress, he would have said "Vandegroot" five times. David had little understanding and even less respect for Big Otto, who had slapped together Heavy Hitting inventions in what was, after all, rather an obvious configuration to produce the Vandegroot Molecular Sniffer. It bewildered David that in the process of this development, Vandegroot had been awarded a series of sweeping patents that gave him broad power over the molecular fabrication industry. The fact that he was Grayer than a district court judge might have had something to do with that.

Really, the road from lab to marketplace was long and arduous enough without Vandegroot and his lackeys crouching like buried mines beneath it. But crouch they did, and on occasion they would rise up to blast otherwise-promising inventions. Not merely block or delay them or subject them to stiff royalties, but literally *blast* them with subpoenas and infringement suits and restraining orders, literally remove them from the remotest possibility of manufacture by their developers or by anyone else.

It was one of the great ironies of the industry that the sniffer, one of its few commercial successes outside the medical and pharmaceutical markets, was a device whose smallest version OSHA had labeled with the words: CAUTION: TWO-MAN CARRY. So much for nanotechnology. A universe of possibilities lurked behind the Otto Barrier, and yet the whole thing was a farce! Vandegroot was a talented administrator, and admittedly a deft hand at manufacturing shortcuts, but his contributions to the science extended no further than that. David and his lawyer had proved as much in the three days of the arbitration.

Certainly, though, the barrier remained. David could commercialize his latest research only so long as he didn't cross another Vandegroot patent, and God knew that was easy enough to do. But he'd swept a few mines off the field, at least, and hopefully other researchers would follow behind him in the fight to clear the path entirely.

"Are we boring you?" Robert G. Shatraw asked David, in a friendly but pointed tone. "You look like you're off in the ozone somewhere."

David smiled, shook his head, made a huffing sound of self-deprecation. "I really am sorry, Dr. Shatraw. Life's been very busy; I've got a lot on my mind. It's no excuse for rudeness, of course."

"We don't all go head-to-head with Big Otto," Elaine Busey admitted. "That's got to be a drain on your mental resources, I would think. It would certainly steal a lot of momentum from your work."

"Yeah." David's grin widened, and he nodded vigorously. "I swear that guy would patent *dirt,* and find some way to put a trademark on the name, so he could sue anybody that so much as mentioned it. He'd patent the carbon atom if he thought he could get away with it."

Elaine Busey's eyes flashed a warning.

"You know," said a gruff voice behind David. He turned and saw standing there, no more than fifteen feet away, the Sniffer King, the Duke of Search and Seizure, Big Otto Vandegroot himself. He wore his usual spider-silk tweeds, his usual greased-back hair and neatly sculpted beard. And his usual sneer, a little exaggerated tonight. In his fist he held a very tall glass filled with ice cubes and amber liquid.

"Otto," David said, nonplussed.

"You know, one thing about me," Vandegroot said, his voice oozing with derision, "is that I have excellent hearing."

Henry Chong held up a hand, palm out toward Vandegroot in a placating gesture. "The boy was just—"

"You little vermin," Vandegroot said, ignoring Henry, brandishing his drink and taking a step toward David. "You haven't got a *grain* of respect. When you were potty training I was changing the world."

A surge of anger ran through David, tensing his muscles. He matched Vandegroot's sneer. "The sniffer? Oh yeah, *that's* been a real boon. Thank you very much."

"What the hell do you know, boy?" Vandegroot's face was bright red.

" 'Boy'? How very Gray of you. You know, two of my friends got mugged last year. Mugged bad, right on the U of Phil campus. Bare fists and a bad case of mean. Can a sniffer detect that, Otto?"

"You don't know a damn thing." He paused, shifted his balance. "You go ahead, boy, build your stupid nanoscale chain drive. We'll see if the world beats a path to your grotty little door."

Vandegroot turned as if to go. Then, seemingly as an afterthought, he looked down at the drink in his hand, dropped an elbow, cocked his arm back, and hurled the glass directly at David. Light from the chandeliers flashed off it as it flew, spinning scotch and ice cubes off in every direction.

Unthinkingly, David stepped back and turned aside,

the standard "when in doubt" move they had taught him in Street Defense. Cold wetness splashed the front of his shirt, followed by a burning sensation, and then a slam of pain where the edge of the glass had caught him and bounced away.

"Hey!" he shouted, his mind completely at a loss to explain or react to this development.

"You cross my path again and I'll take you down," Vandegroot said in his hoarse and gravelly drawl. His eyes burned beneath slicks of hair that had fallen out of place.

David blinked, and then spoke mildly, with surprise and disdain: "You asshole. Don't throw things at me."

Otto Vandegroot's face reddened further, his scowl deepening to an expression of active rage. Suddenly, he moved his right arm horizontally, as if straightening his shirt cuff, then snapped the hand downward in a whiplike gesture. Then, somehow, he had an object in his fist, a little white rod about half an inch thick and five or six inches long. He turned his hand in a peculiar way. The rod made a clicking and scraping noise, and something sprang from the front of it, growing. In less than half a second the rod had snapped out to a length of three feet, with a narrow taper at the end. No, a sharp *point* at the end.

Something else was happening at the wide end of the device: it was puffing out, like a balloon—no, like an *umbrella.* A conical handguard had unfolded just in front of Vandegroot's fist, locking into place with a final snap. And all at once, David recognized what Vandegroot had in his hand: it was a "drop foil," the newest weapon of choice in the circles of the well-to-do.

Spring-loaded, readily concealable in an ejector that strapped to the forearm, the drop foil was fashioned from ordinary plastic and could therefore pass through the security detectors that marked the entrances of most public buildings. But drop foils were *sharp,* and expensive, and (he'd heard) very intimidating to the average street thug, who had no interest in getting poked full of holes for the contents of one man's wallet.

Drop foils were illegal, of course, and very much against the spirit of public helplessness the Gray Party had worked so hard to foster. They were the sort of thing snobby college kids showed off to their friends, with a swagger and a little tough talk, and not at all the sort of thing David expected to see dropping from the jacket sleeve of a puffball like Otto Vandegroot.

"I'll teach you some fucking manners," Vandegroot spat, taking another step forward and brandishing the newly sprung weapon. He'd arranged his feet into a fighting stance, drawn his left arm behind him, the hand hovering six inches off his hip. His right arm straightened, and the tip of the foil dropped until it was pointing directly at David's face, only a couple of feet away.

David felt his eyes widening, sensed his vision growing narrow, his breath growing shallow and quick. He tried to step back but found he was up against one of the buffet tables. Working on its own initiative, his left hand reached behind him and grabbed at whatever was nearest, coming forward with a load of small, soft objects, candies or berries or something. He lifted them up as if he might throw them, then thought better of it and opened his fingers. Small things pattered softly against the carpet. The room, all four and a half acres of it, had gone deathly silent.

"Professor Vandegroot, wait," Da3vid said, in what he hoped was a conciliatory tone. Shit, where was hotel security *now?*

"Oh. So now it's 'Professor Vandegroot' again, is it? That's good. I may just carve it into your forehead so you don't forget."

David dodged to the side, colliding with a knot of people. He felt someone thrust something into his open right hand, and then the knot gave, the people fading back, avoiding the scuffle. Vandegroot took a sliding step sideways, arranging himself in front of David once again.

David let his glance flick down for a moment, and he saw what had been placed in his hand: a little white cylinder, much like the one Vandegroot had so recently held. It was much heavier than he would have expected, much springier, much more *squeezable* in his hand. He squeezed it.

Instantly, the thing jerked in his grip and sprang out to its full length.

"Ha!" Vandegroot called out, seeing the three-foot plastic blade, stepping forward, and slapping it aside. "The mouse has teeth, does he?" Vandegroot's own blade lanced in and out quickly, piercing David's shirt, lightly pricking the flesh beneath it.

"Ow!" Startled, David tried to pull back again, came up hard against the buffet table again. There was nowhere to *go;* there was no way for him to step out of reach of Vandegroot's foil. He was struck all at once by the absurdity of the situation—here he was, twenty-five years old and striving desperately for the respectability of adulthood, yet somehow he was having a *sword fight* in front of all the people he most wanted to impress. And he was losing, badly!

Vandegroot lunged forward again, lithe and strong despite his bulk, his blade coming straight in toward David's heart. *I have to block; I have to parry,* David thought, but by the time he'd brought his blade around, Vandegroot had pricked him again and stepped back. David didn't know how to parry. David didn't know how to fence at all.

"It's a difficult lesson," Vandegroot said, and David saw the bastard wasn't even breathing hard. "It's a *pain*ful—"

Vandegroot lunged forward again, his front leg moving out, his body sliding down and forward above it. Arm projecting straight out from the shoulder, elbow locked. *The extended arm is both a target and a lever,* said the voice of David's Street Defense instructor, and suddenly David knew exactly what to do.

His right arm was forward, the elbow up, the sword pointing vertically downward in his grip. A useless, ludicrous pose, but now he rotated the blade upward with a vicious, snapping gesture that brought it around hard against Otto Vandegroot's drop foil. The two swords, crossing with a plastic CLACK, were jerked to the right, so that Vandegroot's sword now pointed off past David's shoulder.

Without pausing, David stepped forward with his left foot, pivoting at the waist and bringing his left hand forward as he did so. His fingers closed around the wrist of Otto's sword hand. His right hand disengaged the sword, came up and around in a wide, graceful arc as he turned on the ball of his left foot. The movement was mechanical and yet fluid, loose, like a dance step. In half a second, David had swung around until he was back-to-back with Vandegroot, both arms extended as if in a ballet parody of crucifixion. His right hand held the sword out loosely, while his left took a tighter grip on Vandegroot's wrist. His chin was high, and for a moment he saw the astonished faces of Henry Chong and Elaine Busey, of Yeagle and Quick and the other Heavy Hitters.

But the dance had not yet finished. He stepped out and sideways with his right foot, then put his weight down on it and turned, sliding his left foot and pivoting until he faced Vandegroot once again.

This was Wrist Twist Number Three, one of the first moves they had taught him in Street Defense. David was not doing it as quickly as it should be done, but then again he was young and long of reach and he hadn't been drinking, and he could do this much better than he could fence.

Vandegroot gaped at him, looking shocked and outraged. *I was ready for you,* his expression seemed to say, *but you didn't make the right move. What the hell are you doing?* And then, comprehension dawned as David applied the pressure. Like magic, he had jerked Vandegroot off-balance and danced his wrist around until the sword pointed off in a useless direction. The position was awkward at best, and when the victim's hand was pushed and twisted in the Street Defensive way the pain was sudden and excruciating.

"Aah. Aah!" A look of alarm flashed across Otto's face. This hurt. This *hurt.* Good.

"Drop the sword," David said. He sounded remarkably calm, much calmer than he actually felt.

"Let . . . You're . . ."

"Drop it!"

Otto's face relaxed, and his arm relaxed in David's grip, and his hand opened, and the drop foil tumbled free, bouncing off Otto's bicep and knee on its way to the carpet. *I surrender,* the body language was saying. *I don't know what you're doing, but it hurts me and I would like you to please stop doing it!*

But David did not back off on the pressure. Vandegroot had been all too willing to inflict pain and embarrassment on *him,* and he found he couldn't let that go quite so easily. He twisted a little more.

"Ow!" Vandegroot cried out with more than a hint of panic in his voice.

David sneered angrily. "On your ass, old man. It's the only way."

His eyes were locked on Vandegroot's, and understanding flashed between the two of them like a telecom signal. In order to relieve the pain, Vandegroot must bend his knees and fall backward, right onto his generous rear end. He must drop himself, quite literally, at David's feet. He knew this, and David knew that he knew it, and he saw that David knew and hated him for it. And thusly, he fell.

CHAPTER THREE

David took off his pierced, blood-specked zipper tie and threw it on the dresser even before he'd kicked the door shut. The room was bland, unwelcoming, its colors pale in the harsh lighting. White diode arrays striped across the ceiling, bright and tough and economical, drawing very little current for the illumination they gave. But there was nothing welcoming about them. Comfort was what he needed right now, but the hotel had reserved all its posh splendor for the public spaces, and this room was a place of convenience, nothing more. Actual, soul-soothing comfort was not this hotel's forté; that sort of thing came dearer than even AMFRI would shell out for.

He'd handled things badly; he knew that. Hell, the evening could hardly have turned out worse. He had no doubt that the tale would be told again and again, haunting him down the long decades of his career. *Don't mess with Sanger. He once beat up Otto Vandegroot, you know.*

Yeah, broke his arm right in the middle of a cocktail party in Baltimore. David had not, in fact, broken Otto's arm, but a lot of people seemed to think that he had, and no doubt that was how the incident would be remembered.

This was not the sort of reputation David wanted, not at all, but he couldn't even work up a sense of outrage about it; he had crossed the line, and had done it knowingly. Disarming an attacker was one thing, but publicly dumping a respected scientist on his ass was something else again. Whether or not the scientist had earned such treatment (or worse) was hardly the point. David ran over and over the events in his mind, hunting for the moment of his error, the moment at which he could have chosen differently, defusing the tension and still retaining his pride. Facing down Vandegroot without pissing him off . . . But somehow, the moment eluded him. Each of his actions seemed ordained, inevitable, outside the realm of rational control.

Henry Chong had spoken up for him when the hotel's security guards had finally materialized. He had told them that Vandegroot started the fight, that David had had no way to escape and so had been forced to defend himself.

"I wasn't going to hurt him," Otto had shouted as the guards pulled him away. He cradled his arm and glared poison at David. "Stupid little punk. I don't *respect* him enough to hurt him!"

But the sword and the two dime-sized spots of blood on David's shirt had told them all they needed to know. Congratulations had followed, some of the onlookers stepping forward to clap David on the back, to praise him, to ask him if he was all right, and hey, where did he learn a trick like that? He'd answered vaguely, uncomfortable with the attention, with the juvenile gloating and bravado that lay behind it. Unlike his young colleagues, the Heavy Hitters had withdrawn, their smiles now more polite than warm. Treating him like a dog that had bristled and growled unexpectedly. *Good lord, what else is this young man capable of?* He understood their reaction perfectly, and it made him sad.

And then, without warning the shakes had come, a great and uncontrollable trembling in his hands and body as the meaning of the fight, the danger of it, sank in. To hell with his ruined reputation; he might have lost an eye. He and Vandegroot had been waving *swords* at one another. Jesus, he might have lost his *life.*

It took three shots of vodka to get the shaking under control, and three more to really calm him down. Even then, even now, he didn't feel the least bit drunk. He felt a little bit like crying, or like tearing the TV set off the wall and heaving it through the window to smash down among the city lights.

Instead, he threw himself down on the bed and reached for the vidphone.

Marian Fouts either was or was not his girlfriend, depending on what sort of mood she was in when you asked her. And David was or was not in love with her, depending on how determinedly she was ignoring him that day. Marian's life was, to say the least, a full one; she had been part of the cooperative effort to revive the defunct *Philadelphia Bulletin,* and revive it she had. It thrived now as a free, ad-supported newspaper, and her days were filled with writing and editing and investigative reporting, and with the business minutiae that she, as a major shareholder, could never quite escape.

At night she put her work firmly out of mind but had another vice to replace it: NEVERland. Networked Virtual Reality Simulations were for her like a kind of secret identity, a second life entirely distinct from the first and impinging upon it in no way. She was a "closet sorceress," one of millions, but quite good if David was to believe her stories. So at twenty-six years of age, Marian ran both a newspaper and a magic kingdom—a full plate indeed.

She answered the phone on the sixth ring, her color image appearing on the phone's screen just before her voice mail could pick up.

"Yeah?" she said, her image pushing a VR helmet up off its face with a what-the-hell-do-you-want sort of air. David had flagged the call for priority ring, else she probably would not have answered at all.

"I need to talk to you," he said.

"So talk," she replied, simply and without inflection. "I'm dying for the sound of your voice."

Perversely, this was exactly what David loved about Marian. He had the constant feeling that she'd be happier without him, without the constant distraction that he represented, and this spoke to a part of his brain in urgent tones: Be worthy of her! Hold onto her for another day! And another, and another . . . They had gone on like that for almost two years, now. It seemed a childish sort of relationship, and one which David kept expecting one or the other of them to outgrow. But the sex between them was very good, and anyway, David suspected he wouldn't have time for a girlfriend who actually had time for him.

"You're busy in NEVERland," he said to Marian. The remark was not a question, but a question lay unconcealed behind it: however important your game is, will you interrupt it for me?

In the same neutral tone: "The borders are under attack right now. It's amateurs, I think, thirteen-year-olds or something. I'm dug in for a slow night, so I suspect the guards and wards will take them out without my having to be there." Now Marian peered closely at him through the vidphone screen, and her face softened. "You look terrible. Did something happen?"

"Oh, yeah," he said, and launched into a troubled account of the evening's events. Marian, God love her, seemed fiercely determined not to be impressed with his bravery or his wounds, though her eyes sparkled a little as he talked.

"Do you love me tonight?" he asked her at one point, his voice a bit more wheedling than he would have liked.

"What, after you just trashed your career?" She smirked, to show that she didn't believe that had happened. "After you beat up on the Sniffer King? Boy, you don't make it easy on a girl."

Well, comfort was not exactly Marian's forté either.

David awoke suddenly, with sunlight tearing at the edges of his sleep mask and a loud pounding noise assaulting his ears.

"Police! Open up!"

"Who?" David said quietly, more to himself than to the wider world. He pulled the mask off, letting the light flood in against his eyelids. Where was he? What was going on? Then, squinting against the painful glare, he saw the hotel room around him, and the events of the previous night flashed into his mind like a spray of bitter acid. He groaned.

CLUMP! CLUMP CLUMP! The whole door seemed to shudder with the noise, as if someone were kicking it with a heavy boot.

"This is the *police!* Open the door!"

"OK!" he said, kicking the bedcovers away and sitting up, fighting back his amazement and disorientation. This was a hell of a way to wake up on a Saturday morning. "OK, just a second. I'm coming."

He threw his feet down on the floor and got himself up on top of them. Hopped quickly to the door, unlatched it, opened it. *See how eager I am, Officer?*

Two police stood in the hallway outside: a uniformed

black woman and a white male in shirt and tie, badge dangling from a strap around his neck. The woman's thumbs were hooked at her utility belt, the man's jammed into his front pockets. Both their faces were identically grim and set. David regarded them blearily. "Yeah? What is it?"

"We'd like to talk to you about last night," the female officer said. "May we come in please?"

"Huh?" David blinked, then nodded and stepped away from the door. "Yeah, sure. Is this about Vandegroot?"

The officers shared a look between them, and then considered David, eyeing his jockey-shorted form as if guessing how much he weighed.

"Yes," the female officer said, "it's about Vandegroot. We have about a thousand witnesses that saw you fighting with him last night."

"That's right," David said. "Listen, can we do this later? I already said I'm not pressing charges."

The female officer blinked, as if that remark made no sense to her. Her male counterpart, a beefy man in his late thirties, leaned forward slightly and spoke: "Detective Volhallen, Violent Crimes. You used an illegal weapon against Otto Vandegroot at approximately 7:25 P.M. In the main ballroom downstairs, is that correct?"

The bottom dropped out of David's stomach, as if his hotel room were an elevator that had suddenly begun to descend. Illegal weapon . . . "That wasn't my sword. Somebody handed it to me when Otto pulled out his."

"Who handed it to you?" the policeman asked, his tone suspicious, condescending.

"I don't know. I couldn't see."

"Aha. And after the fight? What did you do then?"

David squared his shoulders. "I drank some vodka. I was pretty shaken up, I wanted to steady my hands. You know?"

"What did you want them steady for?"

"What?"

The policeman sighed, glanced at his partner and then back at David again. "You drank the vodka in front of witnesses, right? What did you do after that?"

"I came up here to my room," David said carefully. His own voice was beginning to sound more than a little suspicious. "I called my girlfriend."

"Did you take the elevator?"

"Yes, I took the elevator. What the hell is this about? Is Otto pressing charges or something?"

The officers looked at each other again, and then the woman shrugged and they both looked back at David.

"Otto Vandegroot is dead," the policeman said, and watched David's face for a reaction.

David didn't have a reaction. He didn't blink, didn't twitch a muscle. *Otto Vandegroot is dead?* What the hell was that supposed to mean?

"At approximately 9:20 P.M.," the detective said, still scrutinizing David, "in a stairwell, somebody shoved a drop foil through the back of Mr. Vandegroot's head. You wouldn't know anything about that, would you?"

David just stood there, stupidly. "What in God's name are you talking about?"

The cop sighed again, heavily this time. "OK, here's the deal: your fingerprints are all over the murder weapon, and nobody that we've talked to saw you at the time of the murder. Can you explain that?"

"The murder weapon?" David said, marveling at the absolute weirdness of the situation. "How would my fingerprints . . ."

Oh, dear God. He had dropped the sword after Vandegroot's surrender, and when he'd looked for it later it hadn't been there. He'd assumed the security guards had taken it with them, or else its original owner had reclaimed it. He hadn't pursued the matter because, well, what was there to pursue? The fight was over and best forgotten.

But if someone had picked it up . . . and killed Otto Vandegroot with it . . .

These days, the police could scan for fingerprints with a device that looked like a penlight, and then consult a national database to receive the ID within minutes. The error rate was supposed to be very low, something like one in a thousand. David didn't feel that lucky this morning.

"I can explain," he said, a bit too quickly.

The policeman cracked a sort of lopsided sneer at that. "I thought you could. Get dressed, my friend. We'll let you explain it downtown."

"Am I under arrest?" David asked.

"What the hell do you think?"

The view outside the window didn't move, didn't change, but David still felt the hotel room descending, like an elevator car on its way down to some dark and unknowable place.

CHAPTER FOUR

The walls of the police station were splashed, unsurprisingly, with campaign posters for the Gray Party. JOE MUGGER DOESN'T WANT YOU TO VOTE GRAY! one of them said. The picture, a watercolor, showed a seedy-looking character shrinking away from a pair of coplike figures, gray silhouettes that looked far more sinister than Joe Mugger himself. It had once been forbidden, David was pretty sure, for politicians to advertise in places like this, but lately the practice seemed common.

The floor here was brown linoleum, the walls paneled in cheap but tasteful falsewood. The desks were immaculate, a late-model computer terminal sitting atop every one. The lighting was bright and cheerful. Here and there sat obvious "perpetrators" of one sort or another, but they all sat quietly, their arresting officers speaking to them calmly across the desktops. Aside from that, and the fact that half the people in the room were wearing police uniforms, David might have taken the place for an insurance broker's office.

YOU DON'T HAVE TO *GO* GRAY TO *VOTE* GRAY, said another, unillustrated poster. And beside that one hung a portrait of Colonel The Honorable John Harrison Quince, U.S. chairman of the Gray Party, dressed up in a dichromatic Uncle Sam suit, white stars and stripes on a field of gray and darker gray. Quince held up a fist, as if in victory. The caption said: AMERICA, THE *SOLID* STATE.

At that, David allowed himself a chuckle despite the circumstances. Government people could be so stupid sometimes.

Once, long ago, "solid state" had been a term of praise in the electronics industry, denoting a system that had advanced beyond vacuum tubes and mechanical relay switches and such. However, thanks to the microtechnology David worked so hard to render obsolete, even the cheapest electronic and photonic devices these days had moving parts, microscale pumps and fans and motors without which they could not perform the miracles that were expected of them. These days, "solid state" was a term used by nanotechnology researchers to denote molecular machinery which, through poor design or rough handling, had ceased to function.

It was a very derisive phrase indeed, one that had provoked more than its share of heated arguments in the ivory towers of molecular fabrication. It was, in fact, precisely the phrase David would have chosen to describe the all-too-vivid dream of Gray America. A friendly cop on every corner, a friendly line trace on every telecom wire, a friendly network of interlocking regulations so tight and so inflexible that society, moving in its slow-motion societal way, would smash to friendly pieces against it.

The Dems want to be your mommy, the joke went. *The Reps want to be your daddy, and the Grays want to be your parole officer.* Most people did not vote Gray, he knew, but a great many did allow their opinions to be swayed and their priorities edited by the Party's unceasing agitation. As with EarthFirst and the ACLU and the so-called Moral Majority, the Gray Party's influence was far out of proportion to its actual size. More to the detriment of society, he thought.

"Sit there," David's arresting officer said, nudging his shoulder and pointing to the chair beneath Colonel The Honorable John Harrison Quince's portrait.

"Can you take the handcuffs off?" David asked.

"No."

"I didn't do it, you know. I didn't kill him."

"That's fine," the detective said, giving him a little shove. "Right now you're going to sit down and give me your personal data, and then you're going to go down to an interrogation room and wait for the FBI."

"I'm due to speak at the AMFRI conference today," David protested, with a sudden stab of fear and anger and frustration. Interrogation room? They were actually going to take him, handcuffed, to something called an *interrogation room?* As if he needed to have bright lights shone in his face, to be kept awake all night while a tag team played good-cop/bad-cop games with his head? "I'm presenting two papers."

"Not anymore," the cop told him. He sat down across from David and eyed him coolly. "Can I have your full name, please?"

"Why do I even have to talk to you if the FBI is coming?" David asked stubbornly. "They'll just edge you off the case, won't they?"

The cop nodded. "Absolutely. I wouldn't have it any other way."

"Why are they even coming? Can't the local police handle a homicide?"

Now the cop cracked a genuine smile, the first David

had seen from him. "Are you kidding? A big international conference like that? Whoever killed that guy—" and here he lowered his chin and peered sharply at David "—sure as hell crossed a few state lines to do it. And in two days the conference ends and everyone goes back where they came from." He laughed. "Yeah, that's a beaut. I'll give that one to the FBI any day."

"Oh," David said. So now he could add jurisdictional politics to his list of woes. Obviously, since he hadn't killed Otto Vandegroot, the cops would ask him a lot of questions, would *interrogate* him, but would eventually have to let him go. But if they were bickering with one another as well as *interrogating* him, it might be a very long day indeed.

The chair, a hard and angular frame of bare wood, was biting into him, already beginning to cut off his circulation. But he settled deeper into it nonetheless, determined to draw from it whatever comfort he could.

The door of the interrogation room swung open, white light spilling in around it, mixing with the yellow incandescents and the pale glow leaching from the two fist-sized windows in the wall behind David.

A man walked in. He was heavyish, baldish, hair gone salty with a dusting of pepper. He wore a yellow dress shirt with a pink-and-blue paisley necktie. A picture ID badge hung from the shirt pocket, the blue letters FBI prominent upon it. David couldn't quite make out the name.

"David Sanger?" the man asked, closing the door behind him without turning around. "I'm Special Agent Mike Puckett. I'll be handling this investigation." He leaned across the table, looked at David in an appraising but not overtly hostile manner. "Are you comfortable?"

"Oh, sure," David said nervously, jerking his chains, letting them jingle. His wrists had been joined together by a foot-long section of steel chain, and joined from there to a ring mounted on a bar that ran along the wall. Like a banister, like the bar along the wall of a dance studio, but shorter and lower down, and painted the same ugly blue-green as the rest of the wall. David had about three feet of mobility in one direction, and about half a foot in the other. And he could not quite cross his arms, or put his hands in his lap, so he let them dangle against the restraints in a way that made him feel he was dog-paddling through the air. He was not, in fact, comfortable.

"I'm sorry about the cuffs," Special Agent Mike Puckett said reasonably. "Standard procedure, I'm afraid, but hopefully we won't keep you in here too long. I just want to find out what happened."

David nodded. "And I'd like to tell you." His tone was a mix of low fear and righteous indignation. Not, he hoped, the quaver of a guilty man, but that of one wrongfully accused.

"Do you need to go to the bathroom? If so, it would be a good idea to get it done before we start."

"They took me about half an hour ago," David said.

"OK." Puckett nodded once. "Let's begin, then."

He pulled out a dictation recorder, one of the very new, very small ones that looked like a short stack of nickels, and set it down on the table between them, a couple of feet out of David's reach.

"You were at a conference," he prompted. "Tell me what that was all about."

David cleared his throat. "Well, sir, it's still going on. I have to go back there once you guys are through with me. I'm presenting a couple of papers."

"On nanotechnology?"

"Right," David said. "Well, generally we like to say 'molecular fabrication,' which is a more inclusive term.

AMFRI has influence over a number of small industries." He paused. "Uh, no pun intended."

The special agent looked blank for a moment, and then smiled suddenly and chuckled with polite appreciation. "Very good. So, you're the guy who puts the little fans on the computer chips."

"Uh, no, you're thinking of microtechnology. We work on a much smaller scale than that."

"Oh. Aha. Now tell me, David, what exactly does AMFRI stand for?"

"Association for Molecular Fabrication Research, International," David replied. "It's like a union. Well, not really, but in some ways it's worse than a union. If you want to do serious work in the field, you have to be a member, and that means you have to conform to the AMFRI Standards and Practices, which are pretty strict. We like to say, 'I AMFRI, therefore I am not free.' And believe me, if you want any hope of advancement or funding or anything, you'd better know how to rub elbows."

"And that's what you were doing last night?"

David nodded. "Yeah, more or less."

"What's the paper you were going to present? What was that all about?"

Were going to present? David didn't like the sound of that. "Uh, well, there were two of them. One was about MOCLU, which stands for 'molecular caulk and lubricant.' I invented it"—by accident!—"in the course of my other research. It doesn't do what it was supposed to, but it does have some interesting properties."

"Oh yeah?"

"Yeah. It was supposed to act as a kind of axle grease for nanomachinery, and in fact on the microscale—uh, that's on the scale of those computer-chip cooling fans you mentioned—it's very slippery and yet also has good cohesion, which makes it easy to work with. Unfortunately, on the nanoscale it acts more like a glue than a lubricant. It wrecked a lot of equipment before I figured out what was going on."

"I see. And what was the other paper about?"

David smiled. He was in his element now, suddenly at ease with his interrogator. "That's my baby. I've worked out a procedure for building chain drives on the nanometer scale. Like a motorcycle chain, you know? Or a bicycle. Only much, much smaller, obviously. To date, my smallest design consists of only about ten thousand atoms."

Mike Puckett pursed his mouth, and looked as if he were trying not to look startled. "Ten thousand *atoms?* I thought . . . You're talking about something much smaller than a human cell, right?"

"Yes, sir. Much smaller."

"You've patented this technology?"

"Well, yes, the MOCLU and the chain drive. Nobody holds a patent on the basic nanotech idea, although Vandegroot thinks he does. *Thought,* I mean."

"Is that why you killed him?"

"I *didn't!"* David snapped, his face growing suddenly hot. Where had *that* come from?

Puckett leaned back and smiled, a little sheepishly, maybe. "I'm sorry. That's a crude tactic, but sometimes it works. I had this guy last month, hijacked a truck and . . . Well, never mind. Please continue?"

"With what?" David asked, his voice edgy.

"You fought with Otto Vandegroot last night, correct?"

"In front of a million witnesses, yeah. That doesn't mean I killed him afterward. And for the record, I did *not* break his arm."

Puckett shrugged. "I didn't say you did. I've read the coroner's site report, and it doesn't mention anything about broken bones. The murder weapon was inserted under the base of the skull, just above the first vertebra."

"Yeah," David said sourly, "and it had my fingerprints on it."

"Otto Vandegroot was a famous man. The Sniffer King, you call him, right? Why did you fight with him?"

"I beat him in court recently. He was upset. He'd been drinking. He pulled a sword on me."

"So you pulled one on him?"

"No!" David snarled, jerking slightly at his chains. "Damn it, how many times do I have to say this? It was *not my sword.* Somebody pressed it into my hand."

"Who?"

"I don't know. I wasn't watching when it happened."

"Looks like nobody was; the eyewitness accounts don't mention it."

"It happened."

"Well, witnesses don't always see everything, and they don't always tell everything. I'll ask around. Have you ever owned a drop foil?"

David shook his head. "I don't even know how to use one. I've never taken a fencing class."

"You won the fight," Puckett said, leadingly.

"Not with the sword. I twisted his arm until he fell over."

"Are you trained in martial arts?"

"Street Defense is mandatory at U of Phil. Too many muggings, too many rapes. That training really sinks in, though. I didn't mean to hurt him, but he was an asshole, and I was upset."

"Understandably," Mike Puckett allowed. "Look, we seem to be going ten directions at once, here. Why don't we cool off for a minute, and then take the whole thing from the top again, OK?"

David licked his lips. "How many times am I going to tell this story?"

"You've been watching too many movies," Puckett

said reassuringly. "These days, testimony from a suspect is not very useful to us. Too many gray areas, too many civil rights issues. For the most part, we let the physical evidence speak for itself."

"But the physical evidence points to me!" David protested.

"Well, that's why I'd like to hear your side of things. It may help my investigation."

David *definitely* didn't like the sound of that; from Puckett's tone and manner, it was clear there were no plans for his release.

"I don't like the way this is going," he said, sitting up straighter. "I want my phone call. My lawyer's in Philly right now, name of T. Bowser Jones. I'm not saying another word until I hear from him."

A look stole across Mike Puckett's face, just a flicker of emotion that came and went in half a moment. *If that's the way you want to play it,* the look had said, *I'll just pack up my sympathetic ear and do this by the book. Too bad, really, because I was starting to believe you.*

"Of course," Puckett said, standing, picking up the recorder, and returning it to his pocket. "You're well within your rights. I'll see that the arrangements are made."

The agent's face was far less open than it had previously been.

CHAPTER FIVE

A vidcell phone was set up in front of David, on the table just out of his reach. Numbers were punched. Tones sounded, and an image appeared.

"Bowser?" said David.

The officers, whose looks and voices went right through David as if he were part of the furniture, left the room, clicking the door very solidly shut behind them.

"Hey, buddy," said the face on the vidphone screen. Bowser appeared to be looking up at David through a distorting lens, making eye contact only intermittently; something out of view seemed to require much of his attention. The colors were weak, the image jerky. Shadows played weirdly across Bowser's face, and his voice came in with a background hiss that the noise filters couldn't quite take care of. "I hear you're in a bit of trouble."

"Bowser?" David said again. "Where are you?"

"I'm on my way; I'm on the interstate. It's about time you asked for me—I've been calling every ten minutes for the past couple hours, but they wouldn't put me through. Hyeon Chong is my only info source, but he doesn't know much. Have you talked to him yet?"

"To Henry?"

Bowser laughed. "I'll take that as a 'no.' He's there in the building with you, chewing his nails in the waiting room. I've also called your parents, by the way, and I left a message on Marian's machine. So that old fuck Vandegroot got switched off, did he?"

Words began tumbling from David's open mouth. "Bowser, I'm in *jail.* They think I killed Big Otto, and they're asking me all these *questions.* . . . I'm supposed to be presenting at the conference today. I'm supposed to . . . God damn, you've got to get me out of here. Can you do that?"

"I'm working on it, buddy; just hang tight. I need you to think about something, OK? Don't answer out loud, but I'm working on a plan right now, and it won't work if you're guilty."

The remark hit David like a slap across the face. He felt stunned, then stung, and then after a slight pause, angry. "Bowser," he said, the fury rising up like hot bile in his throat. "God damn!"

"Hey, relax." Bowser stared earnestly through the screen for a moment before looking back down at whatever lay in front of him. Highway traffic? His image jumped and rippled like the horizon on a hot day, and suddenly David understood the view. Bowser was in his car, his clanky old Jeep, with the video cellular clipped to the sunshade above him. The image fractal-approximated, digitized and compressed and then unpacked at David's end, losing a little resolution in every step. And blurring each time Bowser crossed a cell boundary, every twenty seconds or so. . . . How fast was he driving?

"How can you say something like that?" David demanded, his anger burning a little cooler now, but burning still.

Bowser shrugged. "Privileged conversation—the cops can't listen, and even if they do, they can't use the information. Plus, we're encrypted."

"I did not kill Otto Vandegroot," David said tightly. "I don't have any idea who did."

"Hey, I didn't need to hear that. Sorry to get your blood pressure up—OK?—but I'm trying to swing a deal for you. Do you know what a Fellmer scan is?"

"The lie detector?" David asked uncertainly. Did Bowser still think he was lying?

Bowser nodded. "That's the one, yup. Very sophisticated, very reliable, very inadmissible in jury court right now. But if you say you're innocent and the machine agrees with you, I'm guessing we could sway the judge in a bail hearing, and get you back out on the street. Today, with any luck. Do *not* tell me whether your conscience is burdened with something you'd rather not reveal; just tell me whether you'd like to consent to a scan."

David nodded. "Yeah, fine. Whatever it takes."

"This is a big deal," Bowser cautioned. "They'll inject you with a tracer, which is mildly radioactive, and they'll put this thing on your head, like a giant helmety kind of thing, and it's going to be really uncomfortable. It may even hurt a little, and it'll take some time, about an hour. You'll bare your soul, too; they can scan your brain's reaction to a question even if you refuse to answer."

David thought about that. "So I waive the right to remain silent?"

"Under the Fellmer scan, yes, you do. That's why it's

inadmissible, because you can't defend yourself against a slanted interrogation. And if you've done anything else wrong, the scan will probably dig that up, too, and then the police will have probable cause for search and seizure warrants and they'll level more charges and keep you in court for the rest of your life. The thing comes straight from the Spanish Inquisition, I swear, but in this case, if you're sure you're clean . . ."

He looked thoughtful, troubled. "You know, the more I think about this, the more I don't like it. We set a precedent like this, maybe bail judges will start *expecting* a Fellmer scan. Refusing to take one could make you look awfully guilty."

"I'm not guilty!" David snapped.

"Relax, buddy, I didn't mean *you* you."

"I don't want to refuse," David told Bowser. "Set it up for me, I want to take the scan."

"Gee," Bowser said uneasily. "I wish I hadn't brought it up. I mean, if it was just you . . . Ah, screw it; this whole issue is coming to a head anyway. The Pandora's box is already open, you know? We might as well be the ones to cash in on it."

Bowser looked like a man who'd just decided to put his dog to sleep. What exactly was the big deal, here? Was he David's lawyer, or wasn't he? Precedent, schmecedent, David was not going to let himself get railroaded for a crime he didn't commit. And then an unpleasant thought occurred to him.

"Bowser Jones, how long have we known each other?"

"Twelve years," Bowser said.

David nodded. He'd been in ninth grade, Bowser in eleventh, when they'd first become friends. "Yeah. And you know, in all that time I don't recall you ever trying a criminal case. Hell, how many times have you even been inside a courtroom? Are you calling in help on this?"

At that, Bowser tipped back his head and laughed. "You forget, David, I've seen your bank account. I'll go to the mat for you on account of friendship, and that's good, because friendship is about all you've got to offer, unless you want to suck up your parents' retirement fund. If things get really hot, I can make some phone calls, OK?"

David did not laugh, did not crack a smile. This was *serious,* damn it. He scowled at the screen's jumpy image. "Do you even know what you're doing?"

"Nope," Bowser replied, half seriously. "But I got you through your P, T, and C, and I didn't know anything about that, either."

P, T, and C stood for "Patent, Trademark, and Copyright," the department of Extralegal Counseling Services Corporation that had handled the *Vandegroot v. Sanger* arbitration. And yes, Bowser had swept through that affair with remarkable aplomb, his oration and body language flawless, his case-law memory astonishing, his logic unassailable. Vandegroot's people had been on the defensive almost from the start, and their trenchworks had crumbled rapidly. Afterward, the ECS judge had remarked that had David been the plaintiff rather than the defendant in this case, he might well have won some money. The comment had been intended as a joke, but . . .

But it was true that inexperience never seemed to handicap Bowser all that much. A generalist, a Renaissance man, an expert on the subject of expertise itself, Bowser flitted from subject to subject, from hobby to hobby, mastering each one quickly and then dumping it for other pursuits. He wasn't even a lawyer, not really, not more than a few hours out of every month. He spent more time playing with his rental properties and his stock holdings, building and fixing things, adding to his license collection and his comic-bookish assortment of gadgets and toys.

He was one of *those* people, not idly rich but rather accomplished, fulfilled, self-made and self-regulating, the sort of person who kicked through life like it was one long Saturday afternoon. That was a rare talent, in David's experience, and one that went unnoticed and unappreciated by those few who possessed it. It was annoying as hell, really.

But if it came down to it, if things got really bad and David found himself spending long hours inside a courtroom, fighting for his life, he would rather do it with Bowser's assistance than without. So let the man operate his own way, at least for now.

"I'll set up the scan for you," Bowser said, after David's long silence. "There's a beta unit being tested there at Druid Lake."

"OK." David's voice had calmed and softened. "That would be great. I appreciate it."

"No problem," Bowser said. Static replaced his image on the telephone screen.

The bail judge glanced down at David, and at Bowser beside him. His look was precise, thoughtful, at once critical and impartial. *How much do I trust these young men?* he seemed to be asking himself. *What price can I place on that trust?*

On the other side of the room, the DA's assistant sat with one of David's arresting officers. The two of them looked alert; new evidence had just been introduced, piped to the judge by Special Agent Puckett, and things had swung once more in favor of the defense. It annoyed David greatly, that this seemed to surprise them all so much.

"So," the judge said, leaning slightly over the bench, menacing David with his dark and unsympathetic face, "you didn't leave the hotel room during or after the phone call to your girlfriend. Your testimony indicates you were actually *on* the phone at the time of the murder, but your girlfriend can't confirm this for us, because she hasn't been home all day."

"I, uh . . ." David shrugged, not sure how to answer. Under the falsewood table, Bowser waved him to silence.

"Fortunately for you," the judge went on, "the hotel's phone and door lock records support your story. And we have this . . . brain scan."

The judge looked troubled, as Bowser had. And indeed, after experiencing the Fellmer scan firsthand, David knew they were right to worry about it.

The experience had the same quality in his memory as a long-ago tooth extraction: clinical, controlled and yet nightmarish, smothering and inescapable. And they hadn't given David the injection Bowser had promised, but a whiff of gas instead, which had reinforced the overall dental impression. Details were fuzzy in his mind, but he remembered a machine-generated voice, firm and commanding, low in register but androgynous in inflection. The voice had asked him questions, over and over it seemed, and he had mumbled replies to it, replies that went unacknowledged. Had they listened to his voice at all? Had they needed to?

If this process should fall into the wrong hands . . . David shuddered. Cognitive brain scanning should be a thing of wonder, of healing and progress and understanding. *If I could read your mind, love* . . . But such things were years away, at best. Why did the easiest applications always have to be so awful?

The hotel's door lock records were another example—they supported David's innocence, yes, but why would the hotel care how he came and went? What business was it of theirs? Deterring theft by the hotel's own employees was the only reason he could think of, but it seemed a flimsy pretext. Hell, why not just put them all under Ma Fellmer?

"What we have here is a very public murder," the judge said. He seemed to note David's discomfort, seemed now to be weighing it along with the other evidence. "People don't have much patience with that anymore, so I expect there'll be a lot of pressure for a quick resolution. Is there anything you'd like to tell this court? Anything you've overlooked? Anything that will help speed the process along?"

His eyes, a darker, more penetrating brown than his skin and hair, bored into David, probing his soul. *Are you guilty?* the eyes demanded. *Did you kill the man, shove a drop foil through his brain? Come clean; do it now.*

"No, sir," David said evenly.

The eyes cooled, the muscles around them relaxing. The judge eased back a little in his chair. "That's 'no, Your Honor,' " he corrected. He glanced at the screens and papers in front of him, glanced over at the prosecution, then back at David once again.

I hate being a defendant, David thought. *Or a suspect, or a witness, or whatever the hell I am this time. I hate that look.*

"I don't see anything in here that contradicts your story," the judge said. His voice was gentler now, sounding almost friendly. "The victim had a lot of enemies, and I gather a great many of them were in a position to commit the crime. I support the defense's recommendation that you be released on your own recognizance. Does counsel have any objection?"

"No, Your Honor," Bowser said quickly.

"No, Your Honor," the assistant DA echoed, less quickly and with considerably less enthusiasm.

"Very well then. Bailiff, will you please uncuff the suspect?" He turned once more to David. "Mr. Sanger, we're going to return you to the police station, where your personal effects will be returned to you. Be aware there's some paperwork involved in outprocessing, particularly since the investigation is still open."

"Thank you, Your Honor," Bowser said, elbowing David in the ribs as he rose from his seat.

"Thank you, Your Honor," David agreed. He did not say, "It's been a pleasure."

CHAPTER SIX

"Hey, don't get mad at me," Mike Puckett was saying. "You don't like the paperwork, I'm sorry. We'll be charged penalties if we don't keep the proper records, and I am personally committed to seeing that doesn't happen. Hey, if you go wrong with those papers I need to know about it. We are asking for it for the law, because we need to know the information. You are the law, OK? You and me and everyone else, let's try to make it work."

"That's a nice speech," Bowser said. He was still looking around, still amazed at the splendor of the hotel's lobby. Bowser didn't amaze easily.

"Twenty pages of forms does seem a little excessive," David muttered. "I wonder what you need with all that information."

Puckett shook his head. "Just be glad they let you come back here. They didn't have to, you know."

"They sure as hell did," Bowser said, bristling.

This time, it was David's turn to wave Bowser to silence. Enough. Enough.

He'd emerged, squinting at the late-afternoon sunlight, from Baltimore's Druid Lake District PD, and had vowed at that moment to put the whole affair behind him. He'd traded handshakes and small talk with Henry Chong, who had waited there patiently all day, forgoing the all-important AMFRI conference in his concern for David's safety, and then he and Henry had climbed into Bowser's Jeep and returned, as instructed, to the conference hotel.

It bothered David that the police could "instruct" him where to go, but of course he was still a murder suspect, still required to check in with the investigating officer, still required to log his movements and activities.

"I'm glad you're here," Puckett confided, to David and Henry Chong both. He waved a thick document at them. "I need a hand with this nanotechnology stuff. Someone gave me a copy of the conference proceedings, but I still have no idea what's going on here."

"How can we help you?" Henry asked.

Puckett waved the proceedings in the air again. "Some of these people were the victim's enemies, or detractors, or rivals. Some of these people are working in areas related to the victim's research. Some of these people stand to profit handsomely now that the Sniffer King is dead, and I'd like you guys to tell me who they are."

" 'Simplifying Assumptions in Gene Sequence Programming,' " Bowser read from the document's back cover as Puckett waved and pointed with it. " 'Proteins and Polymers, a Trade Study. Prevention of Ribosome Dissolution in DMSO-Based Suspensions.' Yeesh. David, is this really what you do for a living?"

Henry Chong nodded his head at Puckett. "This murder is a tragedy, Special Agent, and a disgrace on our profession. We will be happy to assist you in any way we can."

"Here, wait," David said, pulling a pen from his shirt pocket and clicking it to highlighter mode. "Give me that book, and we'll go through it. Can we use your table?"

"Absolutely," Puckett said. "Security is setting up an office for me on the second floor, but for the moment, *mi mesa es su mesa.*" With a flourish, he stepped aside, letting David set the book down and spread it out at its contents page. Henry crowded in next to him.

"Once more," Henry said quietly, "let me say I'm relieved to see you free. I never doubted your innocence."

"Uh, thanks." David shrugged uncomfortably. Then, he spied something on the page in front of him. "Fiske. Robin Fiske."

"Ah," Henry said, nodding.

David ran his highlighter over the name, and the title of the associated paper: "New Avenues in Enzyme Switching." "Cool," he said after checking his watch. "Presentation is in forty minutes. Last show of the day. This looks good; I want to go."

He looked up pointedly at Mike Puckett. "If it's OK with you." His tone betrayed his resentment. He hadn't spent two hours on the crowded, run-down train from Philly to get in any swordfights, to get arrested, to spend his time as a murder suspect or an FBI informant. He'd already missed dozens of presentations, including two of his own, but he was here in Baltimore as a *scientist,* damn it, and it was high time he looked at some science.

"Who is Robin Fiske?" Puckett asked neutrally, not visibly fazed by David's ire.

"She is a scientist, inventor," Henry said, looking up from the conference proceedings. "Do you know the word *enzyme?*"

Puckett frowned slightly. "That's like a hormone, isn't it?"

"Similar," Henry agreed. "An enzyme catalyzes a chemical reaction. It, uh, speeds up. Sometimes inside a living organism, sometimes in the laboratory or the factory. One type of reaction, only, per enzyme. You understand this?"

"I guess. How is Robin Fiske connected with this?"

"Fiske invented switchable enzymes. Two shapes, sometimes three, to catalyze different reactions without changing solution."

"And Otto Vandegroot stopped her," Puckett said, catching on.

"Blew her off the map," David mourned. "It sucked; we really needed that stuff."

Henry nodded. "Switching was accomplished with chemical triggers. The American courts ruled that this broke, uh, *violated* Vandegroot's sniffer patents."

"Wait a minute," David said, suddenly uneasy. "What happens now? We've given you her name; does that make her a suspect? Are you going to take her downtown?" *And chain her to a wall?* he did not say.

"We just want to talk to her," Puckett said mildly. "I'll put her name on the interview list. And yes, you can go see her presentation, if you finish helping me with this list first."

"Wow, thanks," David said. "Can I make a phone call, too?"

"Sure," Puckett agreed, his smile crisp with professional courtesy.

"It's the jailbird," Marian said with some surprise. "Are you out? Are you OK?"

"Well, I'm out," David said.

"Did they find the killer, then?" Her expression was alert, interested. Things like this did not ordinarily happen, and perhaps that had awakened the reporter within her, Too, there was likely some genuine concern for his welfare. Marian felt things, he suspected, rather more deeply than she let on.

"No," David said, "they just released me for lack of evidence. Not that they didn't try."

She quirked an eyebrow. "You *are* innocent, I hope?"

"Yes." He felt no more than a flicker of outrage. Why did everyone keep asking him that?

Marian slipped him an easy grin. "The killer is still at large, then? Wow, I bet *that* livens up the conference a bit. You were right, I should have come with you."

"I'll give you a full report when I get home," David said, the sarcasm thick and grating in his voice. "You want pictures with that?"

She paused, her smile vanishing. "Are you OK, David?"

He shook his head. His throat had tightened, his eyes begun to sting. The depth of his own feeling came to him as a shock. His heart was full, as Bowser would say, of maggots.

"They chained me to a wall," he quavered. "They scanned my head with this . . . They thought I was a killer. They treated me like a killer."

Marian's forehead creased up with worry lines, her expression working oddly around guilt and contrition, two features that seemed utterly foreign to it. "I didn't mean to make fun of you," she said.

He just looked at her, puzzled and surprised.

"Well, I guess I did mean to, but I didn't mean it to be, um, mean, you know?" She went on, the words spilling from her mouth, faster and faster still. "After last night, I should know, you know, not to make fun when something's happened, but it's just how I am. I just joke about things. I just *do.*"

"I know you do," David said, taken aback by this rare display from her.

It came to him suddenly that the Marian he knew, the Marian he loved with such exasperation, was a mask: a tough hide wrapped around some different, secret person. Almost simultaneously, he realized that the same could be said of him, could be said of any human who had ever lived. It was one of those moments, those rare, insightful moments when an eye seemed to open up in the side of his brain, taking in the view from an area he hadn't known was blank. He sensed the conference around him seething with people: tiny, misshapen creatures lurching around in suits of adult skin. And on the heels of that came an even stranger thought, a question: what sort of creature had dwelt inside Otto Vandegroot? Secret dreams, secret fears, guilty pleasures hidden away. *What did you dream, Otto?*

"You don't look so good," Marian fretted.

"No. No, it's been a long day." He made a show of checking his watch. "Listen; there's a presentation in a couple of minutes that I want to see. I just called so you wouldn't worry."

"Well, thanks," she said uncertainly. "You should call your parents, too."

"Yeah, I have, thanks. Bye. I love you."

He cut the connection without waiting for her reply.

A hand landed firmly on his shoulder.

"You! David Sanger, who let you out of prison?"

Reflexively, he lowered his shoulder, bent his knees and turned to face the owner of hand and voice. It was a woman, middle-aged and frumpy-looking. One of the Germans, one of Vandegroot's lesser confidantes. At this moment, David couldn't recall her name.

"Get your hand off me," he warned.

But the woman merely dug her fingers in deeper. "Murderer, did you escape from the police? Or perhaps they simply let you go. Did they give you back your filthy weapons?"

He grabbed the woman's hand and *turned* it, then adjusted his fingers and pushed. The elbow locked and the wrist bent back, and suddenly the German woman was crying out and leaning over, her fingers open and away from David's shoulder.

This was Wrist Twist Number One, a simple maneuver that David's Street Defense instructor had called "the most effective pain compliance measure you are ever likely to need." David had done it without thinking, moved as he might move to keep a door from closing, or a bottle from falling over. With a shift of balance he could throw the woman to her knees. Adding a sweep with his left hand, he could cause her permanent injury, dislocating her arm, tearing at the muscles and ligaments that held it in place.

He let go of her instead, staring down into her upturned face. Fear had replaced her righteousness; she had laid her hands upon a dangerous man, her expression said, a killer, and now she was at his mercy. Her wince as she straightened let David know she was expecting a blow, expecting him to ball his right hand and smash her with it, in the face, in the stomach, in some vulnerable and painful place. She held up an arm to ward him off.

David felt a little sick. He hadn't meant to hurt her, not even to scare her. He just wanted her not to touch him.

"The police are here," he said. "Go talk to them, if you want, but leave me alone. I haven't done anything to you."

"You," she said darkly, backing away. "People will know about you. I'll *tell*."

"Just leave me alone," David said again, and turned away.

She wouldn't, of course. No one would leave him alone this conference, would leave him alone at all, ever, until Big Otto's killer was found. The long, long weekend stretched out before him, daunting and demoralizing. He just wanted to talk shop, damn it. His MOCLU, his chain drive, his dissociated ideas bouncing loose through the insides of his skull. And the dissociated ideas bouncing around in *other* people's skulls, waiting for a trigger event to bring them alive. Nucleation, crystallization, the spontaneous self-assembly of complex systems—David had seen it happen a hundred times. Two people are talking and then, suddenly, there is a Grand Scheme where before there was nothing. Like a message from the future, telling you how things would be, how they would happen. Like a message from *God.*

He checked his watch again: two minutes to Robin Fiske's presentation, which he *damn* well wanted to see. He hurried back to the lobby to collect Bowser and the others.

The lecture proved more interesting than David could have hoped. Robin Fiske's original concept, now almost five years old, had involved simplifying natural enzymes by stripping away their excess material and reproducing only the active sites, plus minimal molecular structure to hold it all together. The resulting assemblages looked like children's jacks, and were "switchable" only to the extent that one or two of the prongs were hinged and could, in the presence of negative ions, be induced to pop from one stable position to another. Very clever, but dependent on enormous search and optimization algorithms to find enzyme pairs that (a) could be used together and (b) could be represented conveniently with a single molecule.

Vandegroot, of course, had put a stop to all that.

Some people collapse under pressure, while others harden and prosper. Fiske, it seemed, fell into the latter category. Her new design was controlled by flashes of colored light, a method that would infringe no existing patents, but that was the least of its charms. The new enzyme was a cube, eleven nanometers on a side, with sixteen extendable rods on each face. Like a sort of puzzle box, it seemed to David.

"Conservatively," Fiske said of her creation, her eyes twinkling in the light of the viewgraph projector, "we estimate this design can emulate over sixty thousand commercial and industrial enzymes."

The audience gasped. David's hand shot up.

"Yes?" Fiske called on him, seeing his raised arm in silhouette against the window blinds.

"How close are you to market?" David asked the question eagerly, almost demandingly. This was something he could use, something that represented a giant stride toward real, applications-oriented nanotech. This was something damn near everyone in the *world* could use.

"We're not sure," Fiske replied. "It's RHT at the moment, and while we think we can get that overturned, it's going to take time. I can possibly get you a sample in the next year or so."

"RHT?" David said. "Already?"

She nodded. *RHT* stood for "Recognized Hazardous Technology," a label that would hinder commercial use outside of tightly controlled, high-security laboratories. David doubted his own facilities would qualify.

"That's stupid," he whispered to Henry Chong beside him. "It's just an industrial chemical. Drain cleaner is hazardous. *Bad weather* is hazardous."

"Be quiet," Henry whispered back.

"You're missing the point," Bowser whispered from David's other side. "Technology is power. You can't go around just *giving* it to people. Not if you want to keep your own."

"Be quiet," Henry repeated, "or leave."

But it was moot; Fiske seemed to have finished her presentation. She answered questions for a few minutes, and then formally concluded by switching the viewgraph projector off. Several people rushed forward to speak with her, a uniformed policeman and a hotel security guard among them.

David watched the men flash a document at her, watched the other scientists melt away into the background, uneasy. Fiske frowned at this intrusion, and guilt stabbed at David's heart. She was no murderer—why had he given Puckett her name?

"So," Bowser said beside him, his eyes on Puckett and Fiske. "Looks like they're taking her up to see the big guy. How does it feel to be a stoolie?"

"Terrific," David muttered. "Come on; I don't want to watch this. Is the bar open? Let's go get a drink."

"Buddy, I thought you'd never ask." Bowser looked over at Henry. "Hyeon, are you coming?"

Henry looked blank for a moment, then shrugged, his lips parting to form a narrow and humorless smile. "Why not? After this day, I think we all could use one."

The evening went badly for David, eyes and whispers following him wherever he went. The situation worsened when Puckett rejoined them, having "interviewed" a dozen or so "suspects" and grown weary of his own ignorance.

"I just don't see the point of all this," he said now from across the falsewood lounge table. "I don't understand what you all are trying to build."

"Tools of oppression," Bowser opined cheerfully. An elbow straw extended from his glass to his smiling lips, nudging aside a paper umbrella speared with fruit.

"A better world," David countered, with considerably less cheer. Then: "Can I ask you something? Why are you here? The Bureau must have one or two guys who know a little chemistry, at least."

With quick movements of his eyebrows and neck, Puckett managed to communicate a simultaneous note of respect and contrition, like a debater acknowledging a point. "As it happens, I *do* know a *little* chemistry, but you're right; my degree is in criminology. We have a couple of specialists on a plane right this very moment; they'll be here later tonight. They'll handle some of the more technical aspects of the investigation. But it's still my case, and I prefer to minimize my ignorance."

"Good for you," Bowser said, his tone such that David couldn't tell whether he was being sarcastic.

Henry Chong held up a hand and waved it at David and Bowser. *Shut up, you two.* "Our ultimate goal," he said, "is universal molecular assembly. The control of matter."

"Yeah," Puckett said, "but what *for?*"

"For anything. What do you want it to be for? That is what it's for. Like electricity, what is the purpose of that? When we control matter on a small-enough scale, it becomes possible to reorganize it. It becomes possible to create anything we want, even materials which cannot be fabricated by other means. Foamed diamond is an example, a material with very interesting thermal properties."

"It explodes," Bowser said.

Henry waved him off again. "At high temperatures, yes, but that is hardly my point. You cannot make diamond foam without very fine control over the crystallization process. When you gain that control, the world becomes a very different place."

Puckett pursed his lips, thinking. Slowly, he nodded.

"Hey Sanger!" came an anonymous voice from across the bar. "Plead guilty, asshole!"

Puckett and Chong and Bowser turned to see who had spoken. Silence fell.

David sighed. "I'm going to bed," he announced to the room. "Any further comments can be addressed to Special Agent Puckett, here. Good night." He rose from his chair.

"Oh," Bowser chided, "don't let some no-neck ruin your evening. Sit down."

"It's already ruined," David said. He threw a ten-dollar bill on the table and stalked away, his body language instructing the others not to follow him, not to bother him.

He almost wished, for simplicity's sake if nothing else, that he *had* killed Big Otto. And killed his cronies, too, every last one of them. Slowly.

CHAPTER SEVEN

"You're free to go," Mike Puckett told David glumly.

It was early Sunday afternoon, and the conference was winding down fast, like a tent city about to be moved. Except in this case, the tents were scattering, each loaded wagon heading off in a different direction. Such endings were always strangely sad, it seemed to David, but this time doubly so, as Puckett had failed in his search for a new prime suspect.

"Are you giving up?" David asked with some surprise.

"Not really," Puckett replied. "I've got a list of folks who left the hotel early, and I'll follow up on those. You have to admit, it'd be hard to play cool here all weekend if you'd murdered somebody. Be tough to stick around." His tone was leading, suggestive.

"I wouldn't know," David said quietly.

"Ah." Puckett clapped him on the shoulder. "Can't blame a guy for trying. Listen, you're still a suspect in the case, so check in with me at the D.C. office when you get back to Philly. And don't go anywhere else without talking to me, OK? That's a felony; I wouldn't want to see you get in trouble."

"I never go anywhere."

"I'm taking a taxi to the station," Henry Chong said, suddenly materializing at David's elbow. "Are you coming? The train will leave in about an hour." He turned to Mike Puckett. "He can leave now, yes?"

Puckett nodded. "Yes, please. Take him away. Call me if you hear anything. And hey, thanks for a lovely weekend." He cracked a professional, government-issue smile as he said this.

David hefted his bag, pulled it up higher on his shoulder. "Actually, I think I'll ride back with Bowser. He's got his car up here; it should be a little more comfortable than Amtrak."

"Ah," said Henry. "Well, then I will see you tomorrow morning. I'm . . . very sorry about what has happened. This would have been a very good opportunity for you."

"I know. Tell me about it."

"You understand there will be other opportunities? Many of them, many more than you can count. The future is long."

Tell that to Vandegroot, Bowser would say if he were here. David simply nodded.

"Have a pleasant trip," Henry said, turning to go.

"Thanks, you too."

"The eighteenth-century colonial gov'," Bowser was saying, "buddy, that was all brought down by a bad cold and a rather pathetic encryption scheme. I'll tell you the story sometime; it's not in your history books."

Traffic on the interstate was light, and Bowser was driving fast. Wind noise roared at them through open windows. It was warm outside, the sun shining down through puffy cloud islands low in the sky, and the interior of the Jeep was warmer still, so that David found himself wishing they had the hardtop off, had the wind blowing directly in their faces, ruffling through their hair. Muffling Bowser's incessant chatter.

He turned his attention once more to the cardfile box in his lap: Bowser's license collection. Well, the portable component of it, at least; Bowser had a file drawer full of wall certificates and such in his study at home.

Looking through the collection was always a little eerie, a keyhole peek at the strange world of Bowser's mind. Little plastic dividers split the cardfile into six categories, labeled TRANSPRT, COMMERCE, ADMIN, COMMNCATNS, MISC, and DANGEROUS. This last section was by far the most unsettling. What, for example, did Bowser need with a *License to Handle Class III Explosives?* Or a *Lab Chemistry Permit?* Even David didn't have one of those, and he was, technically speaking, a Doctor of Chemistry.

But with Bowser it was less a question of need than of possibility. Heavy-equipment operator? Just a quiz and a road test and a nominal fee. "You can get a license to do *anything,*" he was fond of saying, and if this cardfile were any basis for judgment, he was probably right.

"What percentage of these do you actually use?" David inquired.

Not surprisingly, Bowser ignored the question, as he always did.

". . . can't even buy a good judge these days," he was saying. "Not even in the private sector. What I wouldn't give for some corruption that worked in favor of the little guy!"

"You know, it's been a long weekend," David pointed out tiredly.

Bowser grinned at him. "One murder too many, eh? Personally, I think the old man had it coming. The Duke of Search and Seizure, you'd better believe he's put a lot of people behind bars. And pulled a lot of contraband out of average people's homes. That kind of thing tends to piss people off."

"Bowser," David sighed, "will you cut it with the politics already? *Professional rivalry* is what killed Big Otto."

"You seem awful sure."

"Oh, come on! He was killed in the middle of an AMFRI conference, in the middle of a thousand people who hated his guts."

"Hell of a cover, eh?" Bowser's grin had widened, and his eyebrows went up and down, Groucho Marx–style. "If I were going to kill him, that's exactly where I'd do it."

"I see," David said. "Obviously, it had to be a giant conspiracy, right? You really should have been a tabloid reporter."

Bowser lost some smile at that remark, and turned greater attention to the road ahead of them, to the cars and trucks he was weaving around. "I don't know who killed Big Otto, my buddy. I don't know who shot Kennedy, either, or who blew up the Golden Gate Bridge. Giant conspiracies are out there, some of them not even very secret. Take the Gray Party."

For a moment, David flashed on the memory, smothering and warm, of the Fellmer scan helmet locking in place over his chin, over his mouth and nose and eyes and ears. The scent of rubber was sharp and immediate in his nostrils, but then a gust of wind puffed at him and the scent and the memory were gone.

"The Gray Party?" he asked, feeling not entirely at ease. "What about them?"

Bowser shrugged. "The way they funded Vandegroot's research, the way they sheltered him. Vested interest. John Quince's name appeared on some of the *Vandegroot v. Sanger* documents that got lost. Witness for the prosecution, never called."

"That's all just rumors."

"Good rumors," Bowser said. "Well founded. Grays love the sniffer; they always have. How else do you restrict half the chemicals known to man? You drive around with a Vandegroot box until you catch a whiff of hemp, or gunpowder, or maybe it's *baby oil* this week, and then *bang,* you've got probable cause. Search and seizure warrant, coming right up, and you haven't even broke the Fourth Amendment."

David opened his mouth for a snide retort . . . and found that he had nothing to say. The Grays had promised to rid the streets of guns and bombs and drugs, and they had done exactly that. Crime hadn't gone away, of course; the armies of the dumb and vicious and desperately poor continued to swell, their rage turning boots and fists and everyday objects into weapons every bit as deadly as those that had gone before.

But things like poisonings and drug crimes and accidental shootings had all but disappeared from the American landscape, and for this accomplishment the Grays were vocal in their pride. They hadn't accomplished it alone, of course, not without the full cooperation of the police and the courts and the media, but the party had been at the center of the action right along. And the Vandegroot Molecular Sniffer had also been at the center, had *been* the center of the Crackdown on Crime. And as Big Otto's star ascended, the Grays had seemed to climb right along with him.

And he'd had all those *patents.* Two years of work, not even on the cutting edge, and Vandegroot had somehow managed to corner the entire classical nanotech market. And to hold it for more than a decade.

He's got friends in high places, people had said. *He's Grayer than a circuit court judge.*

"Aha!" Bowser cried out gleefully. "I made you think about it, didn't I? Didn't I!"

"Jesus," David said, turning to watch the trees and high, sound-blocking fences zip past them on the edge of the highway. "Sometimes I really hate talking to you. *Nobody* likes the Gray Party, Bowser. They're uptight and they're preachy and they've canceled all our favorite TV shows. The *voting public* hates them."

"Well, it's true they haven't won many elections at the national level, but then again they don't really need to. They've got the country by its roots. Any idiot can run for national office, sell his soul to the special interests, get beat up by the press . . . State and local control give you *leverage.* Get enough hearts and minds in your pocket—not a majority, mind you, just a good loud rabble—and the feds will come around to *you,* with that great big Uncle Sam hat held out like a beggar's cup."

David thought of the poster he'd seen on the wall at Druid Lake PD. America, the *solid* state. The stern but smiling face of John Harrison Quince floating gray and white above the words. "They're just a fad," he said quietly. "Like the Nouveau Whigs. Like the Birch Society. These things come and go."

"Most go." Bowser's tone was dark. "Some don't. We've got a disgruntled population facing poverty, facing *crime,* facing a government at least as repressive as the eighteenth-century monarchy it once overthrew. . . . And the government has some scary toys this time around. You remember that twelve-hertz burglar alarm of yours, the one that broke your eardrum? That's nothing, it's a toy compared to what they've got for crowd control these days. *Crowd control,* you think about that.

"Opportunists look for times like these. Balance of power way off-kilter, tensions high, all that. Somebody gets mad, tears things up a little, and *pow!* The headbreakers have an excuse. A few bad eggs in the right places and we'll all be walking around with numbered tattoos. How'd you like to see a bar code scanner on every public building? '*You,* come in; *you,* stay out. We don't like your face. We don't like your number.' "

"Jesus Christ, Bowser." David looked out the window again. His friend got like this sometimes, and there wasn't anything you could do but let him wind down. Arguing with him would just stoke his fires, and agreeing would have no effect at all. Not that David was inclined to agree; as obsessively suspicious as he was of everyone and everything, Bowser made an excellent gambler, an excellent computer programmer, and an even better attorney. He was great with taxes, too, finding loopholes the size of aircraft carriers and typing up long treatises to prove their legality, on the off chance that someone might someday question him. And somehow, he did all this with a wink and a grin and his feet on the table, in spare moments scattered among life's other games.

Only on the subject of politics did he grow serious. Politically, the sky was always falling for T. Bowser Jones, and if he chanced to look up he would crow and cry about it until he dropped from exhaustion. He was looking up today.

"How do you rise to power?" Bowser demanded, a full head of steam behind him now. "Easy; you find a constituency. Old people are good, because there are an awful lot of them, and the retired ones will work for you for free. So, you come up with a name and a story the old people can dig, and you give them what they want. Free money? Free medicine? Well, maybe a little, but those things are hard. Safe streets? Ah, that we can do. And then you're really moving, because *everyone* wants safe streets."

"Bowser," David said, unable to help himself, "I really

don't want to talk about this. I'm a scientist, you know. I do science."

Bowser scowled at him for a few moments before returning his eyes to the road. "Do you think that frees you from politics? Grubbing for funding, complying with regulations, doing only the science they say it's OK to do? My friend, you are a *slave* to politics."

"Excuse me?" Anger jerked at David like a tow rope coming tight, pulling him along behind it. "Do you understand what molecular fabrication *is?* Do you understand what it can *do?* We are talking about reorganizing matter at its most basic level, turning it into anything we want. Free medicine? Free food? Free houses? With nanotech those things are *easy.* We're right on the brink of it: the end of poverty. The end of crime. The end of human suffering as we know it."

Bowser made a noise, part giggle and part derisive snort. "Wow. Wow. I don't know what to say." He paused, looked up at the Jeep's bare metal roof for a moment, and then spoke again: "The end of human suffering."

"Well, more or less," David qualified.

Bowser paused for still a longer time, but after a few seconds he grinned and cast a sidelong look at David. "You realize, of course, you'll never get away with it."

And then, suddenly, they were both laughing.

CHAPTER EIGHT

David rang the doorbell a second time, and checked his watch. It was late for dinner, already past seven and getting toward dark, but Marian had insisted he come by to take her out. So where was she?

The door chain rattled, locks disengaging, and then the door opened, and there she stood. In the porch-light glare her hair was like fine copper, her eyes blue and sparkling.

"Hi," he said to her.

She took a step toward him, grabbed his shoulders, and kissed him. "Hi," she said when she was through.

"Are you ready to go?"

"Yeah. Just let me get the door." She fumbled with her keys, nearly dropped them before managing to lock everything that needed locking. She seemed to avoid eye contact with David as she did this.

"Is everything all right?" David asked her. He had a

funny feeling, suddenly. Like when the cops had come banging on his door, like when they had told him Vandegroot was dead. There was that inner *lurch,* his life switching tracks with an almost audible clatter. What was changing this time?

"Everything's fine," she said, still not meeting his eyes. "I thought maybe we could go to Deux Cheminees tonight, maybe soak our guts in butter and wine. It's kind of a schlepp, but it's still warm out, and—"

"Can't afford it," David said, quickly and automatically. It was something he said often. Then he thought about what she'd said and added, "Are you *crazy?"*

"No," she said quietly. "I'm not. It's my treat."

"Are you *crazy?"* he repeated. "Let's go to McDonald's. We'll get chicken sandwiches and soak *them* in butter; it'll be great."

Marian looked troubled. "I have the money, David. I . . . We need to talk."

"Oh," he said, drawing the syllable out. So *that* was it? *That* was the secret lurking behind her mask?

"No," she said quickly, catching his tone. "It's not what you think."

"Can't be seen with a murder suspect, eh?" David tried to make a joke of the comment, but it came out leaden. "Or is it the time thing again? Too busy for the best things in life?"

"David!" Marian *was* meeting his gaze now, and her eyes were blue as the hard, cold light of early morning. "I'm trying . . . OK, I guess this can't wait. I think there's a problem with our relationship."

"You just figured that out?"

She sighed, closed her eyes for a moment. "There's a certain . . . lack of warmth between us. A certain distance."

This can't be happening, David thought. So many bad things couldn't possibly occur in the space of three days.

It would upset the space-time continuum, hurtling them all into some kind of hyperspatial rift. No, it just wasn't possible.

"I think it's necessary," she went on, "that we move our relationship to a different level, one where we can exchange our feelings a little more honestly."

"It's very kind of you," he told her tightly, "but you don't need to buy me dinner to break up with me."

She blinked, blinked again, and burst out laughing.

David's face grew hot, his body stiff. Was that what she thought of him? Something to *laugh* at?

"Oh!" she said around her laughter. "That's funny! I was *trying* to ask you to move in with me!"

"What?"

"What?" she mimicked, still laughing. "Oh, you should have seen the look on your face. That was priceless. What possible reason could I have for breaking up with you?"

"I don't know," he said lamely. The switch of moods was too rapid for him; he hadn't found his equilibrium yet. She was going to ask him to *move in with her?*

"You'll need a tie," she said.

A tie? To move in with her? "Oh. You mean for the restaurant."

"No, for the zoo. What's *with* you tonight, David?" She held up her hands suddenly, palms forward. "Never mind. Hard weekend, I know, I'm sorry. Forget I asked. Should we stop off at your place? Have you got a tie?"

"Uh," David said, "I did, but it got ruined."

Vandegroot had stabbed him through it at the conference, mere hours before becoming a murder victim. White satin, flecked with blood. It might have passed for one of the newer patterns, despite the hole, but David had thrown it away, eager to be rid of it.

Marian frowned slightly. "It's too late to buy one.

Hmm. Maybe they have loaners there at the restaurant. Do you think so?"

A thought occurred to David. "Wait a minute; I have got another zipper tie. I used it for the dean's presentation last semester. It's at the lab."

"Well hey," Marian said, grabbing him playfully around the waist. "That's not too far out of the way. Let's go."

They walked to the bus stop without speaking, something they rarely did. The night seemed quiet for Philadelphia; he could hear her breath whooshing softly in and out, hear the quiet *clop, clop* of her shoes against the sidewalk.

"So, uh, what's going on at the *Bulletin?*" he asked, just to inject some noise into the evening. He didn't like this silence, the naked feeling of it. Silence implied a bond, a telepathy, a mutual understanding that rendered conversation moot, where in fact he thought of Marian's head as a black box whose inner workings could not be deduced from the inputs and outputs he observed. She wanted him to move *in* with her? Three months ago she'd balked at the idea of his keeping an extra *shirt* in her closet.

"Women are funny," Bowser would say, and really, that was what it came down to. Women were a regular barrel of laughs.

"Muckraking," Marian said, "as usual."

Tracking down corruption on the local scene, she meant, and encouraging public debate on issues beneath the notice of the bigger papers. In its latest incarnation, the *Bulletin* was distributed free, so they had to sell a lot of ads to make enough profit to keep going. So they had to please the small business owners, which meant they had to do a lot of fashion articles and review a lot of rock bands and restaurants and offbeat playhouses. That, and address social problems on the nanoscale, discussing what they meant, not to the city or even the neighborhoods, but to the individual human beings on East Lancaster or South Broad Street.

But muckraking was not a term Marian would normally use to describe this. It was a word other people threw around when they wanted to make a point, when they wanted to upset her.

"Sounds like I'm not the only one who's had a tough weekend," he observed.

"Ooh!" she said, venting sudden anger. "The universities have a hobby, and that's pulling down the *Bulletin.* If we get a positive letter from anyone, we can be sure we'll see another one that has a U of Penn or U of Phil return address, a letter that defines a very long list of reasons we should all go to hell. Universities are so damn conservative these days, hey, let's kill the messenger if we don't like the news. Then we just round up the poor and ship them off somewhere, and it's Miller time."

"Want to talk about it?" he quipped; with a start like that one she'd be impossible to silence. Like Bowser, she had her buttons, and it looked like he'd just punched a hot one.

But what she said was, "Not tonight," which surprised him. He waited for her to elaborate, but she didn't seem inclined to.

"Well," he said, trying on a little smile, "we don't want to talk about *my* weekend."

"It might make a good article," she replied seriously. "Page five stuff, half a column." She held up her hands as if framing invisible headlines. "GRAY BASTARD BITES IT: MURDER IN THE SOLID STATE."

A chill ran down his spine.

He tried to think of something to say, something clever that would make her laugh, that would make *him* laugh, but his mind was cold and blank. He felt the awful silence pressing down again. Surely he had to say something.

But just at that moment, the bus rounded the corner with a grinding of flywheel gears, and instantly Marian was lost, her mind elsewhere, her hands digging for tokens in the lower reaches of her purse.

"So," she prompted as they clomped down the dark, deserted corridor, "will you or won't you?"

"Will I or won't I what?" He fumbled with his keys, got the lab door unlocked.

"You have a short memory."

He opened the door, flicked on the light . . .

"Oh, my God," he said with quiet astonishment.

His lab was a shambles.

The counters had been cleared, the shelves emptied. The floor was covered in loose papers and fragments of . . . of everything. Someone had systematically smashed all his equipment, including the computer, including the SPM. And something else had been done to the computer, as well; a hole gaped in its front panel like a row of shattered teeth. The optical drive! Someone had stolen the optical drive!

He scurried in, his feet shuffling and crunching over the debris. The *backup tapes*. Where were his old notebooks, and more importantly, where were the fucking *backup tapes?* The shockproof, fireproof, burglarproof safe which normally held them stood open, its shelves bare.

What happened here?

A keening noise arose from his throat, a strange and inhuman noise. Five years' work was on those tapes. *Five years' work* had been stolen or destroyed or . . . The sound he heard himself making now was like cats in a fight, like a car engine running with the oil drained out. It was the sound of broken dreams.

Marian's hand touched his arm, and he started. Tears sprang from his eyes and streamed down his face in a steady flow, and he didn't want her to see that. He hadn't cried for Big Otto Vandegroot, hadn't cried for himself in the jail, in the courtroom, in the Fellmer chair. Hadn't cried when he'd thought Marian's love was slipping away. He hadn't shed a tear, for anything, in years.

But this was his *work;* this was everything he'd done since finishing his bachelor's degree. This was a horror beyond his ability to comprehend. He wanted to sit, *needed* to, but even his chair had been broken. Dizzily, he leaned against the counter.

"Who did this?" he managed to croak. "The *backup tapes* are gone. God damn it, who did this to me?"

"I'll call the police," Marian said.

"Do better than that," he told her, his voice still choked. He pulled out his wallet, dug around in it until he came up with Mike Puckett's card. "Call the FBI."

"OK." She took the card from him, touched her fingers briefly to his arm once again. "Don't touch anything, OK? They'll need to scan for fingerprints and things."

He turned on her, eyes blazing. "I know what a fucking crime scene is! Jesus!"

She took half a step back, startled.

"I'm sorry," he said. He cast a look around, and his tears started up fresh once again. "Use the lobby . . . use . . . Oh God, Marian, they even broke my phone."

She was at the doorway now, looking concerned and determined and unflappable. "Come with me," she commanded softly. "It's bad for you to stay here."

He couldn't think of a reply, or a reason to remain behind, so he went out into the hall with her. He carefully closed the door behind him, paused for a few moments to collect himself, and followed her down to the elevators.

"We'd better call Bowser, too," he said to her after she'd pressed the call button. "He loves an emergency. He loves a conspiracy. Maybe he'll know . . . what to do."

But what could be done? Bowser didn't have a magic wand he could wave to restore David's lab. Computer freak or no, Bowser couldn't recover data from tapes he didn't have. *Five years' work.* The nanoscale chain drive, intricate as a music box and smaller than the tiniest virus, was no more. MOCLU, the molecular caulk and lubricant that, unfortunately, jammed nanomachinery rather than oiling it, was no more. Even the propeller/motor he'd designed for his master's thesis, mostly cribbed from the flagellar motors of natural blue-green algae, was gone.

He thought of his off-site backups, a patchwork of optical drive dumps five or six months out-of-date, most likely incomplete. . . . His stomach fluttered. What if those were gone, too? With them, and with enormous effort, he could probably reconstruct a good deal of what was lost. But without them . . . There would be nothing he could do, short of starting over again from scratch. Was such a thing even possible?

Marian said something to him as they boarded the elevator, something about how the police would be here soon and they would do something, make things better somehow. He nodded, not really listening, not planning to answer. What could he possibly have to say?

Soon they were in the lobby. The floor tiled with waxy-smelling blue linoleum, the bare cement walls hung with bulletin boards and framed posters: a DNA molecule, a monkishly illuminated copy of the periodic table, a map of the Schrödinger equation for the porbitals of an atom.

Marian found the phone, punched Mike Puckett's number into it. Waited, introduced herself when he answered, and then explained the situation. David heard the words "laboratory" and "sabotage" mentioned several times. He did not hear "backup tapes" or "chain drive" or "five years' work completely and utterly destroyed."

Puckett asked questions for a while, and Marian told him what she knew. This conversation ran down quickly, though, and Puckett soon asked to speak to David.

"I don't think he's in a speaking mood," Marian said, looking over her shoulder at David, sitting on the floor with his back to the cement wall.

"Let me talk to him anyway."

Frowning, she nodded, then turned and extended a hand to David as if to help him up. The gesture was courtly and fluid, like something from a play, something utterly incongruous with the mood of this night. David accepted her hand, stood with her help. Puckett's face looked startled on the telephone screen.

"Jesus, Sanger, you look like hell."

David nodded. "Yes, hell. That's a good word for it, I think."

CHAPTER NINE

The crime-scene technicians did their work slowly and meticulously, creeping through the wreckage with their rubber gloves and their tweezers, their fingerprint scanners and thermal imagers, and that wheeled sniffer that looked like an oversized vacuum cleaner. Two men moving slowly through the room, and one woman who scurried around looking at everything, speaking into a dictation recorder that was mounted to her wrist with something like a watch band.

A local police supervisor stood by, speaking with Special Agent Puckett on video cellular link. The picture phone looked fat and heavy in his hands.

A smoldering outrage coursed through David, burning away his grief. Even this helpful invasion felt like a rape, the officers' questions like glaring accusations. And there were a lot of questions: where had he been? When had he discovered the damage? Did he know anyone who might have a grudge against him?

"My only enemy is dead," he had told them, and referred them back to Puckett for the details. David couldn't stand talking to them, could barely stand even to look at them. It was all he could do to keep from throwing them bodily from his lab. But the police, of course, were not the real targets of his anger.

When first confronted with Big Otto's death, he'd been stunned that anyone might think him responsible for it. But now he knew better: murder was well within his capability. If the destroyer of his lab were here right now, David would crush the life from him with his bare hands, squeeze the bastard's neck until his fingers punched through the flesh to the red pulp beneath. He understood this as a matter of simple fact, as he understood the pull of Earth's gravity.

"You're not being fair." Bowser's voice drifted in from the hallway. He and Marian were having some sort of argument out there. "There's nothing inherently political about a police force. Society needs to enforce its laws somehow."

"But where do they get off questioning David?" asked Marian. "Stormtroopers! What does he need an alibi for? Nobody could believe he'd do something like this to *himself,* destroy his own work."

"They're *supposed* to be suspicious, budette; they're the police. You want to get mad, get mad at the city council."

"Republicans and Grays," she muttered.

Bowser snorted. "Humanitarians versus everyone else, right? That's how you see the world. Listen, budette, nobody can punish the innocent like a humane, statist social engineer with a lock on the police. The effect is random at the user level."

"You're full of shit," Marian said. "You always act like

you know more than the rest of us, but where does all this privileged information come from? Huh? Name your source."

"Well hello, Professor," said Bowser. "What brings you here this evening?"

There was silence for a moment, and then a new voice. "Hello, Mr. Jones, Ms. Fouts. Special Agent Puckett called me; I . . . heard what happened."

Henry Chong? David looked to the doorway, saw his mentor there. They made eye contact, gaze locking into gaze, the subtle twitching of facial muscles sending high-bandwidth signals between them.

Henry: *Look at all this damage! Are you all right?*

David: *No, of course I'm not. Just think how* you *would feel.*

Henry: *Your point is taken. I am so sorry for you, my pupil.*

David: *That doesn't help much.*

Henry stepped forward, gingerly avoiding the broken glass on the floor. "David," he said.

"It's all gone," David explained flatly. "Every bit of it, five years. Please tell me you have my off-site backups."

Henry looked troubled. "I keep them in my filing cabinet at home. I couldn't find them, David. Nothing is missing; there is no damage. . . . But I cannot find your tapes."

Somehow, this final, total outrage did not seem at all surprising. It seemed logical, almost anticlimactic. David simply grunted. "I really am sunk, then."

"I will do what I can to help you," Henry said. "I am so sorry."

"Yeah, well. Thanks." He'd been fidgeting with the cord from his broken telephone, but now he threw it down on the counter and looked away.

Henry cleared his throat. "David. It's understandable that you should be upset, but I see you are torturing yourself by watching this procedure. I see no point in that. Maybe you had better go home."

"I can't," David said. "I have to know who did this to me. I have to know *why.*"

Henry's face darkened. "I should have been more clear: you are not helping anyone, least of all yourself. I am telling you now to leave. Let these people do their jobs."

"Yes, sir," David snapped.

The scowl deepened. "I will speak with your friends, and they will take you home. The authorities believe this matter is related to Otto Vandegroot's death, and that seems like a good theory to me. But you will not test it by sulking here."

"Did you come all the way down here just to tell me that?" David asked. "No backups, go home?"

"I am the department head," Henry replied. "I will have to explain all this to the dean tomorrow morning. And about Otto, and everything that's happened. But yes, I would have come down here anyway, out of concern for you. And out of concern for you, I am now throwing you out."

"Fine," David said, sliding down off the countertop he'd been using as a seat. "I'm leaving. Thank you for your help."

"You're welcome," Henry said, choosing to ignore the irony in David's tone.

"It'll be OK," Marian said for the thousandth time as David chained and bolted his apartment door, sealing them away from the evils of the night.

"It will not," David said. "Please stop telling me that."

"What I mean is, you'll survive this."

"Probably," he agreed, meeting her ice-blue gaze. "Is that supposed to make me feel better?" He turned away, grabbed his stack of mail and rifled through it as if something important might be hidden there. Nothing ever was, of course, nothing but bills and ads.

"Come on, David," Marian said, "let it go for now. Try to relax. It doesn't help you to get all twisted up right now."

"Something's happening," he said, his attention still on the mail. "I'm caught in something, and I don't know what it is. There's been a *murder*."

Marian absorbed this thought in silence.

"I'm scared," he said, only just realizing this himself. He felt hollow, ringing with loss and confusion and pain, and part of the pain was simple fear, the sharp, glittery edges of it cutting him up inside like bits of cold glass.

Again, Marian said nothing, but she moved in closer, pressing lightly against his back. Where they touched it was instantly warm. Her arm came around his chest, enfolding rather than squeezing. He felt the familiar sparks inside.

Turning, he dropped the mail and kissed her. His urgency surprised them both, and in another minute they were falling out of their clothes, trying to unfold the bed without breaking their mutual contact. The sheets formed an envelope of cool satin, warming rapidly as they slipped inside.

"Command: lights out," he managed to tell the computer before his brain switched off.

In the darkness their lovemaking was fluid and passionate, their bodies blending together in a single warm fog.

CHAPTER **TEN**

The phone was ringing, a limp electronic bleating that sounded twice, paused, then sounded twice more. "Command: no picture; answer," David said, sitting up, opening his eyes to the blankness of his sleep mask. Then, "Hello?"

"Sanger." The disembodied voice came out of David's stereo speakers. "I need to ask you some questions. It's urgent."

David slipped off the mask and rubbed his eyes. "Puckett?"

"That's right. Are you awake?"

Seven-oh-eight A.M., the clock said, sitting in a little pool of fresh, glaring sunlight that made him squint.

"No. What's going on?"

"We have a suspect. We need to know if you've seen him."

Now David was awake. "Suspect? You mean for my lab?"

"Maybe for everything," Puckett said. "I think you know him. It's a young guy, name of Jacobs."

"Dov Jacobs? That's impossible," David said, reaching for yesterday's shirt.

"Not impossible. He checked out of your AMFRI conference about half an hour after the murder, and he came straight back to U of Phil, by car. He was on campus at the time your laboratory was trashed. Credit reports show he's still in the area."

"I haven't seen him. Listen, this is impossible. Dov Jacobs wouldn't hurt anybody; he's a . . ." A classic nerd. Smart, small-framed. Gets bloody noses running down stairs too fast. "He's a pussycat."

"Otto Vandegroot sued him and won," Puckett said.

That was true, but . . . Dov?

"This doesn't make any sense."

"Has he ever been in your lab?"

"Sure," David said, "lots of times."

"How recently?"

"I . . . I don't know. A few months ago, maybe."

"His fingerprints are all over the place. It's not conclusive, but we're certainly going to pick this guy up and talk to him. Do you know where he might be staying?"

"In his dorm room?" David asked, using one stupid question to answer another.

"Nope. His door hasn't been opened since Friday. We dumped the records."

David felt a chill. Those damn door-lock records again. When had doors started turning into police informants?

"I haven't seen him. I don't know where he is."

Puckett paused. "We'll find him. Get back to you later."

"OK," David said. "Command: exit."

A dial tone replaced Puckett's voice, and was in turn replaced by silence.

"What is it?" Marian asked sleepily.

"I don't know." He leaned over, gave her a hasty peck of a kiss. "Stay sleeping, hon; I'm going back to the lab. If the cops are through I can maybe start cleaning up."

"Is it eight o'clock yet? I have to get up. I've got a meeting." Her voice was little more than a mumble. Clothed in blue underpants and sunlight, she lay sprawled, her slender form managing to take up nearly three-quarters of the bed. Absently, she pulled the sheet up to cover herself.

David felt the stirrings of desire, and promptly buried them. Something was going to happen today; he could feel it in the air like crackling static. Anyway, it was Monday morning and he was expected at work sooner or later, lest his grants be endangered.

"I haven't forgotten your question," he told her.

"Mmm. That's good." She opened her eyes and looked at him sleepily. "Just for the record, I'm not talking New Motherhood and joint checking."

"Yeah, I understand that. We've both got our work."

"I just want to be closer to you."

He didn't know what to say to that. It sounded good, but . . . But what? His mind wasn't on this; he couldn't think straight.

"Your place is bigger," Marian said, "and I like the location. But we'd have to get rid of some furniture, and you'd *have* to clean up the files on that house computer. Most of that stuff hasn't been touched in years, and there's hardly any room left for voice mail—"

"Wait," he said, a little too sharply. "This is too fast for me. I have . . . a lot on my mind right now. Give me time to think."

Her face fell. "Time? How much time?"

He forced a smile. "I love you, Marian. Just give me a day or two, OK?"

"OK," she said uncertainly. "Do you want me to come over tonight?"

"Um, sure."

She snorted, half amused. "Don't pull a muscle, David. I'll stay home and dial a movie."

"Well, OK," he said, letting his voice sound disappointed. And really, he *was* disappointed. Sure, he was relieved—it was one less thing for him to worry about today—but Marian understood that and was letting him off the hook, which paradoxically made him *want* to be with her.

Bah, this was twisting his mind all in knots. It was time to face the day, time to face the ruins of yesterday. Where the hell had his shoes ended up?

The air was cooler this morning, the breeze a little chilly against his face as the bike thrummed beneath him. Just over twenty miles per hour, he judged, watching the cement wall whiz by him on one side, the steel framework of the elevated track on the other. The narrow groove that ran alongside the Green Line tracks south of Fairmount Park made an excellent bike trail, smooth and level and uninterrupted by traffic signals. Few cyclists knew about it, however, which was good, considering David had only eight inches' clearance on either side.

A daily fear gnawed at him, that he would encounter another bicycle coming the other direction on one of the curves. High speed, low visibility, nowhere to go . . . What would a head-on bicycle collision look like? Not good, certainly. His other, lesser fear was that he'd lose control on a patch of ice some winter and scrape a hand off on one of the sides.

Still, despite these fears, or possibly because of them, David found his twice-daily ride a cleansing experience, an opportunity to scrub his mind of everything but the basic problems of his work. Feeling the atoms in his mind, fitting them together like Lego blocks, trying to picture what would work and what wouldn't.

But today, his mind would not be cleansed. The only problem he faced was the Ragnarok, the Armageddon of his demolished lab. What could he do on this, the day after the end of the world?

He rode hard, feeding the pain and the fury into every pump of his legs. But the bad feelings seemed to grow stronger, not weaker, as he pedaled. The cement and the metal stanchions flew by, faster and faster. In no time at all, he was out of the groove, rocketing out to the sidewalk of Forty-sixth Street.

Pedestrians suddenly crowded the way ahead of him, but rather than dodging them individually, he spotted a hole, a straight-line course that would carry him through. Two people shouted protests at him as he flashed past, but he didn't slow down at all, even when the light on Leidy Avenue turned yellow ahead of him. The crosswalk sign had stopped flashing, its DON'T WALK icon glowing like the red-hot hand of Satan.

David hopped the curb and shot across the intersection, right between the screeching traffic on the right and the parked cars on the left. He was *faster* than the traffic; he was the fastest thing on the road. *I am utterly fearless,* he thought, and then: *I am riding like an idiot.* The turnoff for University of Philadelphia was there on his right, shaded by maple trees whose leafy green was already giving way to red and gold. He cut between two cars and jerked the handlebars hard over. Too hard. Belatedly, he squeezed his back brake, not daring to touch the front one lest the bike do a forward cartwheel with him still on it.

The back brake was not enough, however, to save him; he laid down a black line on the pavement, skidding, feeling his balance shift. The wheels slipped out from under his center of mass, and he was moving not down the length of Regents Street, but across it at a forty-five-degree angle, right toward the bookstore and its plate-glass windows. Fortunately, a parked car was there to break his skid. He was going a good fifteen miles an hour when he hit it, and his stomach went giddy as he flipped up and over. *It's a blue Chevy Schwing,* he thought irrelevantly. *Dent-proof plastic body. Huh, it feels solid enough.* The *world* was doing cartwheels now, until the sidewalk came up and slammed him hard.

For a time, it seemed he knew nothing.

Then, he knew that it was difficult to breathe, and on the heels of that he learned that his chest hurt, where the roof of the Chevy had struck it.

His arm hurt as well, and his shoulder.

He sat up, and found he was somehow ten yards farther down the sidewalk than he'd thought. A few pedestrians stood by, looking alarmed.

"Hey," one of them said, walking cautiously forward. "Jesus, you OK?"

At least David had been wearing a helmet. He should have had a jacket on, too, but somehow his arms did not seem to be badly scraped. He put a hand to his chest, feeling the ribs there. Pain, a sharp ache. But subsiding already.

"Are you OK?" the pedestrian repeated. He was an undergrad, by appearances, nylon windbreaker tied stylishly around his waist, a heavy-looking book bag slung over one shoulder. Phillies cap with the bill stapled straight up against the brow, the way the younger kids were doing it these days. He peered at David with no small measure of alarm.

"I'm fine," David said, his voice a little wheezy, a little shaky.

Was that true? Was he fine? He put a hand flat on the pavement, used it to push himself partly erect. He winced and cried out when he put some weight on his left knee, and it nearly buckled. But in the end it held, and this new pain was also subsiding.

"Are you sure?" the kid asked worriedly. That was nice of him. The other pedestrians, three of them, had also moved in closer. There was an aura about them, a feeling not of fear or suspicion or tabloid curiosity, but of simple concern. And why not? They said the sense of community was gone from the city, even from the college campuses, that street crime had driven it all away. But the most dangerous thing on the streets this morning seemed to be David Sanger himself.

He winced and grunted again, bending and unbending his knee, working the blood back into it. "Just a routine bicycle smash," he said, making a sickly attempt at a smile. He pulled a yellow maple leaf from the collar of his shirt.

"Jesus," the kid observed. "You looked like a soccer ball, bouncing off the wall, there. How could you not get hurt?"

"Street Defense," David said, wondering if it was true. They'd taught him how to fall; that came on the first day. Tuck and roll, spread the impact over as much of your body as you can. . . . But they had not taught him how to flip over a parked car at fifteen miles an hour. Of course, biking had been David's main mode of transportation for a long time, and he'd had his share of spills. Maybe he was just getting good at it.

"Anyway," he said, "it *did* hurt. It does."

"I'll bet. See the doctor, man. And for Christ's sake don't ride so fast."

David nodded. "Thanks; I'm fine. But I think I'll walk the rest of the way."

That turned out to be necessary anyway; he'd popped the front tire and bent the rim beneath it in the impact. But he couldn't find a mark on the car he'd struck, so he simply walked away from the scene, dragging the wounded bicycle with him. His building was only a quarter-mile away, anyway, and the walk and the time would give his aches and pains a chance to die down before he got there. He'd have bruises, of course.

Stupid. What had he been doing, riding around like that? Was it some deeply buried suicide wish? Was he trying to prove something, like the world would somehow give his five years' work back to him if he proved himself worthy? Worthy of a broken arm, maybe.

Sheepishly, he locked the bike up in front of the Molecular Sciences building, then limped up the steep wheelchair ramp, digging out his keys to unlock the front entrance. A thought struck him: *Dov Jacobs had a key to this building.* Someone had gotten all the way in to his lab, and then out again, without triggering any alarms.

Dov?

No, it really was impossible. He unlocked the outer door and went inside, passed the mail room and the lounge, entered and exited the sniffer, then unlocked the inner door and stepped through to the lobby. Someone had done all this on the way to his lab. Carrying what: a black bag and a crowbar? The intruder had placed a black sock over the lens of each security camera along the way, without being seen by any of them. Almost as if he knew in advance where they'd be, what route he could take to avoid them.

Probably an inside job; these things usually are. Had Mike Puckett said that? Or was it from some old movie, some ghostly sound bite kicking around in his head, waiting for a chance to be relevant? He couldn't remember.

The elevator carried him up to the fifth floor, what he considered the "real" molecular sciences floor. His lab and office were up here, and Henry's, and the communal facilities shared by half a dozen doctoral candidates. The intruder had left those other rooms alone.

His lab's door was locked when he got to it. That was usual and proper, but the yellow tape crisscrossed over it was not. CRIME SCENE, it said. DO NOT ENTER. In smaller letters, it went on to discuss the potential penalties for breaking the tape, which could include a fine of up to $70,000 or a prison term of up to seven years.

He blinked at the tape, waited for a moment, as if it might go away. He was sealed out of the lab? *His own lab?* His hands stiffened at his sides. Enough shit had happened to him these past few days; were they trying to tell him he didn't even own the wreckage in there? The thought seemed monstrous.

He did not break the tape, though. Instead, he backtracked past the elevators and down the other wing, to the department secretary's office. Greta would know what was going on. They would tell her, and if somehow they hadn't, she would call them and pester them until they did.

The office was literally a hole in the wall, a recessed niche with a counter and window that couldn't be closed. The "monkey cage," Greta sometimes called it, though she looked more hyena-like, hunched perpetually over her keyboard, her light brown hair spiking upward like a bristly mane. David rang the little bell on her counter, and she turned around.

"Oh, David," she said, nodding when she saw him. "I've been trying to reach you at home. I didn't know if you'd be in."

"I'm in," David said unhappily. "Listen; they've got my lab all sealed off. I need to get in there and clean things up."

Greta looked pained. "No, David, no. They said it would be a couple of days. You can use the other lab until then."

"I want to clean up the mess," he insisted. "I want . . ."

His voice trailed away. What he wanted, the police couldn't give him.

Greta looked up at him with kindly concern. "To rebuild everything that you lost. That's what you want, right?"

He nodded.

"You can do that, David. I know you well enough. This time next year you'll be filing patent applications for something even better."

He snorted. "That's nice of you to say. I think it's wrong, but thanks."

"Well," she said, turning back to her desktop for a moment. She plucked up a scrap of paper and held it out to him. "You have a message. A Michael Puckett called from the FBI about fifteen minutes ago. He said he'd like you to go to the campus police station at your earliest convenience. They want you to identify someone."

"Right now?"

She shrugged. " 'Earliest convenience,' those were his exact words." Her eyes narrowed. "I heard about Friday night. It's awful. Are you . . . still in trouble?"

"No," David said. "But Dov Jacobs might be."

"Dov?" Greta sounded shocked, offended. "Little Dov, over in Microbiology?"

"They think he might have killed Big Otto."

"Well, that's ridiculous."

David nodded. *But Dov had a key. And he hated Big Otto; everyone knew that.* "Yeah. Ridiculous. I'd better get down there and see what's happening."

"Well, it sounds like you'd *better*. Straighten them out for us, please."

"I'll, uh, I'll do my best."

CHAPTER ELEVEN

David had never been to the campus police station before, and although he knew more or less where it was, it took him five minutes of searching to pinpoint the exact building. It was across the street from the campus, rather than actually on it, and it looked like an ordinary house. The words UPH POLICE were stenciled in black on the door, in letters slightly too small to read from the street.

Inside, it looked nothing like a house, and yet also nothing like Baltimore's Druid Lake PD, home of the world-famous Fellmer scan. Well, beta-test site for it, anyway. This place looked more like the driver's license bureau, standard and simple and institutional. It looked like the front entrance to the bursar's office in Regents Hall, with its white floor and orange walls and ceiling of white acoustic tile. David found himself before a windowed-off desk, in an alcove with two doors leading deeper into the building. Both were closed.

"Can I help you?" asked the officer behind the desk.

David suppressed a startled grimace; his experience with the Baltimore police was still quite fresh in his mind, thank you, and he couldn't quite think of the police as his friends and protectors anymore. He thought it might be a while before he could.

"Um," he said, "my name is David Sanger."

"Ah," the officer said. He was white and bulky beneath his uniform, and he jiggled a little when he nodded. "Our star witness. We've got some questions for you about your friend, Dov Jacobs."

"Is he here?"

The officer nodded again. "Yep. Down at interrogation right now. His girlfriend, too. You need to go down the hall until you come to Bill Orbison's office. Here; I'll buzz you in."

"Girlfriend?" David said. He didn't know Dov had a girlfriend. He'd never seen him with one.

"Yeah, she's down in the cage. Have a *nice* day."

A buzzer sounded behind one of the doors, and David grasped the unturning knob and pulled on it. The hallway on the other side was short and very brightly lit. He entered, and the door clicked shut behind him. Bill Orbison's office was the first on his right, its door propped open with a chair. David stuck his head in, saw the room inside: small, crowded with furniture and a geyser of loose office supplies, and quite empty of human beings.

Huh. Should he go in uninvited, sit down and wait? Should he walk around, looking for someone named Bill Orbison? Should he just stand here until something happened? No, he should walk around. He was here on his own time, and the sooner he got finished, the sooner he could get out of here and . . . do something or other. That part of it wasn't quite clear yet.

"Hello?" he called out, starting down the short corridor. He looked in the other open doors, seeing similar offices, similarly empty. Where were all the cops? A few more steps carried him to the end of the hallway, where he faced a staircase going down. Shrugging, he followed it.

"Hello-o?"

The stairs creaked beneath him acccusingly. Should he be going down here?

"Hello?" another voice called back. A female voice, close by.

He went forward, coming to an open doorway, its door of orange-painted wood and frosted glass locked back against the wall with some kind of clip. Visible through the glass was the backwards message:

HOLDING
INTERROGATION
RECORDS
ARMORY

Holding, Interrogation, Records, Armory.

"Hello?" the voice called out again.

He went through the doorway. The hall suddenly widened out to a room. The floor was of bare cement, the walls of cinder block, the ceiling of smooth plaster striped with white diode lighting arrays. He respected those: no filament, no gas, just a shockproof sandwich of metal and plastic. Expensive, but they drew little current, and might well burn for centuries. He would have gotten some for his apartment by now, if they just weren't so damned ugly, but here they seemed appropriate.

One side of the room was walled off with iron bars, behind which stood a young woman, or an old girl, in a beige dress and dark brown spidersilk vest. *An undergrad,* he thought automatically.

"Hello?" she said uncertainly, eyeing David as he came in.

It struck him, suddenly, that he knew her from somewhere. He couldn't place it, but she squinted back at him with the same sort of recognition.

"Hi," he said. "Do we know each other?"

She nodded. "Yeah. Aren't you the guy who invented that MOCLU stuff?"

"David Sanger," he admitted. "Yes. Who are you? And why are you in there?"

A look of anger flashed over her features. "I don't *know.* They won't tell me. They keep acting like I know what it's all about, but I *don't.*"

"What's your name, again?"

"I'm Jill."

Jill. Huh, that did sound familiar. "Were you at the AMFRI conference? Are you Dov Jacobs' girlfriend?"

Her anger dried up, a look of unhappiness taking its place. "Yes and maybe," she said. "Ask Vandegroot."

David took an involuntary half-step backward. *That* was a scary thing for her to have said. She'd delivered the remark flatly, without the sort of tone and inflection he'd expect someone to use when talking about the recently murdered. It seemed, suddenly, not such a bad idea that she was on the other side of the bars.

She watched his reaction, and frowned. "What? *What?* Why does everyone keep acting that way?"

"I know who you are," David said. "You're from Boston. Research assistant. Scholarship."

She nodded uncertainly. The whole world was Vandegroot country, but no place more than Boston, where his home and offices were located. Jill Whatever-her-name-was was one of those unlucky undergrads forced to work in the Big Man's shadow, to labor like serfs at his behest.

"You know something," she said, eyeing him.

He did? Fine hairs tickled on the back of his neck. This girl was *creepy.* What was Dov doing, hanging around with her? "Maybe I do," he said quietly.

"He introduced us," the girl said. "I mean formally, you know? He bought us both a drink, and then he took me aside and said, 'Help me out, honey: be nice to this man.' When he says 'help me out,' it means your scholarship is up for renewal, and when he says 'honey' . . ." Her voice trailed away.

David simply stared at her, wide-eyed. What was she talking about? It was important, it *sounded important,* but it didn't make any sense.

"Go on," he managed to say.

The girl reddened. "Do I have to spell it out? He said, 'Take him back to Philly,' so I did. My scholarship was up for renewal. I mean, he doesn't even know my name or anything, he doesn't even care, but you know he'd find out if he wanted to. If he was mad."

"If who was mad?" David asked, wondering whether he should speak at all. No, that was wrong; he *knew* he shouldn't be having this conversation, knew he was mucking with police business. But damn it, he just couldn't stop.

Dov Jacobs was not a friend, exactly, but he was a nice guy, and one of the few "good" molecular fabricators David knew personally. He'd come from the molbio side, of course, and his primary interest was in designing antibiotics. But he knew good tech from bad, and in his plans the "drugs" looked more like vicious demolition machinery than strings of goopy protein. If only Dov would *build* a few of these things, he too could be a Serious Heavy Hitter in the molecule business.

But no, that wasn't it. David wasn't doing this for Dov's sake, wasn't doing it for justice or even for vengeance. He just wanted to *know.* This girl knew something, and he was by-God going to find out what it was and what it meant.

"If *who* was mad?" he repeated, in a louder voice this time.

"Vandegroot!" Jill shot back. "Big Otto Vandegroot! Do I have to spell it out? He told me, 'Honey, take this guy back to Philadelphia, and keep him indoors for the weekend.' That's pretty unequivocal, don't you think? And, I mean, I liked Dov anyway, so it wasn't like . . . like . . ."

Whoring. The word hung unspoken in the air. Jill burst into tears.

Oh. Oh boy. Sexual blackmail, using scholarship money as the lever? *Otto and Dov?* No, they couldn't possibly be partners in crime; they hated each other.

"When did this happen?" he asked, as gently as he could.

She sobbed. "Friday. Friday night."

"What time?"

"I don't know! It was right before the party started. Who cares?"

David nodded. Jill didn't yet know about Vandegroot's death. Or at least that was the story she was sticking to.

"Hey!"

David and Jill both turned toward the new voice. A cop stood there in the back doorway, hands braced against the frame as if he might launch himself into the room.

"What the *hell* do you think you're doing?" he demanded, favoring David with a look of outraged authority.

Think quickly. Think *quickly!* "Uh, I'm looking for Bill Orbison. Are you him?"

"You weren't looking for me," the cop said. "You were talking to the suspect in there. Is that your job? No, it's *my* job."

"I'm sorry."

The cop sneered at David's tone, at his attempted reasonableness. "Oh, you're *sorry,* are you? It's funny, I've been talking to this girl's boyfriend, and *your* name's been coming up about every five seconds. You're David Sanger, right? Whatever went on this weekend, you're about as tied up in it as a person can be."

"I haven't done anything. I'm the *victim,* remember?"

The cop, Orbison, looked hard at him. "Maybe. You're a busy guy for a victim, though. Get your ass upstairs and we'll talk about it."

"Sure." David's tone was not so reasonable, now. Orbison, like Mike Puckett, seemed able to convey the idea that David's time was of little value here. He wouldn't be ducking out for lunch any time soon, wouldn't be going home until Orbison was tired of hearing him say the same things over and over again. *I am innocent. I am innocent. God damn it, I am.*

"Nice meeting you," David said to Jill as he turned and headed for the stairs. Over her quiet sobbing, he didn't hear a reply.

The sun was low in the sky when David finally got out to the bus stop. Fortunately, his bus was not long in coming. He boarded when it stopped, and took a seat near the middle, sitting down just before the bus *chunked* back into motion with a grinding of flywheel gears. *Transit Revenues Up,* he thought, recalling a recent headline of Marian's. Everyone claimed to hate the new buses, with their padded-cell interiors and their thick, shatterproof windows, and yet everyone seemed to be riding them, and paying the newer, higher fares that came with them.

Bus, schmuss, was his own personal feeling on the matter. He'd thought about calling Bowser, getting him to bring the Jeep around to pick up David and his crippled bicycle, maybe stop off for a new front wheel on the way home. But in the end he was just too goddamn tired.

Orbison had bad-copped him for a couple of hours, and then another guy had come in to be the good cop, and they'd gone around and around again. But David didn't know anything more than he'd already told, and eventually they seemed convinced of this. Or maybe just frustrated, convinced he was too stubborn to crack.

Everyone was so damn suspicious of him. *You're about as tied up in this as a person can be,* they were all thinking. And it was true, but how could it be any other way? The AMFRI telecom directory was jokingly titled, "A VERY SMALL WORLD," and indeed, it held fewer than five thousand names worldwide. In a community that closely knit, there could be no isolated incidents.

Still, didn't that mean David should know what was going on? A death, a break-in, a robbery, all connected to him personally. Who was behind it all? Someone he knew? A faceless stranger? A cabal of trench-coated supervillains?

Open your eyes, buddy, Bowser would say. *Let's look at the facts: One, Vandegroot gets Dov Jacobs a date for the weekend, even though he hates him. Two, you fight with Vandegroot. Three, Vandegroot gets killed, and somebody tries to pin it on you. You, personally and specifically. Four, someone trashes your lab. Somebody doesn't like you, bud. Five, someone tries to pin the lab job on Dov.*

Hey, David protested, taking up his own part in the imaginary debate. *Dov could still be guilty. He was in the right place and time. . . .*

He pictured Bowser shaking his head sorrowfully, disappointed with David's naïveté. *Give me a break. Somebody set him up to take a fall.* Vandegroot *set him up, and then died a couple hours later, right about the time your lab door was getting jimmied open.*

David sighed. He never could argue with Bowser, even in his own mind. And it was true, there had to be more than one person involved in this, and there had to have been some planning in advance. Someone had dealt two simultaneous blows to AMFRI's very small world, and had so far done a good job of obscuring the tracks and circumstances. And David was right in the middle. He was struck suddenly with the knowledge that this wasn't over yet, that his own part in it was not complete.

He was a gnat, buzzing through some great clockwork mechanism, watching the wheels turn, the gears mesh, the pendulums rock back and forth. Too close to see the patterns, too close to make any sense of what was happening around him. How long before the gears pulled him in and crushed him?

You're being silly, he told himself. Indeed, the cops were all over this case, chipping and forcing their way through. Like MOCLU: both lubricant and glue, good cop and bad. Seeking out the mechanism's vulnerable points and penetrating them, each molecule oozing in and then locking to its neighbors, freezing the machinery solid.

The criminals, the conspirators in this grotty little affair, were no doubt scrambling for cover, scrambling to distance themselves from everything that had happened. Who could make trouble in an environment like that? Who would dare?

He looked out the window, saw the sun flashing through buildings and treetops, looking vaguely bruise-colored through the heavy, blue-tinted riot glass. The light of day made his worries seem a little ridiculous. *But the light of day will be gone in an hour,* he thought, and had to suppress a superstitious shudder. Maybe he should have invited Marian over after all—this would be another tough night for sleeping.

CHAPTER **TWELVE**

David frequently slept with an eye shade, just a cloth mask shaped like a floppy pair of oversized sunglasses, to block out the faint echoes of light that would otherwise leave him restless. Tonight, though, it wasn't doing its job. Tonight he tossed and turned and got his feet all tangled in the sheets and *still* couldn't sleep. So he hauled out the big guns.

When he really needed his sleep and was having trouble getting it, he completed the sensory deprivation with a pair of earplugs to keep out the noise. They were Malaudio brand, meant for factory workers and army gunners and such. Slick polymer over soft, pliant wax, they wormed deep into the ears for a 65 dB filtration that let you sleep right through the alarm clock and the telephone and the garbage truck banging Dumpsters outside your window.

When David put these in it was like reentering the womb; the only sound his own breathing, in and out, in and out, hypnotic in its regularity. Combined with the sleep mask, they could put him under in about two minutes, and keep him there for ten hours and more, utterly dead to the world.

The combination was so effective that three men were able to break into his apartment and walk right up to his bedside without disturbing him. The first David knew of it was when one of them grabbed his right arm and pinned it to the bed. Sluggishly, he opened his eyes, and saw nothing. Another intruder grabbed his left arm and pulled it tight, flopping him over onto his back. Now he was definitely awake, though still blind, and he knew that something was happening, but not what sort of thing it might be. Had Marian come? Was she doing something strange to him?

He didn't feel even a tickle of fear until the third man leaned over him and, with gloved hands, jerked the eye shade off his face.

"Ow!" he said, and heard almost nothing of his own voice through the filter of the Malaudios.

Silent as a trio of wraiths, the men stood over him. They were cops, he saw, motorcycle cops or something; white, gray-visored helmets with badge decals on the front and sides. Dark blue or black uniforms, tool belts, nightsticks. Guns.

Now the tickle of fear came, and right on its heels an explosion of terror and incomprehension. He jerked his head from one side to the other, confirming his peripheral vision, filling in the details of the scene around him. This was not a dream! There were dark, faceless figures looming over his bed, pinning him, holding his arms!

One of the wraiths, the one not holding onto him, appeared to be speaking. David could hear him, vaguely, but couldn't make out the words. He stared back in blank horror.

The wraith leaned over and slapped him, hard, a backhand that one might use to propel a racquetball or crack a whip. It cracked against David's jaw instead. The glove felt solid, as if it had been padded with lead shot.

"Ow!" David shouted again. "Jesus!" His flesh stung and swelled where the hand had connected.

". . . the girl!" the wraith demanded, this time in a voice almost loud enough for David to hear. He grabbed the nightstick from his belt, raised and brandished it threateningly.

"I can't hear you! I can't hear you!" David replied. Jesus, what the hell was going on? Why was this guy hitting him? Was he going to use the stick? "Don't hit me!" he added.

The policeman said something else, something David didn't quite catch, and then drew back the stick as if for another blow. Good God, if that stick came down where the hand had struck, David's skull would crack! His teeth would shatter! What the hell was going on? Why were they doing this?

Suddenly, the police-wraith drew back, jerkily slamming the nightstick back into its holster. His hands went to a different spot on the tool belt, made small, mysterious movements in the darkness. Opening a pouch? In moments, something glittered between his black leather fingers.

"Oh, God," David said, in what sounded to him like a fairly ordinary tone of voice. "What's going on? What's going on? What are you *doing?*"

The men holding David's arms were strong and immobile, like figures from a nightmare. He pulled and twisted his arms, trying vainly to free them. What had Street Defense taught him about breaking holds like this? Nothing. Nothing! In Street Defense you were always on your feet, always in motion. Not Home Defense, not wake-up-in-the-middle-of-the-night-being-beaten-by-goons defense.

"Command!" he yelled at the ceiling. "Dial 911!"

The wraith countered impatiently with an almost-audible command of his own. Exit, probably.

He came forward, the glittering thing in his hand catching in a beam of moonlight. It was glass. It was a piece of glass, a shard of it, like from a broken window. It moved, scalpel sharp, toward David's open hand.

"No!" David screamed, drawing a fist to protect his palm. "What are you *doing?* Nooo!"

He heard his voice more clearly now; his thrashing had dislodged one of the earplugs. It hung half out of his ear like a warm, soft slug crawling out to face the world. Presently, it fell out onto the pillow beside his cheek.

"Shut up," the wraith said. Then, to the goon beside him: "Get his hand open."

There was a pause, a drawing of breath, and then the Left Heavy was shifting his grip on David's arm, freeing one hand and using it to pry open David's fingers. David fought him, to no avail. His hand was curled back roughly, exposing the palm.

What happened next was strange. He expected to be cut, to be stabbed or dismembered somehow by the razor point of the glass shard, and, in fact, the edge of it did slice lightly through the skin of his fingers. Cold and sharp, too sharp to be immediately painful. He felt the flesh separating, felt the blood well out. But the cut was shallow, nothing like what he'd braced himself for, and it seemed accidental. Or incidental, anyway; the intruder seemed intent on pressing each of David's fingers against the surface of the glass.

When this was done, the intruder, the police-wraith, returned the shard to the pouch at his belt. The heavies never loosened their grips on David, never really moved much at all. They seemed accustomed to this sort of work, almost bored by it.

The telephone rang, its sudden, shrill bleating so much

out of context that David at first didn't recognize it. Then suddenly he did.

He shouted, "Command: answer! Hello! Help me, call the police!"

He struggled once more against his immovable captors. They absorbed his efforts. Not moving, not reacting. Why weren't they reacting?

"Help!" he screamed at the ceiling. "Help me!"

A voice clicked on through the speakers: "Hello, David. I am so sorry."

"Henry?" David said incredulously. There was no mistaking that voice. It seemed impossible, and yet it seemed to be true, and David did not have the time just now to figure out exactly what was what. "Henry! Help me! Somebody's—"

The voice cut in, sadly, softly: "A good many people outside China have used catastrophe theory to model events at the nanoscale. But this way leads to increasingly complex equations, and only the Chinese have made progress in solving these analytically. You understand, we Chinese are no strangers to chaos."

"Henry?" David said again. His fear had seemed absolute, but now he found there were new depths, unimaginable before this moment. He had never before heard a tone like that from his mentor, a tone of such icy and fatalistic calm. "Henry? Can you hear me?"

"The scholar is lonely," Henry Chong said with slow precision, "because he has no time for personal affairs. The spy is lonelier, because in his foreign land he has no counselors. In China they are always concerned with Marxism and Confucianism and Taoism, but they have not forgotten the value of material force. If we wish the world to be a certain way, it must be constructed by our own efforts."

No, David thought. *This can't be right. This can't be anything but a dream.* But the ham-hands gripping his arms were real enough, the weight and breath of the goons around him, the slight chill of the night air.

"This is more difficult than I had guessed," Henry said, and now he sounded maudlin, another tone foreign to his nature. "I thought if the police had you in custody you would be silenced, but now everything has . . ." His voice choked off for a moment. "I am so sorry, David Sanger. I have been a poor teacher."

The speakers clicked and crackled, and a dial tone emerged and then was silenced.

"What's happening?" David asked, uselessly, of his captors.

Silently, the police-wraith dropped a hand to his holster, pulling forth a service revolver. It shone blackly in the moonlight as its muzzle came around to point at David's face.

Fear hit him like a cannonball, disintegrating his thoughts, his mind, his awareness. Disintegrating even the fear itself, leaving nothing of David but a throbbing core of indignation. He was a *scientist,* dammit, he had *things to do,* but these goons were going to put a stop to that, were going to steal his life and everything that went with it.

It wasn't acceptable; it wasn't something he could allow to happen. With almost no thought at all, he opened his mouth and spoke.

"Command: run program, twelve-bad-twelve."

The result was instantaneous and shocking.

A few years back, he'd been noodling around with the house computer, getting it to generate a twelve-hertz harmonic through the stereo subwoofer. Burglar alarm, he was thinking; just one of those things, killing time on a snowy Sunday in February when no one was around. He'd heard things about that particular frequency, that it had an effect on the brain and the body, that the army was experimenting with it as a crowd-control measure.

He'd expected something calm, something low and soothing like the rumble of waves against a beach. What he'd gotten instead was not a sound but a physical sensation, a gut-wrenching, tooth-loosening, brain-jamming sensation like heavy steel marbles raining down from above. He'd called out, trying to stop the computer, trying to shut it down, but *command: halt program* was a sequence he could barely frame in his mind, much less in his mouth. Fortunately, he'd been sitting right beside the house computer and had managed to turn it off manually. He'd found out later that one of his eardrums was broken.

"Hell, that sounds useful," Bowser had said later. "I'd keep it if I were you."

At the time, that had sounded like exceedingly bad advice, but cleaning old files off the house computer was not something he often did. His life was full, the incident forgotten as soon as his ear pills ran out. Forgotten until now.

Now, the twelve-hertz tone hit him like a bag of doorknobs. The three goons fell away like puppets whose strings had been cut.

David writhed for a moment, not in pain, exactly, but in an awfulness that was like pain. He snatched at the earplug on the pillow beside him. Would earplugs even help? He didn't know. He grabbed the thing and jammed it in his ear, jammed again when it refused to go in straight.

The vibration didn't seem to abate.

Fighting nausea, he sat up, kicked at the covers, freed his legs. The effort was almost too much; he almost collapsed back into the bed, but instead he forced his balance to shift so that he fell forward. Boneless as a jellyfish, he oozed onto the floor, onto the struggling, grunting form of one of the goons.

"Go to hell," he whispered, or perhaps only thought about whispering.

The sound was shaking his guts apart, now. It was like sitting in one of those vibrating massage chairs, one that had gone horribly wrong and couldn't be turned off. With tremendous force of will, he rose up on his hands and knees and crawled away from the bed, away from the invading goons. Toward the door.

The vibration seemed to lessen a little as he approached the door, but his resolve weakened at the same time. He collapsed on the cool tiles, gasping for breath. Such a simple, homespun trick, and such an awful one, like a splash of drain cleaner full in the face. He felt the shaking might well kill him, and right now that sounded almost inviting. Good God, this was bad.

He managed to grab the doorknob and pull himself up by it. The door swung open with his weight; the goons had left it unlocked and slightly ajar. But though he wobbled, he got to his feet and did not fall. He took a pair of lurching steps that carried him out into the moonlight. Instantly it was quieter. Instantly he felt less ill. He took another step, and pulled the door shut behind him.

The night air was cold, the sort of biting, damp chill that said summer was over for sure. David had only his pajamas. The cement porch felt icy beneath his feet. He took a breath, and another, feeling the strength flow back into him.

Removing one of the earplugs, he could hear commotion in the apartments around him: doors banging, voices growling and snapping. He could call for help right now! He could run to a neighbor's door and demand admittance, hold out there until the cops came.

It took him about two-tenths of a second to flag that as a damned foolish idea. He took off running instead, flying toward the staircase, hurling himself down it with only the lightest of grips on one banister.

Where's the girl? they had asked. Cop decals gleaming on cop helmets. And Henry's voice: *I thought if the police had you in custody you would be silenced . . .* What did that mean? On one level, David knew that he'd been betrayed in some way, that once-friendly forces had somehow turned against him, taking advantage of his lowered defenses. He also could not ignore the fact that his attackers were police, or police impersonators. That was important, somehow. It was difficult to know whom to trust; indeed, trust seemed a bitterly alien concept at that moment.

Such was the background of his thoughts, roiling chaotically beneath the surface. Translated through the adrenalized filter of his emotions, it came out roughly: *Run! Speak to no one!*

He hit the bottom of the stairs, his feet coming down on sharp pebbles and the asphalt of the parking lot. He ducked left, looked for his bicycle under the stairs—

But his bicycle was gone, damaged, still locked up outside the Molecular Sciences building. Damn it!

His instinct would not be denied. Ignoring the cold, ignoring the jabs at the soles of his feet, he pushed away from the staircase and ran on, racing past the parked cars and the empty slots of residents who could afford only the bus. Out onto the empty street, his feet slapping and slapping against the pavement as he whooshed through yellow-orange pools of lamplight.

Run! his mind insisted. *Get away from here!*

And run he did, until he was well away and the night swallowed him up, one more homeless man gibbering in the streets.

CHAPTER **THIRTEEN**

When David passed his third telephone booth, he calmed down enough to stop and get inside it. His hands were shaking so badly from the cold and the adrenaline, he could barely hold the receiver against his ear. His feet were like lumps of cold clay.

Where's the girl? they had asked. He was sure that's what they had said.

He punched in his long-distance code, but then he couldn't immediately recall Marian's number. Then he did, but had trouble entering it, and then she wouldn't answer it, despite the priority ring he'd keyed in. Eight rings . . . nine rings. Ten rings! A fresh bubbling of fear broke through the crust of the old. And then, suddenly, she was there in miniature on the telephone screen.

She wore a bathrobe, her static-charged hair standing out in all directions. Bleary annoyance projecting from her features.

"What."

David took a breath. Where to begin? No, no beginnings! No time!

"Marian!" he said quickly. "Get out of the house; you're in terrible danger!"

She blinked. "David? What happened? You look terrible; where are you?"

"No time to explain," he insisted. "There are bad guys coming, looking for you. I don't know what they want. Get out of the house, now! Stay hidden!"

He cut the connection without waiting for her reply. She'd want to know everything, she'd *demand* to know everything, and by the time he got done explaining how little he knew, the goons could be breaking her door down looking for . . . for him? Yes, surely for him. He was about as tied up in this as a person could be.

But tied up in what? *What?*

He needed to call Bowser. *Crisis Man,* Bowser sometimes jokingly called himself. *Cooler than a speeding cucumber, able to leap tall bullshit without getting stinky.* They'd grown up in the same neighborhood, attended mostly the same schools, shared the same bookish white-bread suburban background, and yet Bowser had somehow come out streetwise. One of the great, annoying mysteries of life.

David couldn't remember that number, either, until he recalled the last four digits spelled out "SLID." After that it was easy, and the phone was ringing a moment later.

"Yello," Bowser said, his image appearing on the screen after a negligible delay. *Up at this hour?* David thought irrelevantly. What hour was it, anyway?

"I'm in trouble," David said, falling into Bowser's own staccato speech pattern, sans introduction.

His friend and attorney squinted out at him, paused, nodded. "Yes, you're in a phone booth in your pajamas. What happened?"

David started to speak, but drew a solid blank. What *had* happened? He still hadn't gotten around to sorting that out.

"I don't know," he said, giving his head a quick shake. "I need you to come pick me up. Right now!"

"OK," Bowser said, sounding only mildly surprised. "Where are you?"

"I don't know," David said, fighting down nameless panic. *Don't let them pin you down!* "It doesn't matter, I'm not going to say it over an open line. Somebody might be listening!"

"Huh. Paranoia's usually a good thing, but it certainly . . . comes as a surprise from you. How about . . . if I meet you someplace? How about—" He paused, then flashed a sly, knowing grin. "Can you make it to Lillet's place?"

"Yes! Yes, that's an excellent idea! Meet me at Lillet's place!"

Now Bowser looked a little concerned, a little suspicious. "You're not yourself tonight, buddy. What sort of trouble are you in, exactly?"

"I don't know," David repeated, trying not to hyperventilate. "I really don't. I think some cops were trying to kill me tonight. In my sleep, in my home. I think, maybe, Henry Chong put them up to it. They're still after me, I'm sure! And Marian, and maybe you, too."

"Oh." Bowser hesitated, but only for a moment. "You mean *serious* trouble. That's OK; I'll bring the serious trouble bag. See you in a few, OK?"

His image winked off.

David was alone once again in the cold, fitful light of the phone booth. His hands were shaking badly when he set the handset back in its cradle. *Lillet's place. Lillet's place.* He opened the door, stepped out once again into the night. He barely felt the bite of cold pebbles in the asphalt against the numb Play-Doh of his feet.

What about Marian? She wouldn't know to meet him at Lillet's. Damn, what an idiot he was! Turning the woman he loved out into the dangers of the night with "Stay hidden" as her only instruction! And of course, it was too late to call her back now. She'd seen his face, heard his tone; she would know this was serious. She would do what he said. And, too, calling her now might tip his hand. He pictured goons answering Marian's phone, glaring out at him with their blank, visored faces. Reading the caller-ID number . . . No, no way.

He needed to get with Bowser, talk this whole mess through and figure out what was going on and what they could do about it. Bowser would know how to find Marian, too; he was good at that sort of random, spontaneous insight.

So, David needed to get to Lillet's place. He looked around him, trying to get his bearings. Streetlights, street signs . . . Jesus, he'd run farther than he thought. And he'd fortuitously fled in the right direction; Lillet's place was barely ten minutes' walk from here. He was winded, dizzy, viewing the world as if through a filter of nightmare.

He kept to the shadows, making his way onward in a dreamy, loping walk that covered ground slowly but safely. Watching ahead of him, watching behind. Already he'd hid from a couple of police cars, and he would no doubt hide from many more before the night was through. Philly was *crawling* with cops these days, and gee, weren't they just doing a swell job of keeping the public safe?

He followed the smell of water, the distant roar of I-76.

Lillet's place was under a bridge, where a dozen storm drains let out into the Schuylkill River. *A prime interface between the upper and lower worlds,* was one description of the area, delivered in Lillet's creepy, nasal-whiny, pseudo-intellectual parlance. Lillet was once a Doctor of

Philosophy, if you believed her line. David didn't believe it, but she was a kind of philosopher nonetheless. Ethical Advisor to the Hidden Kingdom, was her preferred title.

Marian had done a whole series of articles on the homeless, topping off with a full-page spread on Lillet's tribe and their lawsuit against the city. Police brutality was driving the homeless underground, the group had charged. Driving them into the sewers and the storm drains and the old network of tunnels that linked so many downtown basements. The Patriot Tunnels, Lillet called them, though in reference to what David had no idea.

That wasn't what the suit was about, though; the key issue had been timing in the city's use of toxic pesticides. "They sweep the streets," Lillet had said. "Demons with swords of fire, sweeping the unhomed before them, driving them Under. Then, before dawn's light breaks, they spray the tunnels full of rat poison, and blame the deaths on tuberculosis. The Final Solution to the problem of urban indigence."

The story's hallucinatory imagery and tone had proved a little far out for the *Bulletin,* with its constant struggle for respectability, and in the end Marian's partners had overridden her objections and killed the story. And the lawsuit had been dismissed as frivolous, anyway.

The reference to "Lillet's place" would be understood by at most a handful of people. A few cops, maybe. A few county bureaucrats and just possibly the judge, if he had a good memory. And the *Bulletin* staff, and David, and Bowser. And the area was secluded, safe from prying eyes of all varieties. The perfect rendezvous point, courtesy of T. Bowser Jones, Esquire.

Twice more, he ducked away from cop cars, ducked into narrow, stinking alleys and pressed himself flat against brick walls. Then loped on in the chill and darkness, crossing under the interstate, coming to the river and following it into the railyard district he needed.

Soon, Lillet's bridge came into view, and the little grassy terrace beneath it and to one side. He hurried onward. Maybe the homeless would take pity on him, recognize him as one of their own and find a jacket for him, and maybe an old pair of boots. He'd pay them back a hundredfold when he got the chance.

He slowed, found a hole in the chain-link fence, crawled through. The concrete slope of the riverbank was colder than pavement against his feet. A slight breeze was blowing down here, chilling him even more. Up ahead was silence and darkness. Odd. He'd never been down here in the dark, but he'd expected campfires and conversation, some kind of hobo camp like you'd see in the movies. But the place looked empty.

He reached Lillet's grassy front lawn, looked around him. Empty. The grass had grown knee-high in places, and looked like it had never been stepped on. Water trickled from the man-high drain pipes ahead, running down the slope and into the river with low, gurgly noises.

"Hello?" he called out softly. His voice echoed off bare cement corners.

Alone. No one to share his homeless terror, to share even the chill of this September night. How long 'til morning? He looked up at the urban blankness of the sky, finding no clues there.

Finally, he chose a spot in the tall grass and sat down in it, hugging his knees to his chest for warmth. The ground seeped damply against his pajama bottoms. The wind whistled by with faint, tuneless music, carrying along with it the soft growl and chatter of the city.

"David?"

The voice came to him as if in a dream: distant, sourceless. He sat up, rubbing his eyes.

"David?"

"Bowser?"

He looked around, saw nothing at first. Then he made out the silhouette of a man coming toward him down the slope of the riverbank, with an oversized gym bag swinging heavily from one hand.

"Bowser?" he repeated.

"Hey, buddy," the voice came back. "You look like a stray dog."

David had no reply for that, so he simply waited until Bowser got down to the lawn.

"I brought you some clothes," Bowser said, fishing in his bag as he came to a stop. "It's that one-size-fits-all crap from the J. J. Brooks catalog. Very stylish."

"Thanks," David said softly, accepting the bundle.

"Put 'em on, man; you must be freezing."

David nodded. Fumbling, he pulled the oversized shirt and trousers on over his pajamas, cinching them into place, then slipped on a pair of black, stretchy "deck shoes" that were essentially socks with stiff vinyl bottoms. There was a jacket, too, but after he shrugged into it, he found his hands too numb and shaky to work the zipper. *Never mind it,* he thought distantly. He felt no warmer with the clothes on, but at least he was no longer hemmorrhaging his body heat into the night.

"I have some other stuff in here, too," Bowser said when David had finished dressing. "You need a disguise? I've got a wig and a hat, and I think maybe a clip-on earring."

David shrugged. "I'll take the hat, I guess."

Bowser nodded, and after a brief search pulled a baseball cap from the bag. In the darkness, David could not judge its color.

"So, like, what happened to Marian?"

David shook his head, feeling empty inside. "I don't know. I just told her to run; I didn't say where. I don't know where she'd go."

"Oh. Well, I guess she'll turn up. She can take care

of herself a lot better than you can." Bowser made an overhand gesture, beckoning David to follow him back up the river's slope. "The Jeep is right up there, still warm."

They climbed back up to the chain-link fence, then hopped over it, David's hands partially numb but still strong enough for the task. The Jeep was right there, and they got inside it, and Bowser started up the engine and put the heater on. Warm air flooded through the vents.

"Oh, God," David said, holding his hands up in the flow. "Thanks; I really needed you to come."

"That's OK," Bowser said. "You want to tell me what happened?"

"Yeah." And so David told him what he knew of the night's events, and those of the day before it. It made a pretty confusing picture.

"Hyeon did this?" Bowser asked skeptically. "I can believe he'd kill Otto Vandegroot, but not *you.* Jeez, he likes you. And he's got no ties to the cops that I've ever heard of."

"I know; I know. It doesn't make any sense. But he sounded so *strange* on the phone."

"Huh. Are you sure it was him?"

"Oh, absolutely. Bowser, let's get out of here. I want to call the FBI or something."

"You want to trust Mike Puckett? Remember, you trusted Hyeon, too."

David sighed. "I don't know. No way I'm going to the regular police with this, but I can't think what else to do. I mean, my *life* is in danger."

"Yeah, well. We'll see about that. Let's find a hotel room, so we can sit down and hash this out. Calling Puckett seems like a good idea. He's so much an outsider in all this, even *I* can't imagine he's on the wrong side. He's just a bystander."

"He's going to arrest me again," David complained.

"He'll maybe call it 'protective custody' or something, but what's the difference?"

"Oh, hey, I didn't say we'd tell him where to find you." Reaching into his pocket, Bowser removed a thin, rectangular object and presented it to David with a flourish. "I gotta protect the interests of my client, after all. You want a piece of gum?"

CHAPTER FOURTEEN

I signed in as Tom Jones," Bowser said, pulling the door shut behind him.

David shrugged, not sure what kind of answer was expected. "Thomas Bartholomew Jones" was Bowser's real name. Using it here didn't seem like such a good idea, but Bowser had his own way of doing things and was not easily deflected.

The air in here smelled vaguely of sweat and cigar smoke. The bedcovers were on the frayed side, and the graying carpet had seen better days. And the ceiling was of cheap acoustic tile, not at all like you'd expect for a motel room, but the place was bright and warm, and importantly, it had no windows. David moved over to one of the beds, and sat down tensely on the edge of it. He did not in any sense feel secure, but he felt a whole lot more comfortable than he had in the past few hours.

Bowser set his heavy black gym bag down on the table and unzipped it. He looked pointedly at David. "Why don't you take a quick shower or something? I've got some equipment to set up; it'll be a few minutes."

David just nodded, too tired to argue. He didn't know why Bowser needed "equipment" to place a simple phone call, but at the moment he didn't much care. And a shower sounded like entirely too much trouble, but he did get up and shuffle into the bathroom—washing his face would probably help a little. Roaches scrambled for cover when he flipped on the light, dragging their hard carapaces over the tiles with clickety-click noises. In the mirror over the sink, David's face looked drawn, wary, unfamiliar. He closed the drain and filled the basin with tepid water, soaking his hands in it for a few moments, watching grime dissolve into murky clouds. Frowning, he emptied the sink, washed his hands with the complimentary soap bar, and started the process over again.

When he shuffled back out into the room, Bowser had set up a laptop computer with a green plastic box sitting next to it, winking with green and red LEDs. A nest of wires ran between it and the computer, and a single fat cable snaked from its front to a telecom port in the wall beside the table. The hotel room's phone, one of the old voice-only jobs that looked vaguely like a droopy-eared Mickey Mouse, completed the ensemble by connecting to the laptop's modem port.

"What is that?" he asked incuriously.

"Telecom substation." Bowser didn't look up when he spoke. He fiddled with the wires, and a few more of the green box's lights winked on. "It's sort of crude, but I think it'll do."

"You're going to get us in trouble," David said, glaring at his friend's back. He should have expected this; Bowser favored extreme, elaborate solutions to the problems of life. But damn it, this was not a game.

Bowser barked out a laugh. "We're already in *trouble,* David. Anyway, I'm pretty sure I have a license for this."

"What are you going to do?"

"I'm blinding the return signal from this port. If we bounce a phone call through a couple of anonymizers, nobody can trace it back to the source with any precision. If they're good, they'll get ID on the first legitimate substation we jack through, but that'll maybe pin us down to a five-block radius. On top of that, I'm instructing the substation to block caller-ID signals, and as an extra precaution I'm limiting this call to sixty seconds, because I've never done this before and I'm not really sure what'll happen."

David sighed, and pulled up a chair next to Bowser's. "Do you want me to dial the number?"

"No, the computer's doing a callback flash. Just pick the phone up when it rings."

Presently, it rang. David picked up the receiver, put it to his ear.

"Hello?"

"Hello?" demanded the voice at the other end.

"Puckett?"

"Who is this?" The tone was tight, verging on anger.

"Puckett, this is David Sanger. I have to talk to you. Something's happened."

"Yeah," Puckett said, not questioning but agreeing. "And you're going to explain it. Where are you?"

David's heart clenched. "No, I'm not telling you that. Somebody's trying to kill me, I'm not trusting anyone." His voice wavered, thick with outrage. "The cops tried to kill me tonight. *Henry fucking Chong* tried to kill me tonight!"

"Easy," Puckett commanded harshly. "You're not making sense. What's your story on this, self-defense?"

David paused. Of *course* he had defended himself. Of *course* he had. "The twelve-hertz tone," he said. "Somebody died, didn't they."

"Somebody died, yes."

Uh-oh.

"Puckett, you have to understand, I just wanted to get out of there. It was self-defense, yes. They were trying to kill me!"

"So what were you doing there in the first place? It was two A.M. on a weeknight; you had no legitimate business."

"What do you mean," David snarled back. "I *live* there. They broke in!"

"No," Puckett told him, "*you* broke in. Your blood and fingerprints are all over the goddamn glass. I've been . . . slow to react on this case, but it stops here. I want to know *why you killed Henry Chong.*"

David froze, feeling the dizzy sensation of the world inverting around him. Henry was dead? That didn't make any sense.

"Henry called me," he said shakily. "The cops broke in, and they put this piece of glass in my hand, and then Henry called, and he said he was sorry. And then they tried to kill me."

"You're out of control," Puckett said. "You're not making sense."

Bowser, looking alarmed, tapped his wristwatch and mouthed the words "fifteen seconds!"

"Where are you right now?" David asked.

"I'm still in D.C. But if you turn yourself in at the campus police station, I'll be there by sunrise."

"No, listen to me. Check out my apartment, you'll see, what-do-you-call, 'signs of a struggle.' The guys who broke in were wearing uniforms. I'm not crazy, and I'm not out of control, but there is no way in hell I'm trusting the police with my life tonight."

With an exaggerated gesture, Bowser pulled a plug from the front of his green box. "Cut!" he said. "Good stomping grief, what the hell's going on here?"

David held the phone, now dead, in a limp hand.

Absently, he let it slip, to hit the carpet and bounce back up, twirling at the end of its cord.

"Someone killed Henry?"

"Someone killed Henry," Bowser agreed. "I'll be damned. My buddy, this has been a hell of a night."

CHAPTER FIFTEEN

"Just so you know," Bowser said over his shoulder, "at this point, we are definitely breaking the law."

"Oh," David said. At this point, he definitely didn't care. "Why, what are you doing?"

"Hacking into Hyeon Chong's voice mail system. I figure it can't hurt to know who he's been talking to." Bowser cast a sidelong look at David, then bent to pick the black gym bag up off the floor. "Here, take this. I want you familiar with the equipment before we pull out of here."

"What equipment?" David accepted the bag, setting it down on the bed next to him. He pulled the zipper down, letting the sides of the bag peel back like grinning lips. Beneath was an assortment of colors and textures, from glossy orange to matte black and camouflage. Sizes and shapes were equally varied, creating a visual jumble that rivaled the insides of Marian's oversized purse.

His eyes fixed on an object, a slim white cylinder

caged in rings and plates of black plastic. A drop foil. Like the one Big Otto had used to threaten him. Like the one Big Otto had been killed with.

"Jesus Christ," he said.

"It *is* impressive," Bowser agreed. "I pay for a particular item because I see a possibility, at the federal or state level, to criminalize it. A lot of this is contraband right now, but I can prove in court every item was obtained legally. If anyone asks, I just collect old stuff for the investment value. Gas mask? It's Soviet surplus; I got it when I was ten."

Gas mask. Drop foil. Kevlar body armor. Wigs, makeup, costume jewelry. Fat wallets bursting with documents. And some ordinary items, as well: a box of matches, a flashlight, a Walkman stereo. But knowing Bowser, even these simple things were no doubt more than they seemed.

"Jesus H. fucking Christ," David swore again. The phone gear had been in there, too, and the clothing he was now wearing. Bowser hadn't thrown this stuff together on his way out the door, that was certain. *I got it when I was ten,* he'd said. Bowser had been waiting all his life for a night like this.

There was even a giant can of coffee in the bag. Can't tackle a serious emergency without a cup of Java, right? Except that Bowser's ulcer wouldn't let him drink coffee. David fished the can out, hefted it. It weighed rather more than a can of coffee should.

"What's in here?" he asked, his tone undecided between awe and disgust.

"Oh, leave that," Bowser said, making put-it-down motions with his hands.

"What's in it?"

"Well, it's airtight, and it was sealed exactly nine years ago, and if you open it, every cop in the state will be breaking the door down in about twenty minutes. Is that enough of a hint?"

David dropped the can. Most sniffer alarms would provoke a routine inquiry, with search and seizure warrants to follow if the circumstances so dictated. The kind of swift, decisive response Bowser was talking about was for counterterrorism. High explosives, neurotoxins, gunpowder.

Nine years ago. Nine years ago. David searched his memory, came up with the image of his father's face, looking on in dismay as a patrol car pulled away, his hunting rifles locked securely in its trunk. David himself, some sixteen years old, clutching a pink ticket in his hand. POSSESSION OF PYROTECHNIC DEVICES, FIRST OFFENSE. They had confiscated a box of sparklers.

"Jesus," David said, "it's your old Markov."

"Makarov," Bowser corrected. "And it's my grandfather's. Picked it up in Cuba, no papers."

David could not think of an appropriate reply. This was so typical of Bowser, why should he be surprised? And yet, he was not merely surprised but *shocked.* This was serious, serious trouble if anyone ever found out about it. What was the penalty these days, ten years? Fifteen?

"Don't look so offended," Bowser said, with uncharacteristic coldness. "What's wrong, you swallow too much propaganda? Remember, your life is in danger."

"I remember."

There was an uncomfortable pause. Then Bowser said, "Look; you asked. Just put it back and forget about it, yes? Believe you me, I hope that can never gets opened, because if it *does,* that means the country's gone totally postal."

David put the coffee can back where it had come from. "I'm not getting 'familiar' with that, Bowser."

"That's fine. Play with the drop foil, OK? I've got some work to do, here."

The drop foil. David eyed it uncomfortably. A tool for

intimidation, for murder. And yes, for self-defense. David had been lucky tonight, roaming the streets alone, but lately his luck had been flaky. He could just as easily be bleeding in a gutter right now, or lying cold on a slab.

With an unease that bordered on nausea, he picked the weapon up. The straps and buckles puzzled him at first, but soon it was clear how the thing was intended to go, how one strapped it to one's forearm so the foil could be dropped into the waiting hand below. He moved to the bed, stretched his right arm out on his leg, and, with slow reluctance, girded himself for battle.

He was not pleased to discover how *good* the weapon felt snugged against his flesh, how *safe* it made him feel. Street Defense was all well and fine when you had your wits about you, when your opponents were drunk and slow and all you wanted was to make them fall over so they would leave you alone. But people who fell over could still shoot a gun, whereas those who'd been run through with swords generally could not.

Wincing against imagined shock, he raised his arm and then gave it a downward jerk, springing the ejector mechanism. The drop foil shot into his hand, and his fingers closed on it automatically, and squeezed. The handguard unfurled like an umbrella of stiff plastic vanes, and the blade sprung almost instantly to its full length, coming within two feet of the back of Bowser's head.

"Be careful with that thing," Bowser advised without turning around. He had flinched and hunched at the noise, but only slightly. He seemed intent on his computer screen now, descending into the "geek trance" he favored for computer-related activities.

David studied his grip on the weapon. It was awkward and weak; a stiff parry would spin the foil out of his hand entirely. He grasped the silver knob on the foil's pommel end, and began turning it, slowly cranking against springy resistance, ratcheting the blade and handguard back into the hilt. When he was done, he stepped back to a safer position and tried the *en garde* maneuver again. He remembered the fighting stance Big Otto had used against him, and he tried his best to imitate it.

On his fourth and fifth tries, arm and hand and spring and blade worked together in a single fluid motion, the drop foil snapping to full extension as he stepped forward into a crouch, his elbow slightly bent. His reach, and the speed with which he achieved it, were astonishing. Clearly, Vandegroot had been toying with him at the AMFRI reception; he could have pierced a vital organ in a single, shocking lunge from seven or eight feet away.

David tried it again, and again, ten or fifteen times. He screwed it up a couple of times, but the basics of the maneuver were locked in, fused with that part of his mind that knew dancing and Street Defense. Finally, he retracted and locked the blade, returned the weapon to its ejector, and rolled his oversized, J. J. Brooks sleeve down over the whole assembly. He felt disgustingly pleased with himself.

"How's it coming?" he asked Bowser, ambling back over to the table to give himself something else to pay attention to.

Bowser was lost in a fog. He looked blankly at David and said, "Fine, I think. The first record header contains the checksum of the login ID of the local administrator. The ID itself is encrypted, but with the checksum in hand I can just run the combinations. Believe it or not, the way to get into these systems can be protected under federal law, because in the United States the password is considered intellectual property rather than real property. I call it 'the notary public loophole.' That's my defense if we get busted for this. Anyway, if I delete line 802 in this stupid program of mine, I can simply scan for both street encryption and market-level. Bang-bang, we give the secret knock and we're in, simple as that."

David uh-huhed and nodded. Bowser tended to talk like that when he was working something out in his head. When he was doing taxes or administrative stuff, his banter was even more obscure.

"Are you almost done?" David thought to ask.

"A few minutes," Bowser said, his eyes once again riveted to the screen.

David went back to the gym bag, looking for something else to familiarize himself with. He came out with a hard, vinyl-coated plastic case that looked like it might hold eyeglasses. It didn't seem likely to explode or anything, so he opened it, and found inside, surprise surprise, a pair of eyeglasses. The frames were thick and black, like the nerdy glasses Dov Jacobs wore. Something was odd about them, though; they bulged oddly on the sides. The earpieces were also unusually thick.

He took the glasses out and examined them closely, and then had to fight back the urge to say "Jesus Christ" yet again. The bulges were tiny CCD cameras, and the thick frames were Lasing Linear Stacked Arrays, or "Lisas," capable of projecting images directly into the eye. This stuff was RHT contraband in a big way, and *cutting-edge* contraband at that. Wherever Bowser had gotten these, he hadn't gotten them cheap.

David found an "on" switch, activated it, and slipped the glasses over his face.

He found himself suddenly in a different world, one filled with purple numbers and messages and diagrams that scrolled and shifted, some continuously, others with the movement of his head or his eyes. Bowser, for example, had acquired a sharp outline and a diffuse cartoon glow overlaying his body, and, connected to these by thin purple arrows, a number of annotations hovered near him in the air:

R:	2.9m
T:	36.8°c
ID:	HUMAN

A number of regions, more brightly haloed than the rest of the body, were tagged with the label STRIKE ZONE. With a sick feeling, David realized he could run the drop foil through that purple haze and kill Bowser instantly.

This new, enhanced world had rearview mirrors as well, a pair of palm-sized fish-eye circles that seemed to hover about a foot and a half ahead of David's face, low and off to the sides so they didn't block his forward vision. They didn't really look much like mirrors—the reflected images were a weird chromatic negative of purple on white, difficult at first to make out, but by swiveling his head back and forth, David was able to confirm the fish-eye mapping, which gave almost the full view behind his back.

There were so *many* indicators in the air around him, it seemed he walked through a purple blizzard, a forest of digital telltales, of linear and circular numbered scales. He identified a thermometer/barometer pair, a horizon indicator, a compass that seemed to hover, horizontally, just below his left rearview. And near the top of his vision, a digital calendar/clock readout.

Wristwatches are obsolete, he thought, awed by the spectacle. What was all this information for? *Who* was it for? He now carried with him a cockpit instrument panel, a news bureau, a set of eyes in the back of his head. A lot more than watches were obsolete, with technology like this.

Experimentally, he switched the glasses off again. Reality returned to the motel room, rendering it drab and dark and mute. *How alone we are, with our puny senses.*

Shuddering, he switched the glasses back on again. The world of purple commentary sprang to life around him.

His mind expanded, conceiving its own existence in a new way. Was this what NEVERland was like for Marian? Would the whole world see like this, someday? The prospect seemed both great and terrible, a literal "end to life as we know it." He switched the glasses off once more.

"Oh," he choked, blinking at the barren world. "Wow. These glasses are . . ." He couldn't think of a word that would capture the experience.

"Pretty cool, huh?" Bowser noted distantly. "Those are called Hud Specs. They can see in the dark, by the way. Monochrome thermal imaging, or MTI. Just don't run the batteries down; they only last a couple hours."

"Huh." Maybe that was good. Maybe that would keep people from losing themselves in that world forever, the way Marian had lost herself in the magic kingdoms of Networked Virtual Reality.

Marian is lost in this world, too, he reminded himself. It was a bleak thought. Despite Bowser's assurances, Marian was better at *acting* like she could take care of herself than she was at actually doing it. The nights were so dangerous, these days, Gray propaganda notwithstanding. . . .

"We're in," Bowser said. "I've got a list of deleted messages."

David looked over at his friend, still hunched before the notebook computer. "Can you undelete them?"

"Yup. Listen to this."

Bowser took the telephone handset off its cradle, adjusted a control on his green box. David heard a crackling noise, and then a voice:

"Henry, this is Otto. I notice your boy Sanger is on the schedule for Baltimore. I thought we discussed this. Fix it." Click.

A pregnant pause followed, David simply too surprised to say anything. Big Otto Vandegroot had talked to Henry? About *him?* The rolling, grating voice was unmistakable. *Fix it.* What a strange thing to say.

"Here's another one," Bowser said.

Click. "Henry? Otto. Your boy is still on the agenda. I suppose you've probably got a personal relationship you're worried about, but I'm warning you: if you don't take care of this, somebody else will. Call me." Click.

Click. "Henry? Otto. Call me, you son of a bitch."

"Well," Bowser opined, "this is damned interesting. What do you suppose all that's about?"

David pulled his chair out, sat down next to Bowser. "I don't know. Is there more? Keep playing it!"

"There's more," Bowser said.

Click. A musical wash of language. Chinese? The message lasted nearly a minute, then clicked off.

Click. More Chinese, a female voice this time.

Click. No answer.

Click. "Henry Chong? I don't have to tell you who this is—"

"Whoa!" Bowser called out. "Do you recognize that voice?"

"Shut up, shut up!"

The voice clicked off.

"Shoot. Play that again."

Click. "Henry Chong? I don't have to tell you who this is. What the hell happened in Baltimore, mister? You've got some fancy explaining to do. Screw the usual channels." Click.

The voice was familiar. Stern and paternal, the kind of voice that made you feel guilty for not snapping to attention. David couldn't quite place it.

"That was John Quince," Bowser said, clearly surprised and impressed, and maybe a little bit scared.

"Play it again," David said.

Click. "Chong? I don't have to tell you who this is. What the hell happened in Baltimore, mister? You've got some fancy explaining to do. Screw the usual channels." Click.

Yes, Bowser was right. That *was* John Harrison Quince, or someone imitating him flawlessly.

Click. "Chong? Do us all a favor and call me back. Bye!" Click.

That one was Quince again. Jesus, what was he doing talking to Henry Chong? What possible connection could the two of them have?

"Well, well, well," said Bowser. "I had no idea our Hyeon was such a bad boy. In bed with the Grays, and I never once suspected."

David's head was buzzing. He felt as if he might pitch forward in his chair, unable to support the weight that had just settled onto his shoulders. Henry and Otto? Henry and Quince? Henry and a uniformed police death squad? The combinations were too complex, too unexpected. Like chopping up a simple molecule and finding a chaos undreamed of in the whirling bits and pieces.

Whatever had happened these past few days, Henry and Otto had given their lives to the effort. And David, too, had nearly been killed. By the *Gray Party?* That was just too weird, the idea that they would know him, mark him, despise him in some way. David Sanger, the apolitical recluse. If not for the nagging of Bowser and Marian, he probably wouldn't even remember to vote.

Bowser was at the keyboard again. "How 'bout those Chinese messages?"

"Uh. What about them?"

"Well . . . what say we run that . . . through . . . this language glosser. I'd like to hear what they're saying."

Despite himself, David was intrigued. "You can translate Chinese? Really?"

"Well, kind of. The language glosser just breaks the

speech up into individual words and translates them in place. 'The wine is muscular, but the meat has spoiled.' That kind of thing. Occasionally, though, you'll get something useful. Here, watch:"

He made a series of keystrokes, then worked the trackball to click on a screen icon. A window appeared, and text began scrolling up along it.

用 (USE, BUSINESS) 心 (MIND, CORE, HEART) 深 (DEEPEN, MAGNIFY, INTENSIFY)
[IDIOM: Use Caution] [85% Confidence]
PROPER NAME: Hyeon
私 (I, MY, PRIVATE) 達 (REACH, ARRIVE AT)
[IDIOM: We] [90% Confidence]
[[?]]
知 (KNOW)
灰色 (GRAY COLOR) 党 (CABAL, CONSPIRACY, POLITICAL PARTY, FACTION)
[IDIOM: The Gray Party] [65% Confidence]
[[?]]
暴 (ACT VIOLENTLY OR CRIMINALLY, RAGE, EXPOSE) 露 (BRING TO LIGHT, EXPOSE) [IDIOM: Blackmail] [70% Confidence]
[[Full Stop]]
[[?]]
急 (URGENCY, CRISIS)
決 (RESOLVE, DECIDE, SOLVE)
PROPER NAME: Hyeon
[[?]]
問題 (PROBLEM, QUESTION, SUBJECT)
[[Full Stop]]
•
•
•

Bowser took in a sharp breath, and let it out in a grunt that was part laughter, part shock and dismay. "I'll be God damned. Bend me over a church pew, my buddy; Henry Chong was a goddamn Red Empire spy! Look at this caller-ID tag; this comes from the Chinese embassy in Washington. 'We know the Gray Party has been blackmailing you.' God hairy damn it!"

"This is crazy," David said, feeling as if all the blood were draining out of his head, pooling thickly in his gut.

"No," Bowser insisted. He shot to his feet, making broad, enthusiastic gestures in the air. "It makes perfect sense! The Chinese get all the AMFRI data, but they want fresher news than that, something they can use to scoop the competition. Who better than *the* Hyeon Chong, trusted by everyone in the business?"

His hands spread apart, dramatically. "But wait! The Sniffer King gets wind of it, and snitches to his Gray Party friends. Being true patriots, they jerk Henry's strings instead of turning him in. Gotta make a buck in this world, right? But the story leaks, somehow, and Quince has everyone snuffed as a safety precaution. I'll be damned."

"Well, what would that have to do with *me?*" David demanded.

Bowser looked down at him excitedly. "They probably figured *you* were the leak! Oh, this is great. We have to find Marian, get this story out in tomorrow's *Bulletin.*"

David sighed. Bowser's entire life had been building toward this moment. He'd kept his skills sharp, hypothesizing conspiracies of every sort, woven through every aspect, through the very *fabric* of modern life. And parts of what he'd just said did indeed make sense, given the message glaring out from the computer screen. But something was missing, something vital and central and huge. Bowser's speculation was the hollow shell of some grander and simpler explanation.

"Your boy is still on the agenda," Big Otto had said. "If you don't take care of this, someone else will." Clearly, his interest in David had been more than simple anger. He hadn't wanted David to speak in Baltimore, and in getting that wish, he had paid a very high price indeed.

Answers tickled at David's brain. It was like a molecular fabrication problem, in some ways: information spread out before him, seething with the Brownian motion in his mind, trying to come together into a coherent whole. He sensed, somehow, that most of the puzzle pieces were now in his possession.

"Let's read the other one," Bowser said, sitting back down again and putting his hands to the computer. He rattled off quick sequences on the keyboard, working the trackball impatiently with his thumb.

"Hello," he said. "Hello. Oh, *crap,* there's been a *trace* on this line. Who the hell puts traces on a dead man's voice mail?"

David sat up in alarm. "I thought you said this telecom port was blinded."

"Well, yeah, for the *phone* call. We're in *maintenance* mode right now. You can't run blind in maintenance mode; it just doesn't work that way. Crap, crap, we've got to get out of here." He looked behind him at the trouble kit, looked back at the computer equipment arrayed in front of him. "Go watch the door, David; I've got to pack this stuff up real quick."

His heart hammering, David rose from the chair and moved to the motel room's only exit. He put an eye to the peephole, then jerked back in annoyance when the Hud Specs clacked against the door and against his face. He was about to remove them, but in a flash of inspiration he switched them on instead.

Everything went warm and purple once again, and when he closed one eye and looked out the peephole, he could see the world outside like another of his rearview mirrors: a disk of purple shapes on a white background, fish-eyed by the peephole lens. After brief disorientation, things snapped clear in his mind.

He could clearly make out the cars in the parking lot, some of which were annotated AUTOMOBILE and some not, some marked with elevated temperatures and glowing auras over their hoods, indicating they had been driven in recent hours and were still warm. One particular vehicle, a van, seemed to glow purple-white hot, a cloud of brilliant exhaust blossoming behind it. POLICE CRUISER, its annotation read. 31.8°C. The bubble lights on its roof confirmed the analysis.

"Oh, shit," he said. "There's a cop car out there. And cops!"

He saw them now, piling out of the van, guns and riot sticks at the ready. HUMAN, 36.8°C. HUMAN, 37.2°C. HUMAN, 36.9°C. Heads and faces concealed beneath smooth, visored motorcycle helmets. A familiar terror stabbed through him.

"Bowser! It's the guys from my apartment! They're heading this way!"

David heard a crashing noise, turned to see Bowser sweeping his telecom equipment to the floor, lifting the table. His face was tight and expressionless as he moved toward the door, nodding his head sideways, urging David out of the way. David stepped aside and watched Bowser drop the table, jamming one edge up under the doorknob.

There had been no delay at all in Bowser's reaction, no pause for reflection or regret, and David was struck once again with the realization that his best friend had spent his life dreaming of, possibly even *hoping for,* a night like just like this one. "A crisis lends real weight and meaning to your actions," he recalled Bowser saying in a long-ago, drunken conversation. "Everything else is just a game, and kind of a dull one."

Still in motion, Bowser swept past the bed, scooping loose articles into the trouble kit and lifting it. "Come on," he said, striding purposefully toward the bathroom as he zipped the gym bag shut. Through the Hud Specs, David had watched Bowser's temperature rise from 36.8 degrees to 36.9, then to 37.0, where it now seemed inclined to hover. He followed into the bathroom like a wad of paper drawn along behind a speeding truck, ignorant of destination or purpose, but helpless in the draft nonetheless.

Bowser slammed the toilet lid shut, and stepped up onto it. His face curled with displeasure, and he jostled for a moment before regaining his balance. "Crappy cheap plastic," he muttered quickly. "Don't stand on the center."

"What are we doing?" David asked, bewildered.

A crash resounded from the motel room's front door, startling both of them. A second crash followed, and a third. Splintering noises accompanied the last.

"Come on, come on!" Bowser shouted, weaving his fingers together and dropping them to knee-level.

"What are we *doing?*" David repeated.

"Climb through the ceiling!"

David looked up. Yes! The ceiling was acoustic tile; he could just push his way through it! Eagerly, he put a hand on Bowser's shoulder and another on the wall for balance, and stepped up into Bowser's cupped hands. His horizon indicator wobbled for a moment, but he ignored it, straightening his leg, shooting himself upward toward the ceiling.

His head was now within inches of the acoustic tile, so, trusting his balance, he released his hands and shoved them upward, bursting a large rectangular tile from its frame to spin up into the ceiling somewhere. Without waiting to be told, he got his arms up into the hole, scrabbled his hands around for something to hold onto, and heaved himself up. The tile frame groaned ominously, but held.

It was darker up here, the glasses compensating with an information-dense fog of purple and white. He saw the tile stretching in all directions like a floor, a trembling unstable floor supported by coat hanger–thick wires and thumb-sized crossbars. Bright patches flared where air vents led up from the warm rooms beneath.

He hauled his knees up behind him, waited for balance, then turned around as quickly and carefully as he could.

"Take the bag!" Bowser shouted up at him, shoving the trouble kit into his hands. David accepted it, pulling it in beside him and then lowering his arms once more, to help Bowser up behind him.

"Hurry!" Bowser snapped, gripping David's arms tightly and pulling himself up.

A helmeted policeman swung through the doorway, nightstick cocking back, ready to strike. Three more police boiled through behind him, pushing and urging him forward. The nightstick swung, connected.

David watched it happen in purple-annotated, slow-motion horror. The club struck Bowser in the ribs of his left side, so hard it bounced, leaving behind flesh that rippled liquidly in a way a human rib cage never should.

Bowser screamed, a piercing shriek more of surprise and outrage than of pain.

Below, the police helmets gleamed lacquer white, stark against the navy blue of their jackets and gloves.

Bowser's fingers convulsed with the shock of the blow, releasing their hold on David's forearms.

He fell. Like a fragile thing that had been dropped, a fumbled dish that could be clearly seen on its way down to shattering impact, he fell, maintaining eye contact with David all the while. His feet brushed the lid of the toilet, but at a bad angle, legs crumpling, shifting his balance forward, toward the opposite wall. His arms smashed against a towel rack, and he hit the floor face-down.

Amazingly, he was turning himself over the very instant he struck, throwing himself back onto his knees and turning to face his attackers. David caught a glimpse of blood on his face.

The service revolvers were out already, aimed already, cocked and in the process of firing already.

"Hey, *fuck* you," Bowser said, in what David's later testimony would call "a voice of calm defiance."

The pistols went off like cannons, hurling Bowser hard against the shower. The splash of brain tissue was noted, highlighted and thermally mapped by the Hud Specs. Bowser slumped, boneless and nearly headless, against the shower's glass door.

"Oh my God!" David screamed.

The visored helmets turned up to face him.

In that instant, both thought and emotion fled. He simply picked up the trouble kit, turned to one side, and scrambled. Acoustic tiles came apart beneath his churning feet and knees, but he kept ahead of them, his body's instincts optimizing and economizing, hurling him forward at maximum speed.

The service revolvers exploded again, sending barely felt shock waves up past his legs. They went off still again, and this time he heard the bullets smacking the metal roof and punching through it, but well behind him this time. He continued forward as far and as fast as he could, until he came up against a cinder-block wall that marked the far end of the motel.

Again, without a single conscious thought or feeling, he shoved down hard against the tile which now supported him. It came apart with squeaky eagerness, dropping him to the room below. He missed, by inches, the soft landing pad of an oversized bed, but he did come down on his feet, retaining his grip on the heavy gym bag.

The room was dark, and a bright figure stood out clearly on the bed; HUMAN, 36.4°C. The man sat up, pulling away from David in confusion and alarm.

Wordlessly, David turned away from him, ran for the door, undid the latches with a speed that astonished him. This completed, he threw the door open and hurled himself outside, where he vaulted a railing to land, catlike, on the cracked asphalt of the parking lot. To the east, dawn had begun to break, but his body turned him in the opposite direction and, running at a full-bore, muscle-tearing pace that would leave him sore for weeks, left the Twilight Motel behind and pursued the cool darkness of the night.

CHAPTER SIXTEEN

David awoke, shivering, to the sounds of traffic above him. He was wedged under a bridge, up where the sloping concrete met the bottom of the roadbed. There was no disorientation, no moment of realization or shock; last night's events were burned vividly into his brain, images that he could never possibly forget, even for a moment. Even in sleep.

Dreams, fitful and horrible, had plagued him despite his exhaustion. He felt he could sleep a lot longer, simply close his eyes and sleep the clock around. But it was full daylight, and out beyond the bridge the telephone poles cast very short shadows. Ten or eleven A.M., he guessed, and about ten degrees above freezing. Autumn was setting in hard, this year.

Rummaging in the trouble kit, he found an energy bar and consumed it greedily. It left his mouth sticky and dry, but there was nothing to wash it down with. Even Bowser Jones couldn't think of everything.

The thought alarmed him with a wave of profound sadness. *My best friend just died,* he thought, stringing the words together to see how they sounded. Very strange and very bad, he concluded. Not words he'd ever thought he'd need.

Jesus. What the hell was he going to do now? Go to the police? Arrange a surrender to Mike Puckett, in person? Give up and die, here, under this bridge? No, not that, certainly. What would Bowser do?

Find Marian, you putz.

Oh, of course. And all at once, he knew just where to find her. But to get there, he would need money. He checked the trouble kit.

The wallets held mostly paper documents, and a driver's license for someone named Wayne Schlagel, a bearded but otherwise-nondescript man who wore black-framed glasses and looked, rather remarkably, like a digital touch-up job of Bowser. Wayne also had an ATM card, its PIN number foolishly scrawled across its plain yellow face. BERMUDA PROVIDENT BANK LTD, the card said in stiff type below Wayne Schlagel's name. There were some other documents pertaining to that bank, documents which referred, cryptically, to something called a "triple-blanked bearer account."

David also came up with a money belt whose secret compartment contained five gold coins the size of dimes, sealed in a strip of clear, flexible plastic. They appeared to have been minted in a place called "Fürstentum Castellania." One face featured an elaborate crest of lions and crowns, the other a stylized cross and the message: "1998 5g 999.9." No immediate clue as to their value.

The only cash he found was a roll of dollar coins,

twenty of them. Not enough to accomplish anything, though it might buy him a cheapie pair of actual shoes.

He zipped up the money belt and threaded it through his own belt loops, buckling it about his waist, and he cleaned most of the garbage out of one of the wallets and pocketed it, along with the roll of dollars. Then, he unzipped his jacket and reversed it, swapping sky blue for Scotch plaid, and performed a similar maneuver with the baseball cap. He thought about putting a wig on under it, but decided against it, at least for now.

I can't believe this is happening, he thought as he zipped up the trouble kit and, standing, slung it across his back. It was the first time that day the thought had occurred to him, but he sensed it would by no means be the last.

Squinting, shielding his eyes with a raised hand, he stumbled out into the sunlight. There was a sidewalk right on the other side of the fence, with people hurrying along it every few seconds. There was no hole in the fence, so he simply dropped his bag on the far side and climbed over after it, ignoring the glares of passersby. So far as he knew, he was breaking no law, certainly doing no harm.

Once over, he snatched the bag up again and merged with the crowd. He supposed he did look a little dirty by now. That would have to be remedied eventually, lest he draw unwanted attention, but it was hardly the first order of business. *Money* made the world go 'round, and it definitely had some going 'round to do this morning if he was going to get his affairs in order.

David had always been an obsessive planner and scheduler, feeling comfortable only when the foreseeable future had been structured, like a road paving itself ahead of his footsteps, zipping out toward the horizon, showing him where he had to go. Under current circumstances, it seemed frighteningly impossible to plan anything, but nonetheless a picture of the day ahead began to coalesce in his mind. And the more he saw of it, the more he knew that, yes, laying hands on some money was the only way to begin.

For safety reasons, automatic teller machines were never installed in secluded locations; too easy for the customers to be beaten and robbed. So it was right out in the open, on the Wharton Street sidewalk bustling with pedestrian traffic, that David tried Wayne Schlagel's bank card. It wasn't at all a casual thing; he expected someone to stop him at any moment. He expected lights to flash, sirens to scream, passersby to whip out guns and badges and warrants of arrest. He tried switching on the Hud Specs, but the visual clutter did nothing good for his paranoia. After a few seconds he switched them off again.

When he'd been standing by the machine for over two minutes, and now really did look suspicious, he gritted his teeth and made his move. His hands shook so badly he could barely punch the keys, and the sweat rolled off him in chilly rivers.

In the end, though, it was easy as falling down, and he walked away with $300 in crisp, new bills. He'd have taken more, but the machine informed him he'd withdrawn the daily limit. Well, then. His planned shopping trip would have to be at the Friends of Jesus store, his lunch at Cheap Mike's, his night, when night came, at another fleabag motel.

It wasn't so bad, really; as a longtime student, what Bowser called a *terminal* student, David was no stranger to living cheaply. In fact, despite everything, he felt a peculiar, cloak-and-dagger excitement at what he was doing. Trusting no one, speaking to no one, moving through the city like a ghost, cut off from everything he'd previously known and, in return, rendered transparent to the eyes of those around him. Philadelphia seemed new and strange, a pulsing, vibrant matrix of danger and suspicion and, yes, opportunity.

The drop foil, cool against the flesh of his arm, seemed to hum with power. *I am also carrying a gun,* he realized, and that thought filled him with equal parts fear and black, righteous joy. Bulletproof and bespectacled, he bore the weapons of his enemies and the knowledge of what they would do if they caught him again. He had seen them gun down Bowser with hardly a second glance, like stepping on a bug.

They wouldn't step on David like that, no sir.

He walked past Wharton Square, eyeing its splashes of autumn color, and then past Twenty-second and Twenty-first Streets, until he came to Cheap Mike's Hoagie Shack. The place would be called a fast-food restaurant, except that it wasn't part of a chain and didn't have a big flatscreen menu hanging up over the kitchen, didn't, in fact, have a "menu" at all.

He pushed the door open and went up to the cashier, who smiled at him. He half-smiled back at her, and said, "I'll have the cheese steak sandwich," which was kind of a joke; Cheap Mike served nothing else.

"Did you want chips with that?" the clerk asked brightly.

"Yes."

"Onions and peppers?"

"Yes, please."

She quoted him a price, and he paid it, and half a minute later he was carrying his tray off to a white plastic table in the corner of the room. It wasn't really lunchtime yet, so the place was not crowded. But then, maybe it wouldn't fill up at mealtimes, either; the popularity of the city's native sandwich had nosedived with the dairy poisonings of '04, and its recovery had been slow and incomplete. Nobody was eating red meat these days, anyway, except the poor who took advantage of its declining price. Marian had done a piece last year called "Cheese Staked: The Death of a Philly Tradition."

"Leaves more for us," Bowser Jones would have said, clamping his jaw down on an enormous bite of sandwich and chewing hugely.

That was a sad thought. A sheen of tears sprang up in David's eyes, and he pressed a napkin to his face to blot them away. He hadn't shed any tears before now, so in a way, this came as a relief—he was not, in fact, a callous bastard, unable to cry at the death of his best friend. It was just that he had so much else on his mind. . . .

Shot him down like a dog, like nothing at all. His brain, home of facts, schemes, ideas, and passions that existed nowhere else, no more than a bit of paint to be splashed across the shower curtain.

He wiped his eyes again. That was a hard way to end a life, very unfair. His eyes continued to drain, the tears coming faster and harder now. But it was right, it was proper, that he should cry at a time like this. It was only when he raised his sandwich and attempted to take a bite that he began to worry—he wasn't breathing right; he was gasping like a fish.

It occurred to him after a moment that there was, in fact, nothing physically wrong. This was *grief,* the brutal sledgehammer of emotions, destroyer of hopes, the ancient darkness that had impassioned so much of history and literature. It was a novel sensation for David—nobody close to him had ever died before. At age twenty-five, he still had four living grandparents! And yet, in the past five days he had lost his best friend, his worst enemy, his faculty advisor, his work, his laboratory, and his home. His life was a windblown tent with half its grounding stakes flapping in the breeze.

That's it, God damn it, no more. Nothing else would

be lost, no one else would have to die for the sake of this grotty little affair. He would see an end to it, a *just* end, even if he had to remake the world in the process.

Indeed, molecular fabrication *would* remake the world, and right here, right now, was as good a time as any to decide what form the change should take. "Even death may someday be a curable ailment," Henry Chong had said once in a lecture.

The comment had been intended as a joke, but right here, right now, it struck David as being in ghastly poor taste. The tears splashed down on his hand, cool and wet where it lay on the plastic surface of the table.

Oh, Bowser, God damn it.

CHAPTER SEVENTEEN

Clouds, white and fractal-puffy with recursive features echoed in smaller and smaller detail, scudded across an amber-colored sky, its sun shining like a silver coin through the layers of haze. A jagged fractal mountain range rose high and purple in the distance, the snowline cutting ruler-straight across the peak tops. Below, the river valley was lush with greenery, patches of leafy forest thick as jungles. He could see a city down there, and a number of small towns and villages scattered like crumbs. Somewhere up ahead, a whipporwill sounded.

Visible here and there, standing out on rounded hilltops, were castles of fantastic design. Even miles, even tens of miles away, he could see their towers of colored glass, their lava moats, their shimmery bubbles of protective magic. These were the strongholds of the Sorcerers, and this was Llyr, the corner of NEVERland that was Marian's dominion and second home.

The journey to get here had not been a long one—he'd simply plugged his charity store VR rig into the motel room's telecom port, picked his way through five layers of menu selection, and waited a few minutes while the front-end software was downloaded. Easy as falling down. And yet, the illusion of otherworldliness was quite good. No physical textures here, not without *really* good equipment, but the sights and sounds were detailed enough to seem real. He had jumped dimensions, found his way into a simplified realm where good and evil hashed things out with the unself-conscious glee of a Saturday morning cartoon. If there was subterfuge here, it was at least a known and expected quantity in the game.

Which of the castles was Marian's? He'd never been here before, never listened closely to her descriptions of this unreal place. Unimportant, yes? Unless you were chased in here by murderers and goons. He made a mental note to listen, henceforth, to everything everyone said to him.

He made a window-washing gesture with his hand, bringing up a status report of his magical abilities. If Marian were here, contacting her shouldn't be too hard; she was the queen of this particular valley. Even if she weren't here, he should be able to nail a message to her throne or something. In fact, he could probably whisper her name on the breeze, and let enchantments carry it until it found her waiting ear. But no, alas, his status report showed his *Potentia Numen* at zero. He had entered the game as a beginner, without power or knowledge, without so much as a map of the territory.

Jesus. In actual peril for his actual life, he would nonetheless have to tramp up and down these pastel hills, asking directions to the palace of the Queen of Llyr. Well, maybe that was what he got for stupidly turning her out into the night. "Meet me at Lillet's," he could have said. Four little words.

He started forward, clomping down the hillside with faint clickety-click noises. Looking down at his virtual body, it was easy to forget he was actually sitting in a chair, working the VR rig's foot switches to simulate leg movement. With modest effort he was able to jog at a heady pace, maybe twenty miles an hour. Turning, however, required a difficult heel-toe-heel movement for which he had to slow down almost to a stop.

The verdant forests approached. He passed a tree, and then another, and then he stopped before a whole grove of them, looming darkly above him like a wooden cliff. Within, the hazy sunlight filtered darkly through the canopy of leaves. Shafts of gold pierced the gloom here and there, and between them, on the forest floor, he thought maybe he could see some movement.

It was dumb, it was just a game, but his breath quickened a little. He drew his sword and backed away. Better to go around. Getting eaten by some slobbering creature would not get him any closer to his goal.

He drifted for a while between the stands of trees. The landscape was as green and groomed as a golf course, and as convoluted. By appearances, the city had been no more than a few miles from the top of the ridge, but distances could be tricky. Fractal theory was an important part of his work at times, and he knew well the problems of measuring the edges of a non-Euclidian structure—run your ruler around every nook and cranny, every subnook and subcranny, and your distance measurement quickly went asymptotic.

What is the circumference of Britain? Unknown, irrelevant. Properly measured, all nonlinear paths were infinite. He could end up wandering here for a very long time indeed.

The forest began to seem more and more like a maze, the same every direction he looked. There were no landmarks down here, no directional cues aside from the silver-dollar sun hanging up there in the sky. He reasoned that moving downhill would eventually take him to the river, but his path was convoluted enough to make even that a difficult task.

Eventually, though, he came upon a little pool of water, a spring, with a picturesque stream running out of it like a gently sloping mirror of blue glass. Flowers surrounded the pool, bright red and yellow against the unbroken Astroturf shades of the ground itself. *This is a game,* he reminded himself. He could follow the stream down to the river, but the spring itself, standing out so sharply against its background, appeared to have some significance.

He stopped, bent over to peer down into the water. He was momentarily surprised by his reflection—a brightly painted doll's face in place of his own. He touched a finger to the water's surface, disturbing the image with spreading waves of tiny concentric rings. Then the rings were gone and the pool was still again. The illusion was plausible, if not entirely convincing. Welcome to NEVERland.

He noticed a strange momentary shimmering, a blue-white aura that flickered faintly around his hand as he withdrew it from the spring. Huh. Curious, he called up a status display, and saw that his *Potentia Numen* had jumped to three points. Was that a lot? Would it be of any use? More than zero, definitely, but he still had no idea how to tap and control the magic forces of this place. It was rather a complex art, if Marian's comments were any standard to judge by.

The water in the spring began rippling again, though David wasn't touching it. There was a heaving in the water, and then . . . something leaped out of it toward David, something the size of a dog, but green and leggy, glistening in the amber light. It flopped at his feet, glaring upward, and he staggered back, brandishing his virtual sword. It was, he saw, a giant frog.

"HELLO," it croaked, blinking its frog eyes at him.

David suppressed a scornful giggle. This fairy-tale gimmickery was supposed to be entertaining? Adults paid money for this?

"HELLO," the frog croaked again.

"Hello," David sighed, resigned to playing out the scene. "Do you live here?"

"YES. DON'T WANT TO. ENCHANTED."

"Oh," David said, with some genuine surprise at the lifelike inflections on the voice. "Are you a real player?"

"YES."

"Someone changed you into a frog?"

"YES. SORRY. DIFFICULT TO SPEAK. TAKES *NUMEN*. WHAT IS YOUR MIDDLE NAME?"

"I beg your pardon?"

"MIDDLE NAME. IS IT 'HAPGOOD'?"

A chill ran down David's spine. David Hapgood Sanger. How would a cartoon frog know that? He'd felt safe in this anonymous world, more or less, but now he felt that security ripped away. Were his enemies *here?* Were they *everywhere?* It sounded crazy, even after everything that had happened. But how did the *frog* know his *name?*

In a flash of mindless fear, he stepped forward and pierced the frog with his sword. The blade entered between the creature's eyes.

"HEY!" it croaked in belated alarm. "I WAS TRYING . . . OH GREAT, THAT'S A MORTAL. THANKS A LOT, KILLER."

The frog shimmered, sparked, turned transparent, and then vanished. David stepped back, raising his sword, eyeing the spot where the creature had been. Guilt tugged at him.

He had messed around with virtual reality back in high school, mostly exploring moonscapes extrapolated from his microscope images, or wandering through the simulations on the atomic scale, the world gone Brownian in a hailstorm of colored tennis balls. He'd played a few games, off and on, but never the networked variety, never with real people as opponents. He hadn't seen the point, hadn't fathomed the protocols of an imaginary interaction that nonetheless involved real people.

Had he just inflicted unwarranted harm on another human being? Stripped him of virtual life, robbed him of some status he'd worked hard to achieve? Someone had turned the guy into a frog; was that any worse? People took these things seriously, he knew. *Marian* took it seriously.

He looked up at the forest around him, listened to its sounds. Stupid game or no, he was in a foreign place, governed by foreign rules, and very much at the mercy of forces beyond his control. Trigger-happiness was not likely to help the situation. Damn.

How had the frog known his name? Why hadn't David simply *asked,* instead of skewering the creature in panic? Damn, damn, was he vulnerable here, or wasn't he? Should he pull out, yank the helmet off his head and jerk the plug out of the wall? If he did, how would he find Marian?

Fear gnawed at him like a vicious, hungry little animal as he started forward once again, following the stream deeper into the valley. The forest canopy closed overhead, shutting out the sunlight. He gripped the (real) pommel of his (imaginary) sword tightly, holding the weapon out in front of him like a talisman.

He walked for ten minutes, then another ten, until his calves ached with the working of the foot switches and his hair hung damp and sweaty beneath the VR helmet. This environment presented an actual, physical ordeal, and there seemed to be no way around it. No doubt there were broomsticks and magic carpets and such in the game, but he had to *find* them to use them, and he had to *get* somewhere in order to find anything. The walk continued far beyond the point of discomfort.

Then, blessedly, he came upon a path, with a little stone footbridge arching over the stream. He stopped, leaned over to massage his sore leg muscles. The sensation was strange—the game projected his legs in a different position than they actually had, so his fingers seemed about to close on empty air. And yet, the air was filled with the nerves of his own invisible flesh. It made him dizzy, made his head ache.

"WHO GOES THERE!" boomed a voice from under the bridge.

David's heart sank as a dark, hairy creature unfolded itself from beneath the bridge. When it stood, it was half again as tall as David, and twice as big around. Of course, every bridge had to have a troll under it. Jesus H. Christ.

"I'm, uh, just a player. I'm lost; I'm trying to find my way to the queen's palace." David's heart banged fearfully as he spoke.

"NONE SHALL PASS HERE, WITHOUT THEY SHARE A MAGIC OR A TREASURE. TEACH ME A SPELL, OR I SHALL EAT YOU."

David sighed. "Look, I just started here; I don't have anything to share. It's very important that I speak with the queen. Can you tell me how to find her?"

"YOUR SCREECHING WILL NOT SAVE YOU. TEACH ME A SPELL, OR I SHALL EAT YOU."

"Are you even a player?"

The troll stepped toward him, spreading its arms. "PREPARE TO BE EATEN."

Wonderful. An idiot system-sprite was going to knock him out of the game. In anger and frustration, David leaped forward, extending his sword arm and snapping his wrist down. With a real sword, the move would have been awkward, but the virtual blade was weightless, its light pommel balanced perfectly in his hand. He lopped off the troll's left arm with a single clean slice.

"AAIGH!" the troll cried out. "YOU HAVE WOUNDED ME! PRAY, ACCEPT THIS GIFT AND HURRY ON YOUR WAY."

The creature's face, brown and lumpy as a rotted pumpkin, seemed to split open at the wide, toothless mouth. A shimmering, blue-white ball leaped from the opening, striking David in the chest and splashing, spreading there, fading.

"Hey," David said, stepping back worriedly. But the sparkling did not seem to have harmed him, and presently the troll retreated, stooping down to fold itself back under the bridge again. Ripples glided down the stream where its feet disturbed the water, and then all was still and quiet once again.

Huh. David waved up a status report, and saw he'd received the gift of two more *Potentia Numen,* and a spell called "Temporary Bubble." The name hung before him, in frilly black letters. Curious, he touched the words. They flashed red, then vanished along with his *Numen* indicator. A whole series of words filled the air, now, hovering in front of him as if painted on glass. Nonsense words, he thought, or maybe some old language like Sanskrit. OH LEI SHAH STEKKI JOMJAH STEKKI BREIJAH . . .

He touched these words one by one, but nothing happened. He tried speaking them aloud, though, and that made them flash and disappear each in turn. When he finished the last one, a burning palm print appeared. Taking the hint, he raised his hand and pressed it against the image. It flared brightly for a second or two, then darkened, then disappeared.

The message -2 NUMEN flashed in the air and vanished, and then the bridge in front of him began to shimmer in a strange way. A bubble appeared around it, rainbow-transparent, like a soap bubble. Its purpose was not immediately clear, and nothing else seemed to happen as a result of it. Huh. What was it supposed to be for?

Well, enough of this crap. He stepped over to the flagstone path, and followed it down the gentle slope of the valley.

His next encounter came after a thankfully brief interval; he found himself staggering out of the forest, back into the silver sunlight. The path stretched on ahead, over green-carpeted hills, toward a Slavic-style castle that seemed constructed of red-lacquered copper and brass. Or . . . could it be gold?

He hadn't taken five steps toward it when he suddenly froze in his tracks. The world flickered and sizzled around him, and he found his cartoon body locked, immobile, no longer registering the movements of his head and hands, no longer listening to the foot switches.

"You have entered the domain of Woodruff," said a soft, feminine voice in his ear. "Please state your business."

"Uh," David said, taken aback, "I'm, uh, looking for the Queen of Llyr. Is Woodruff a sorcerer? Can he help me? Or she? Are you Woodruff?"

"I am the master's gatekeeper," the voice answered softly. "I will convey your message to him. Your message has been conveyed."

"Yeah, so?"

David remained frozen in midstride. He realized, with some vague sense of alarm, that he could in fact be trapped here permanently, like a fly in a spiderweb. He could be forced to abandon this body and start the game all over again, aching muscles and all.

"Woodruff!" he called out, trying not to sound angry.

"The master has agreed to an audience," the gatekeeper murmured.

The world sizzled and flashed again, and suddenly

David was standing indoors, on a stone floor, in a dome-shaped room walled in bookshelves. Light spilled in through a pair of narrow, Gothic-arched, glassless windows. Before him, a bearded man in yellow robes stood within a chalked circle on the floor. David himself stood within a pentagram, strange characters marked beside each vertex.

"Woodruff?" he demanded.

"Yes," the man said, in a theatrically patient and confident voice. "Welcome to my home. For what reason have you chosen to disturb me?"

"Cut the crap," David said. Then, more politely: "Listen; I'm not here to play this game. I'm a friend of the queen's, and I have to get a message to her right away. It's urgent."

"You are Hapgood," Woodruff said, in that same annoying tone.

David didn't bother denying it.

"Elishandra has been looking for you," the sorcerer intoned. "She's posted a generous bounty, even by my standards. Be honest with me: this has some effect for the future of Llyr, does it not?"

Elishandra? Oh, yeah, that was what Marian called herself here. VR people didn't like to use their real names.

"Elishandra, yes. She's been here, in the game? Can you take me to her?"

"Answer my question, if you please."

David flared. "Kid, you take yourself pretty seriously. I can really use some help here, but I'm not going to wade through this garbage to get it. I'm not impressed, OK? Drop the act."

Woodruff smiled a patient smile. He gestured in the air, mumbled something quietly, gestured again. Casting a spell? Nothing happened that David could see.

"You're fresh from the Other World, my friend. Things

here are not mayhap quite the way you imagine them. Is it fake? Am *I* fake? I seem to have some power over you, to give you what you want, or not to. Is *that* fake?"

"How old are you?"

"It hardly matters, my friend. If I said a thousand, what would you think?"

There was a pause. David glared at the sorcerer, who looked back impassively. Or maybe not; the range of facial expression was pretty limited. What was this guy thinking, really? Did it matter?

"Look," he said, "I'm not into this game. I'm sorry to trouble you; I'll just be on my way."

"You may find that somewhat hard. Believe it or not, you really are in my power here. I want to know what Elishandra is up to."

"It's not a game thing. She's in trouble in the real world, and I'm trying to help her."

Woodruff's eyes lit up. "Trouble? What kind of trouble?"

David felt a chill. "Who are you?"

"I am Woodruff. I am one of the most powerful sorcerers in Llyr. Give me what I want."

"Are you . . . Gray?"

"What? I am Woodruff. Gray is not in this world anymore. She was never very good, anyway."

Confused, David tried to rub his eyes. He rubbed the front of the VR helmet instead.

"Gray is a person?"

"She was. You ask a lot of questions for a man in your position. You *will* give me what I want."

"What do you want?"

Woodruff's eyes glittered like cut glass. "I want the throne of Llyr. Elishandra has held it long enough."

"Oh!" The tension ran out of David's body. Of course the Grays were not here. Why would they waste their time playing games, important folks like them?

It was the sorcerer's turn to look confused. "You will help me, then?"

David cracked a smile, then wondered if Woodruff could even see it. "I don't give a rat's behind what happens here. Just take me to the queen, and I'll put in a good word for you." Watching his opponent's body language, a projection of uncertainty and indecision, David realized he had somehow broken through and gained the upper hand. He pressed the advantage: "Listen, Woodruff, there's a lot more going on here than you know about, and I don't have the time to get into it right now. You want to collect that bounty, right? And believe me, if, uh, *Elishandra* finds out you've been detaining me, you're going to regret it. Take me to her *right now,* and we'll all still be friends."

"You would betray her?"

"In a small way, I suppose. I won't tell her what we've talked about, you and I."

The sorcerer nodded. "Yes, I see. Let us go, then, with no delay."

He gestured and mumbled. The air shimmered, and the scene changed yet again. David found himself standing in a cathedral-like chamber, on a red carpet, before a throne. Woodruff stood next to him, half a pace in front. The throne was occupied by a woman in flowing satiny white robes, who leaned forward with an intense expression.

"Woodruff," she said quickly, icily. "How dare you enter here unannounced. Have you tampered with my security demons again? I could *destroy* you for that!"

"Forgive me, Your Majesty," Woodruff said, removing his hat and sweeping through a deep, theatrical bow, "but I did not wish to hinder the delivery of the man you seek."

"This is Hapgood?"

"It is."

"What club do you belong to?" the woman demanded, glaring piercingly at David.

"Uh . . . Oh, you mean AMFRI?"

"Correct," she said, more softly. "You may approach the throne."

David walked toward her, stopped a few steps away. Whispered: "Marian?"

"David?"

"Oh, God, I was so worried!" He rushed forward, threw his arms around her. The virtual arms stopped at the surface of her cartoon flesh, while his real arms sank through her, invisible and intangible as those of a ghost.

Apparently, she was having the same trouble. Her face contorted strangely, her mouth opening and closing to emit low squawking sounds, and David realized that she was laughing and crying at the same time. And so, to a lesser extent, was he.

"Are you all right?" he asked urgently, holding his lips near her intangible ear.

She nodded.

"Are you hiding somewhere? Are you safe?"

Again, she nodded.

He took a deep breath, inflating his chest with false courage. "Marian, listen to me. Bowser is dead."

"I know," she said, sobbing and sniffing quietly. "And Henry. It was on TV."

"It was?"

"David, they're blaming it on you!"

He sighed deeply. "I guess they had to. I'm just about the only one still alive."

"What's happening, David? Who the hell is doing this to us?" She turned sharply. "Woodruff!"

The sorcerer blinked innocently. "Your Majesty?"

"Get out of here! This is private!"

He smiled. "Of course, Your Majesty. I am simply waiting for my bounty *Numen.*"

"You have it," she said, gesturing in the air. "Now go."

"Is . . . there a problem I can help you with, Your Majesty?"

"No," she said emptily. "There is no problem."

"As you wish." The sorcerer worked magics in the air before him, then sparkled and vanished like an old Star Trek transporter effect.

"Who's behind all this?" Marian demanded, turning back to David. "Who's killing our friends?"

"The Gray Party," he said.

"What?"

"I'm serious. They tried to keep me from presenting my papers in Baltimore. Big Otto was helping them, but they ended up killing him. I don't know why. They've tried to frame me; they've tried to frame Dov Jacobs. . . . Marian, they shot Bowser at point-blank range. He never had a chance."

"What about Henry?" she asked, in a tone of forced calm.

David shrugged. "I really don't know. I think maybe he was with them, too. Why are they killing their own people? It's me they're after."

"You?"

He turned to glare at her. "Is it *so* shocking? It has to do with my work in some way. People are dying over it. Something I was working on must have scared them, bad."

"The MOCLU, I would think."

David froze. "What?"

"MOCLU," Marian repeated. "It jams up nanoscale machinery, right? Maybe including the molecular sniffer?"

"Oh. Oh, my God, that must be it."

Gray-haired volunteers, an army of them, had built an organization to further their own interests: senior citizens' benefits, a return to "Three R's" education and "decent" TV. Changes to insurance law, stuff like that. And then came the Crackdown, "gray" transforming into a symbol not of age and wisdom, but of law and the enforcement of law.

And the Vandegroot molecular sniffer was the key to it all.

He tried to picture the sniffer's guts, the whirling, fractal array of nanomachinery sprouting from micromachinery sprouting from ordinary, everyday machinery on the macroscale. A crude device, really, lacking any sort of technical elegance. A few micrograms of MOCLU worming around in the gears . . . God, the machine would stop dead in a microsecond.

Taking with it the ability of the Gray Party to keep its campaign promises.

Good God. To the likes of Colonel the Honorable John Harrison Quince, David's MOCLU must look like the end of the world.

"We have to break the story," Marian said. "Can we go to the police?"

"Not a chance. Cops killed Bowser; I'm sure they'd do the same to us."

"What about Puckett?"

David shrugged. "I don't know. I don't want to go to jail, Marian. I don't think I'd ever get out."

"Can't you at least call him, share your theory?"

"No! Look, it was a phone trace that nailed us last night. They tracked us, broke in, and blew Bowser's head off. I don't know who they *were,* I didn't see their *faces,* but they were dressed like cops. For all we know, they could be listening right now. We've got to dig in and hide somewhere."

Marian's gaze was bright and sharp. "Until when, David? You want to hide forever? We have to get the story out, don't you think? Feed it to the newspapers, TV stations, get it out on the Internet . . . The electron is mightier than the sword; you *know* that."

"No. The sword is mightier," David said, thinking of Otto Vandegroot.

Marian sighed. "Fine. You're such a genius, what do *you* think we should do?"

"If we lift a finger, they'll find us. Pick up the phone, mail a letter, they'll find us. You don't think they'd watch the newspapers? Shit, I'll bet they've got spies all over the place."

"David, that's crazy."

"They kept a line trace on Henry Chong's voice mail, even after they killed him. These guys are so paranoid they make Bowser look like—" He choked on the words. "Marian, we don't dare stick our necks out right now."

"So what do we do?" she repeated. Her voice was soft, and her hands rested intangibly on his own.

"I don't know," he said. "Something subtle. We can't talk here, though."

"We sure as hell *can*. I'm the Queen of Llyr, David, and one of the most powerful players NEVERland has ever seen. *Nobody* can eavesdrop on me, not here."

He shook his head. "We're talking over an open telecom line, aren't we?"

"Not really." She made a grimace, plastic-stiff and yet vaguely predatory. "Voice signals are encoded and buried in the game data, very well hidden, along with information on where we're calling from. Anonymity has to be guaranteed or the whole game falls apart. Bribes, threats of violence, that sort of thing."

"They can decrypt it," he assured her.

"No," she said gently. "They can't. The volume of data flowing through NEVERland is so huge that if you captured just a second's worth, it would take a supercomputer over three months to crack all the code keys. That's the figure I'm always hearing. Anyway, you have to understand what a sorceress *does*. I've got a hundred geniuses after me twenty-four hours a day, and none of them ever get anywhere. My precautions are just too elaborate. Believe me, if the Gray Party even *tried* to spy on us, I would know about it."

David grunted noncommittally.

"You have to tell me what you're planning," she insisted.

He sighed. "OK, but there's not much to it. We have to get lost. Right here in the city, I think, because Amtrak's probably got our pictures taped over every ticket booth. So how do we get lost? Are there any neighborhoods where you don't need a housing ID?"

"Sure, lots of them. They never could enforce those regs in the low-rent districts."

"We need an apartment or something. And a computer, and some time to think. Somewhere away from the university, away from the cops . . . Away."

"This city can embed itself so deeply up its own asshole, it's not even pathetic," Marian asserted. "I can name a dozen mixed neighborhoods the police never touch. Did you ever see my crime rate map? It's a much more localized phenomenon than they'd like you to believe. Little bubbles of anarchy all through the city. Fishtown, down by the river, is practically a third-world nation."

David held up a hand. "Don't say any names. We'll talk it all over when we meet."

"Denny's?" she suggested. "Over on Walnut?"

His eyes narrowed, lips pursing, but the expression brought no visible response to Marian's plastic face.

"Meet me at Lillet's place," he said.

Light filtered in through the stained glass above them, casting flat rainbows across the floor.

CHAPTER **EIGHTEEN**

"Won't you carry me across the threshold?" Marian asked as David sank the key into the apartment door's lock. Off to the right, the staircase was an exercise in peeling layers of brown and blue paint. The hallway was done all in waterstained paper, faded images of the Liberty Bell still visible on it in places, oozing down the wall in filthy, brown-white columns.

Don't go out at night, baby. It doesn't get any more Fishtown than this.

"Ha ha," David had been about to say, but when he looked at Marian, he saw no humor in her eyes. He got the door open, then solemnly scooped her up in his arms, and carried her inside.

The "furnished" apartment turned out to have a puke green rug on the floor, and a puke yellow sofa against one wall of the living room. The bedroom was empty, the kitchen so bare even the doors had been removed from the cabinets. But as advertised, there were telecom ports in every room.

"Not much, but it's home," he offered neutrally.

Marian grunted as he set her down. He kissed her lightly on the cheek.

"Hello?" At the sound of knocking, they both turned to face the doorway behind them. A woman stood there, leaning forward against the doorjamb with her right elbow. She was black, heavy, clothed in baby blue sweatpants and a sweater of pale green. She was grinning the sort of open, guileless grin that David had always associated with women who wanted to copy his homework.

"Can we help you?" Marian asked, not quite politely.

The woman's smile broadened. "Maybe t'other way around. Y'all look like some folk could use a hand."

"Haind" was the way she pronounced it, her drawling accent so thick David could not at first make sense of it. Louisiana? Not a local accent, certainly.

"Oh," Marian said, more kindly now. "Well, that's very nice of you. Would you like to come inside?"

"Surely would," the woman said. She stuck out a puffy-fingered hand, like a brown glove filled with pudding. "I'm Bitty Lemieux, and I guess I'm kind of the local Welcome Wagon. Such as it is."

"Marian . . . Jones." They shook hands.

"I'm Don," David said, extending his own hand.

"No last name, this'un," Bitty Lemieux chortled, winking. "You a man in trouble if ever I seen. I won't even ask, is what I won't do."

Her grip was firm, but not excessively so. Her smile looked as if it were held up by invisible hooks, as if it had never left her face and never would.

David eyed her closely. Her friendliness seemed genuine enough, but it worried him nonetheless. To pounce on them so quickly like this, she had to have known they were coming. And he had the idea she wanted something from them, though what it might be he couldn't imagine. It wasn't like they had much to offer.

This is a real black person, he thought. No, not black: *Afriatic* was the word these days; but whatever the label, she was it. Race had never been much of an issue for David—he tended to think of people on the molecular level, where differences like that were all but invisible, and anyway his world, the world of molecular fabrication research, was necessarily a mixed bag. The heavy-hitting Denzl Quick, for example, was black, or rather Afriatic. Still, David was not so naive as to believe that racial inequality had vanished from American life. The real blacks, he knew, the *statistically representative* blacks, did not work in high-profile scientific applications research, did not live in university-subsidized student or faculty housing.

They lived right here in Fishtown, and thousands of other neighborhoods like it. And they were all just as real and solid as Bitty Lemieux, and not one of them had an ATM card from T. Bowser Jones.

"What is it you want?" he could not help asking.

"Ho!" Bitty said, making an "o" of her mouth and slapping her thigh. The gesture conveyed a certain sense of approval. "Listen to you! They teach you manners like that in your lily-white upbringin'?"

David said nothing.

"Well," Bitty allowed, "I can't exactly expect y'all to ask me to dinner, given you ain't even moved in yet. I'm a pushy ol' bitch, though, and ain't making no apologies. I live down the hall, number twenty-nine, and I believe in knowing my neighbors. Sometimes we do favors for one another."

"Favors."

"Uh-huh. Like, let's say you needed something and, maybe, didn't have time to go out and get it. Well, maybe

I have time. Maybe you need a question answered, and I know the answer."

"Just like that?" David asked skeptically. "No strings attached?"

Bitty looked surprised. "No strings? I'm talking about a business arrangement! Strings, yes! I am the official *business lady* of the building, and I don't mean none of that horizontal business, neither."

Oh! David suddenly felt better—this was something that made sense to him. Back in his dormitory days, he'd done a lot of his chores and errands through middlemen and middle-women. Hustlers, they called themselves, poor kids squeezing every possible dime from scholarships and Work Study and still not quite able to make ends meet. Truth be told, they were pretty convenient to have around.

"How much would you charge for a . . . favor?" Marian asked, a thoughtful look on her face.

"Well, now. That would all depend, wouldn't it? We all have a soft spot in our wallets for folks who's our friend."

"I see," Marian said. She had started work on a shallow smile. "I don't suppose you'd like to join us for dinner? We can order a pizza or something."

Bitty grinned and clucked. "Child, you're in a different world from what you think. There ain't no one gonna deliver a pizza in this neighborhood; get stabbed and robbed is what they'd do. Now just maybe, as a favor to my two new friends, I could shake my ass down the block and go *get* us all a pizza. But I ain't got the money to buy one myself, you see what I'm saying."

"I believe I do," Marian said. She reached out for the older woman's hand, took it, held it for a long moment, and then released it.

Bitty's grin opened wider, showing off the straight ivory whiteness of her teeth. "Marian Jones, I believe you and me are gonna get along just fine."

She turned then, and with a grace that belied her pillowy bulk, strutted out the door, closing it behind her.

"No onions!" Marian called after her.

Only then, seconds after the fact, did David realize what had happened: Marian had discreetly palmed a folded bill into Bitty's hand, the gesture between them so smooth and unrehearsed it might as well have been coded in their genes.

"One good thing the government done, is got me off the drugs," Bitty was saying. She sat on the couch next to Marian, and gesticulated with her pizza slice as she spoke. "I about thought I was gonna die back in the Crackdown, but I guess I wouldn't go back."

Marian offered a disapproving frown. "It looks like they haven't done much else for you. This city doesn't need more and better cops; what it needs is a conscience."

"I thought you *were* its conscience," David said.

Marian didn't seem to find that funny.

David didn't blame her—not much was amusing him right now, either. He couldn't shake the feeling that eating the food had somehow sealed their fate, like Persephone with her pomegranate seeds. Like it or not, the pizza marked the passage from one phase of life to another, making them *actual, functioning residents* of this ghetto. And it wasn't even good pizza.

"You know," reflected Bitty, "you two are about the most out-of-place folks I seen in a long time. Must of been some hard luck drug you down to a place like this."

David nodded, and took another sip from his tepid beer. It tasted like plastic. Technically, he hadn't been old enough to drink beer when they phased out aluminum cans, but those had been looser times, and the frothy taste of Budweiser chugging out over cool metal was something he hoped he'd never forget. But plastic was the thing alcoholic beverages came bottled in these days—a sealed metal can could hurt someone, if you threw it hard or dropped it out a window or something. Never *mind* the hazards of a glass bottle in the hands of a drunk.

"Welcome to Nerf World," Bowser would say when subjects like that came up.

"I got the feeling," Bitty went on, "that there's something y'all hiding from, down here on the riverfront. You ain't plannin' on stayin' around too long; that much is plain as day. But y'all waitin' on something, and I'll be plucked if I know what that is."

David snorted. "How about an 800-kilohertz laser nanoassembly workstation?"

"Really? Is that what you waitin' on?"

Marian leaned forward. "If it is, this is the first I've heard of it. I take it you have an idea?"

"I do?" He thought about it, then shrugged. "I'm just thinking out loud, about the MOCLU. If that's what this whole thing is about, we really should have our hands on it, don't you think? Leave a copy with . . . Well, you know. Use it as insurance. Maybe it can help prove . . . stuff."

He'd almost said "leave a copy with our lawyer." He'd almost said "prove my innocence."

"Aha," said Marian. "And why do you need a workstation for that?"

"Well, *because*." He glared at her defensively. "I have no notes; I have no simulation data; I have no *laboratory*. . . . It's a complex molecule with about a thousand steps to fabricate it. If I'm going to resurrect the recipe, I'll need a good computer at the very least."

Indeed, parts of the MOCLU structure had come from the biochemistry department, and had been incorporated with only the briefest of inspections. "I need something long and flat," he had once told Dov Jacobs, "with an alanine group at one end and something with a slight negative charge at the other." Four days later, he'd received a glass beaker full of clear fluid, which Dov had told him contained approximately 80 trillion copies of the desired molecule. Of these, David had used maybe five or six in constructing his templates.

"This workstation could fix all your troubles?" Bitty asked, sounding skeptical and confused.

"Well," David allowed, "it would be a start. We also have to figure out how to get in touch with some people, without exposing ourselves in the process." An angry sadness descended upon him. "God damn them, Bowser would have known what to do. That's *exactly* why he's dead right now."

"So," Marian urged, "use your brain; pretend he's here. What *would* he do in a situation like this?"

David shook his head and looked away. "Hell, I don't know. He'd probably be playing poker with the neighbors by now, and he'd know them all by name."

Marian's eyes remained tired and sad, but her mouth managed a smile. "Yeah, that sounds about right." She killed her beer and finished off the slice of pizza in her hand.

"Y'all wanna meet the neighbors," Bitty said, "I can arrange it no trouble. *I* know 'em all by name."

"No," David said. "I don't think that's such a good idea."

The fewer people who knew they were here, the better. God, they were vulnerable enough as it was. And yet, Marian was right; Bowser would be out meeting the neighbors right now, knowing the trustworthy among them as if by scent. God damn him, he had no right to be dead.

Bitty favored David with a sympathetic look as she rose from the sofa. "You miss your friend pretty bad," she observed, her voice gentle and kind.

"Yeah," he said. "Yeah, I do."

"I guess prob'ly you loved him, don't know how in the world you gonna get along without him. Maybe you feel a little guilty, too. I guess he must have died some bad kind of way."

"You could say that, yes."

"We all lose somebody sometime," she told him. "I done lost my share, and then some. This a mean world; we just all do our part to nicen it up. You can't replace a friend who's gone, but God loves you, child. You can make a new friend."

I think I already have, he did not say, but he smiled at her, and accepted the handshake she offered.

Out on the street somewhere, a crowd of teenagers bubbled into laughter.

CHAPTER NINETEEN

Sounds coming in from the living room; he opened his eyes to darkness. His first thought was that something awful had happened, *must* have happened, and he sat up sharply. He knew exactly where he was: he'd been sleeping on the floor, on the tattered mattress he and Marian had removed from the foldout sofa and dragged here into the bedroom.

He knew exactly where the drop foil was, too—reaching for it was the first thing he did. It popped open in his hand, with umbrella-like sounds.

Rising, freeing himself from the covers, he crept out into the living room, tiptoeing silently on his bare feet. A yellow-white, urban nighttime sort of light leaked into the room around the edges of the window shade, a warmer, yellower light coming in through the front doorway. A figure hunched there, pushing something along on squeaking wheels. An empty hand truck, it looked like.

"Who's there?" David demanded, brandishing the sword. He felt for the light switch, found it.

"Ah! God," a familiar voice said. "you scared me half to death."

"It's mutual."

He flipped the switch, flooding the room with light and revealing a drawn-looking Bitty Lemieux, still dressed in yesterday's clothes. Or was it still today? He checked his watch—11:42 P.M.

"Oh, goodness," Bitty said, turning the hand truck and leaning it up against the closet door. "Thanks for the light. I didn't think y'all would be in bed yet; didn't mean to wake you up."

"What are you doing in here?" David asked, not lowering the sword.

She nodded at the hand truck. "Thought you could use this. Theresa let me in."

Theresa was the name of the building manager. Now David lowered the sword.

Marian crowded in beside him, rubbing her eyes. "Bitty? What's going on? What's the cart for?"

"An 800-kilohertz laser nanoassembly workstation," Bitty said in a deprecating, singsongy tone. "The *doctor* has been doing a little *operating.*"

David went cold inside. "How did you know I was a doctor?"

Bitty leaned against the door frame, hands on the small of her back, massaging. "Oof. My poor bones ain't so young anymore. Doctor?" She eyed David up and down. "I'd say you're a little young for that." Her eyes brightened. "Oh, not a *medical* doctor. I get it; you're that college boy I heard about on the radio. Your name's not Don; it's *David.*"

"No," he said, "that's not true."

White teeth flashed broadly in Bitty's dark face as she opened her mouth to laugh. "You about as transparent as a frog's egg. You can relax; I'm not turnin' no one in. Never have done; don't see a need to start now."

David turned to Marian. "Get your things."

"David, wait."

"No, it's time to go."

Bitty was still laughing, "Hee! hee! Child, if I was in the habit of turning folks in, I'd of done it this afternoon. Don't take no sense to figure out it's the police you two are hiding from. But did I turn you in? No, I brought you a present instead."

"A nanoassembly workstation?" David asked incredulously. "You can't be serious about that."

"I can't? Well, maybe so, 'cause I ain't. What I mean is, I had a talk with my friend Hamilton, a local ne'er-do-well who owes me a couple favors, and he says he can help you out. You tell him where this 800-kilohertz nanoassembly thing of yours can be had, and he will help you go out and get it."

"Get it?" David held back a look of disbelief. "You mean *steal* it, right?"

"Ain't no stealin' in this world. You have a need, and someone has a way to fill it. That's the way."

"And you're going to help me do this. Out of the goodness of your heart."

Bitty clucked and smiled. "You learn slow, my friend; there's always strings attached. I'm in business, here, same as the rest of the world, and you gonna owe me a favor for this."

"I don't want to," he said. "I don't want any part of this. You can't just go around *stealing* things."

"Picked up some scruples, did you?" Marian's voice had a tungsten-hard edge to it, like the sound of a heavy door slamming shut.

He turned to her. "What's that supposed to mean?"

"I mean, you're spending Bowser's money like it's on

fire. Even if his parents don't know about it, that money technically belongs to them. I'm sure they could use it."

David felt a chill. Bowser had been helping him all along—it seemed only natural that he should continue to do so now. Mr. and Mrs. Jones had never entered into David's thoughts, had never crossed his mind even once. God, at some point he was going to have to *face* them, knowing that he had not only killed their son, but robbed him as well. The realization was like a ball of frozen vomit dropping into his stomach.

"We needed it," he said lamely.

"Yes," Marian blazed back at him. "We needed it. We *still* need it. We need a lot of things."

"This isn't right," he insisted. "It's not the same thing."

Marian advanced on him, her eyes like twin blue flames. "You owe me this, David. In case you hadn't noticed, we're in a hole right now, and we have no leverage to get us out. You *asked* for Bitty's help."

"Not on purpose, I didn't. This isn't like a pizza." He turned back to Bitty. "I can't possibly be a part of this. These machines cost a hundred thousand dollars if they cost a dime, and there's no way I'm going to just swipe one. No. Thank you, but *no.*"

Bitty leaned against the door frame, favoring him with a tired but knowing smile. "Child, I've seen a lot of folk in trouble before, but the angels tell me there's something different about you. I don't know what to call it. A specialness. The angels told me to help you out any ways I could, and that much I done. Hamilton's gonna come over here tomorrow night."

"Bitty, I don't want it; I don't want this kind of help."

"I know you don't. It goes against your nature, and that's good, mostly. But listen to Marian, here; you *need* it. Me, I just need some sleep. I know you're . . . planning something big, and I *suspect* that if things work out, you'll be able to pay me back, pay the *legitimate owners* back, do everything in your power to set things right. I feel you're a good person in that way, and so long as you're struggling to preserve your own self, and the young lady here, your conscience don't need to bother you none."

She stepped back, placing a hand on the edge of the door.

David found himself torn. Part of him was itching to *work* again, to submerge for a time in that tiny, tiny world, and to bring something back from there when he returned. Part of him was itching to kick Bitty out into the hallway, pick the phone up and call Mike Puckett. Part of him simply wanted to crawl back into bed.

"I'll have to think about this," he said. "I don't know what to say to you."

"I believe the correct reply," Bitty grumped, looking tired, "is 'thank you.' "

The night and morning and afternoon and evening passed uneventfully, seeming to take forever, and in all those long hours there was no further argument on the subject of theft. David never specifically caved in, but somehow it was mutually understood that he'd been cornered, he had no choice, he was really going to do this. Never mind the risk, because really when you thought about it, the risk of doing nothing was infinitely greater. And yeah, he just plain *wanted* the workstation; on that particular subject, he didn't need any convincing.

So Bitty made further arrangements, and David listened to them without comment, and at 10:00 P.M. when an ancient Ford Econoline van pulled up under the apartment's window and honked, he knew what to do.

"Bye," he said to Marian, kissing her quickly on the cheek. "I'll be back as soon as I can."

She grabbed his hand, held it for a moment. "Be careful, OK? Don't get caught or anything."

"Or hurt?"

"Yeah, that too. This is all so . . . strange."

He nodded. "Strange, yes."

And he left, pulling the squeaky hand truck behind him.

He bumped his way down the stairs, out the front door, around the corner to where the van was parked. The night was chilly, Bowser's one-size-fits-all jacket not quite warm enough for comfort. Maybe David should steal a coat while he was out.

Hamilton's Econoline was a dark blue, painted over with gray primer in the places where rust or dents had scarred it. The back door was split down the middle, the right half sitting open, and there was a bumper sticker high on the left door: I ♣ MY DOG.

"Hello?" David called up to the driver through the open door.

To David's surprise, the man in the driver's seat was white and clean-shaven, and had long, wavy blond hair like some pirate ship captain on the cover of a romance novel. "Are you David?" the man wanted to know.

"I don't know. Are you Hamilton?"

A nod. "Hop in; let's get this over with."

David lifted the hand truck, placed it inside the van, and closed the door firmly behind it. There was another bumper sticker, fresh- and new-looking, on that side. FOR SECOND COMING, it said, USE JESUS AS A DILDO. Yeah, whatever.

Moving around to the passenger's side, David opened the shotgun door, climbed aboard, belted himself in. Inside, the van was all falsewood paneling and dark, ancient shag carpeting, even on the walls and ceiling. Chooka music played softly on the stereo, which was a huge thing with colored lights all over it that stuck out of the dashboard like a separate instrument panel for some other vehicle. There were curtains drawn over the side and rear windows, street light filtering through them to reveal the cargo area, empty but for an oversized tool box, and now Bitty's hand truck.

Looking grim, Hamilton offered a handshake, which David accepted. Firm grip, not crushing, his hand slightly callused. And then, without a word, Hamilton put the van in gear and they were moving.

"We're looking for a warehouse over in Camden," David said, so the man would know which direction to go, though he didn't seem too interested in asking. "Southwest, near the river, just a little ways from seventy-six Company called MFE. They supply laboratory equipment to most of the local colleges."

"Uh-huh," Hamilton said.

David got a bad feeling. "You don't have to do this," he said. "I don't want to make you do this if you're not into it. I mean, if you owe Bitty a favor, that's fine, but—"

"I'm fine. Just a bad fuckin' day, that's all."

"Oh."

The ride continued in silence for a while, Hamilton driving sensibly through the nighttime traffic, sticking to the speed limit even when it would have been easy to go faster. Eventually, they got on I-76 approaching the Whitman Bridge, and Hamilton found his voice again.

"Do you have change?"

David, who'd been studying his hands, looked up. "What?"

"For the toll. I'm a little light on cash at the moment, so you're going to have to pay your own way."

"Oh," David said. He rummaged in his pockets and came up with a hundred-dollar bill. "Here. You can take some out for gas, too."

"I'm OK on gas," Hamilton said. And then, looking at

the bill, "God damn it, don't you have anything smaller?" Calmly and politely, he fought his way across four lanes of traffic, moving into the HUMAN ATTENDANT: CHANGE AVAILABLE lane.

"That's all I have," David said. *And lucky I've got it.* He'd stupidly brought his wallet along, with all his real ID and everything, which would be just *great* if he got caught, but he'd just as stupidly left it empty, cashwise. Hundred-dollar bills were floating all over the apartment, courtesy of Bowser's bank card, but it was plain dumb luck that David happened to have one in his pocket.

But the toll clerk accepted the bill without complaint, and counted over a handful of bills and change in return, which Hamilton passed awkwardly to David before hitting the gas and taking them across the bridge.

"So what sort of favor is it you owe Bitty?" David asked quietly, as the glittering Delaware eased by beneath them and the bridge railings shot past with soft, breezy sounds barely audible above the hoots and drumbeats on the stereo.

Hamilton turned and looked hard at him for a moment before returning his eyes to the road. "Got my mother into a hospice. She died last week."

"Oh. I'm sorry."

"Yeah, well, life's a bitch. Somebody had to take care of her, but both my brothers are in jail. And I will be, too, the way things are going. That's the life, I guess."

No, David wanted to say. *That's not the life. You don't have to be a criminal, you don't* have *to make ends meet by stealing things.* But this man was helping him, and deserved better than to have his lifestyle criticized that way. Come to think of it, David was a criminal now, too: running from the law, stealing money from a dead friend, planning burglaries . . . And if he'd had any choices anywhere along the line, they were not immediately apparent.

"Society does kind of suck, doesn't it?" he said after a while.

"Indeed it does," Hamilton agreed. And then the river was behind them, and the road signs were welcoming them to New Jersey, the Garden State, and David had to stop philosophizing and start giving directions to the business they were about to rob.

"This is it!" David whispered loudly, waving his flashlight beam around to get Hamilton's attention. It flickered off the walls, the windows, the high, girdered ceiling, the rows and rows of metal shelves. David was in heaven, in a warehouse that held lab equipment and scientific instruments he'd kill to obtain. Well, not *literally,* but . . . He'd passed all sorts of probes and microscopes and X-ray crystallographs, still cherry, sealed up fresh in their factory crates, and it had taken some nonnegligible force of will to leave these items where they were and keep searching. And in the end, the only reason he hadn't found the 800-kilohertz workstation he wanted was because MFE Enterprises had already upgraded to the faster model. They had two of them. "Ham, I found it!"

A head popped around corner of the row of metal shelves David had been examining.

"Shut up!" Hamilton whispered back at him. "Jesus. Three things you need to know: One, keep your voice down. Two, don't wave your flashlight where somebody might see it. Three, don't *ever* call me Ham."

"I'm sorry," David said, more quietly. "But I've found the box I need."

And a lot of other stuff, oh yes. He should leave it, of course, all but the workstation, if only to prove he was not really a criminal at heart. But damn, all this stuff was certainly insured, and Hamilton had cut a chain and some alarm cables and pried open a padlocked door on their way in, so there was no way the robbery could remain a secret. The police would know about it soon enough, no matter what was or wasn't stolen.

In fact, taking just the one item might look a little suspicious: one nanotech scientist on the run, one nanoassembly workstation missing. Kind of obvious, really. It might just make sense to steal a whole *bunch* of stuff, or even set the whole building on fire so nobody would ever know what was missing.

Jesus, that was crazy. He was thinking like a maniac. And yet, the logic of it was compelling, almost inescapable. *Reveal nothing, cover your tracks* . . .

"Load it on the cart," Hamilton whispered, stepping forward and covering David's flashlight with his hand. "Come on, do it; let's get out of here."

"Who's there!" a voice called out, echoing off the walls and ceiling.

Suddenly, a figure loomed down at the end of the row of shelves, holding another flashlight and pointing it at David and Hamilton.

Shit, we're caught, David thought with surprising calm. He switched off his flashlight, a heavy aluminum job like cops carried, and tried to decide which way to run.

Hamilton's reaction was rather different: he pointed his own flashlight beam directly at the newcomer (cop? security guard?) and shouted, "They're behind you! Look out!" And then, before he'd even finished speaking, he sprinted forward, raising his crowbar up in the air and then bringing it down sharply on the top of the newcomer's skull.

It sounded just like a slap, like an open hand connecting with somebody's cheek, sharp but not really very loud. The security guard—for in Hamilton's light beam David could clearly see now that that was who had surprised them—crumpled to the floor, grunting. David thought for sure the guy had been knocked out or killed, Hamilton had hit him so hard, but in a moment the man grunted again, and continued grunting. And groaning, and finally screaming, quietly and with great apparent effort, as he lay in the pool of Hamilton's flashlight beam.

David could see a wire—no, a *pair* of wires—connecting Hamilton's bicep to some small object on the floor, beside the fallen guard. A taser? Presently, Hamilton tucked the crowbar under his arm, and reached up to pluck the wires out.

"Ow! Mutha fuckah," David heard Hamilton say in a thick ghetto accent that was not his natural voice. "You put a couple needles in me. I got *holes* in my arm; I'm bleedin'! You lucky you didn't juice me, muthah; you'd *really* be payin'."

He kicked the guard sharply, then turned and looked up at David. "Hey Lerone, grab somethin' and let's get out of here."

Hurriedly, not pausing to think, David grabbed up the heavy box that contained his workstation, and threw it down ungently on the hand truck. Hamilton left the guard behind and ran back toward David, switching his flashlight off as he went. "Come on, come on! Push it!"

Hamilton passed him, and David ran after, pushing the squeaky cart out ahead of him. He followed Hamilton out the exit, not bothering to throw the door closed behind him. Out in the yard, floodlights mounted on the building's sides cast bright pools of light and shadow. David could see his breath in the lights as he ran, so he made for the shadows and pushed for all he was worth, toward the open gate in the chain-link fence, toward the blue van, parked over there in the deep shadows out on the street.

Shit, there could be cops here any second.

Hamilton had the van's tailgate open for him when he

got there, and he clanged the hand truck to a stop against the fender, grabbed up the box, tried now to be gentle as he lifted and hoisted it into the back of the van. It wouldn't do to go through all this and then damage the fucking workstation.

As Hamilton ran around front to get in and start the engine, David slammed the tailgate, then cursed and opened it again, picked up the hand truck, and put it inside. *Leave nothing behind, especially if it's got your damn fingerprints on it!*

Only when they were finally underway and moving safely out of the neighborhood, the dark, curvy streets lined with muddy lots and chain-link fences giving way gradually to storefronts and apartment buildings, did David finally let himself get angry.

"What the *fuck* were you doing back there?" he screamed at Hamilton. In the darkness, spittle flew from his lips, landing on the stereo's brightly lit buttons and dials.

Hamilton looked at him in confusion, as if David had said something stupid, something nonsensical. "What? Oh, you mean . . . If it's dark and you're doing something bad, you *always* pretend to be a Negro. They'll always believe you, right? They'll *remember* you as a Negro; they'll swear they saw your black face looking out at them."

"You hit the guard," David said, genuinely shocked and outraged. He'd hit people in his life, probably *hurt* one or two in the past few days, but in self-defense, always. Criminal or no, you didn't go around whacking innocent people on the head! That was *wrong!*

"He caught us," Hamilton said, not defensively but in exaggeratedly gentle tones: explanations for the idiot. "He would have sent us to jail if we'd let him. You want to go to jail?"

"He was just doing his job!"

Looking puzzled and a little hurt, Hamilton slowed the van down and gave David a hard look. "Are you clear on the concept here, my friend? I don't know what your situation is, and I don't want to know, but you obviously *need* that machine for some reason, and for some reason you can't go out and buy it. Probably it's expensive, and probably you're in some kind of trouble. Bitty asked me to help you, and so I am, and at that one moment, *helping* you meant bashing that guard."

"No," David insisted, "that was wrong. He could be seriously hurt, for all you know. He could die. That was the wrong way to handle it."

"Really?" Hamilton sounded more puzzled than angry. "You need something, and he won't let you have it. That's his job, OK, but what am I supposed to do about it? Let him call the cops? Let him shoot me with a damn taser gun 'til my brains leak out my ears? I didn't hit him that hard, and that kick was nothing, it was just for show, but if it's our needs versus his needs, I tell you, I'm going to vote for ours, even if it means he gets hurt. That's the way it is. You've got a lot to learn about life, my friend."

"Apparently," David said. And they continued the rest of the trip in silence.

CHAPTER TWENTY

"That's so pretty!" Marian exclaimed. Through the diagnostic port on top of the workstation, the laser beams flashed, narrowing and widening as they threw pointillist patterns up on the wall and ceiling in ever-shifting colors.

"Yeah." He closed the port, cutting off the beams. "It can blind you, too. If this little door is ever open while the machine is on, keep away from it."

He'd crawled into bed very late last night and spent the hours tossing and turning, thinking about what had happened. "Did you get it, are you OK?" Marian had wanted to know, and he had simply said yes and left it at that. It would not help her in any way to know the details, so he kept them to himself—a little pocket of infection in his soul.

But despite the misgivings and the guilt and the almost-total lack of sleep, he found he could not keep his good mood down this morning. That in itself was a source of guilt—that he could be involved in something so awful and still go on with his life as if nothing had happened. Well, the human mind was a fickle thing, and as Bitty said, he could try to make things right in the future. If he lived. But however he had come to this point, the fact was that he *did* feel good. After being jerked so forcibly from the life it had taken him so many years to build, he was unspeakably relieved to be back in his element again, in a place where he and he alone was in control.

1.0 MHz Nanoassembly Workstation: Penultimate®, by Zeus Scientific™. The machine hulked atop their little table like a black stegosaurus, filling up one corner of the living room. Incredibly, this was the only spot in the apartment that had access to a polarized electrical outlet. He hoped to God the power was reliable in this building.

"What are the beams for, anyway?"

"To hold the atoms," he said, "like mechanical microprobes, only more precise."

"Oh, I see," she said, nodding in his peripheral vision.

He could have explained further: There were six frequency-tunable lasers, arranged in two groups of three. Each beam passed through a lens which brought it to a sharp focus in the assembly chamber at the workstation's heart. Three beams, with three different points of origin, were made to cross at the same point in space, creating a variable nanoscale volume with an astronomically dense energy flux. If the lasers were tuned to just the right frequencies, the peaks and troughs of laser light could interact to hold a single atom in place, like a trio of firehoses supporting a golf ball. The atoms, hydrogen through zirconium, were stored in the forty mass buffers on the workstation's left side. Anything heavier than zirconium's forty-proton bulk would have to be introduced by special means, but then copper, with atomic number twenty-nine, was generally the heaviest atom in David's personal periodic table. As far as he was concerned, the heavier stuff might as well be bowling balls.

Anyway, of the two laser beam triplets, one would grasp and hold the molecule under construction, while the other trio fetched atoms one by one, stripping electrons off them until they had the proper valence, then slapping them into place in the tiny kinetic sculpture. A precision electron gun could also be fired into either focus, tuning the charges here and there.

Once assembly was complete, the finished molecule was kicked down through a series of electromagnetic airlocks, into the output buffer below. The assembly chamber itself was a tiny bubble, smaller than David's thumbnail. The only sound the workstation made was the faint, gurgling wheeze of the vacuum pump, keeping this tiny space in a state of high industrial vacuum. Because the chamber was so small, the sound was completely unlike that of the pumps on a standard SPM, much quieter and shallower. It was a sound David associated with Heavy Hitters, with prestige, with the rare kind of success that let you order whatever equipment you damn well pleased.

He could have explained all this to Marian, but he did not. She would understand, technically, what he was saying, but not what it meant, how it resonated in the assembly chambers of his soul. Which meant, of course, that she wouldn't understand at all.

The workstation's keyboard, trackballs, and I/O screen were annoyingly small, the kind of things you'd expect to see on a little subnote computer, but they seemed at least adequate to the task. Wiping the diagnostic display, he called up a schematic for glucose, one of the simplest molecules in the machine's ROM library, and began setting up the process that would actually assemble the molecule.

"Is that MOCLU?" Marian asked, sounding intrigued. She leaned forward to peer over his shoulder.

"That's glucose," he said. "It's a simple sugar. There are ten of these in a single particle of MOCLU, and a lot of other parts, besides."

"I thought MOCLU was supposed to be small."

"Oh, it's small, all right. My nanoscale chain drive was a thousand times larger than this glucose, but even that was one of the smallest machines ever built. The ninth smallest, I believe."

"Ninth? Wow, you never told me that."

"Um, yes, I did. I'm pretty sure."

He pressed the INITIATE button. Patterns danced on the screen for a moment, segments of the glucose ring flashing from white to green. In less than a second, the message PROCESS COMPLETE appeared at the bottom of the screen.

Marian grunted. "What happened?"

"I just made a sugar molecule. Um, listen. You wanted me to do this, and starting now, I'm giving you your wish. That means you have to leave me alone for a while."

"Oh. OK," she grumbled, pulling away. He grabbed her hand and pulled her back toward him.

"Give me a kiss," he said. "For luck."

". . . like narcotics dependents," Marian's voice droned from the other side of the room. "With their habits they get deeper and deeper into poverty, whether or not they have access to the drugs they're addicted to."

"Uh-huh."

She seemed to be off on some kind of restless sociological tangent today, every aspect of the ghetto environment revealing itself in pregnant detail to her sharp, reporter's eye. Cabin fever, he thought. She had no way to reconnect with her world, as David had with his. Four days in Fishtown, now. Was it four? Thinking about it, he wasn't sure. MOCLU had become his world. He'd laid down a spine for it and roughed in the core of the mechanism, but that was the easy part. Getting all the widgets in the right places, getting the whole thing to *move,* getting it to *function . . .*

"If we don't enact *major changes* to the city's 'white gloves' policy, the social problems on the east side will just get worse and worse. We have to stop this the way we did nuclear power: play at acceptance and then attack the system from the inside."

"Huh. This ratchet mechanism is too close to the spine. I need . . . I think I need another carbon in the axle."

"Are you even listening to me?"

"Major changes to the white gloves policy," he quoted without looking up.

He heard her move into the kitchen, bang some things around in there, move back out into the living room.

"I'm going out," she said. "For a walk."

"I wouldn't recommend it."

"David, it's broad daylight. Nothing's going to happen."

"They know what you look like. They may even know where you are."

"*You've* been out. I'll wear a hat."

"Wear a wig," he told her, still not looking up. "And sunglasses. And take Bitty with you."

"You're fucking paranoid."

"Only because I love you," he said, and descended back into his work.

There's no right place to put this ratchet mechanism. Why is there no right place? God, I'm an idiot. What the hell time is it, anyway?

"Are you coming to bed?"

To stare at the ceiling, sleepless, running the problems

over and over in his mind, helpless to fix them? Or worse, letting his mind wander, tallying up his losses, his failures, his crimes?

"Yeah, in a minute."

"You said that an hour ago. If you're not coming, just say so."

"I'll be there in a minute."

"Good *night,* David."

CHAPTER **TWENTY-ONE**

Outside the window, snow was falling through the nighttime glare of streetlights, turning to pewter-colored slush on a street and sidewalk that had not yet given up the last of autumn's warmth.

Time had passed with frightening speed, one ghetto night blurring into the next, until the days of their Fishtown exile stretched out into weeks. What was it now, fifteen days? He boggled at the concept. Not only was it October already; it was *mid*-October.

Behind him, the TV was quietly singing to itself. Bitty had brought it for them, and it was so old and huge, not a flat, hanging picture but a great plastic box the size of an oven, that he hadn't bothered to refuse it. Who else could possibly want a thing like that? And so, it ran most of the day, keeping the noise level up so the neighbors wouldn't wonder about them. Right now it was playing a soap commercial David had learned by heart.

It's a dirty world / full of grunge and grime
So when you do your laundry / it's Scrubley time!
(just half a scoop washes out the poop)
In this great big dirty world!

If he had to listen to that song one more time, he was going to heave the TV set out the window.

On the screen before him, the *real* screen, the nanoassembly workstation screen, hung a molecular schematic, at once lean and intricate, possessed of both an alien chaos and a hard, functional inevitability. Beautiful, like a strange, organic form of art. The first internal combustion engines must have looked like this, to the people who'd never seen one before.

He turned to cast a look at Marian, seated in her chair, ensconced in her NEVERland virtual reality gear. She'd barely moved from that chair this past week, just as David had barely moved from his. He tried to keep the outside trips to a minimum, and they'd both grown tired of bickering, and really, aside from sleeping and eating and making love, activities that could fill only a fraction of each day and night, what else was there to do? And so they coexisted, presiding in isolation over their separate kingdoms.

She mumbled something, subvocalizing into the microphones strapped to her throat. "I'm not amused, Woodruff," it sounded like.

He cleared his throat. "Marian."

She continued to mumble.

"Marian!"

She cast a look in his direction, her face blank behind the glossy white VR helmet.

"Just a moment."

She gestured in the air, paused, then gestured some more. Then she reached up, reluctantly it seemed, and released the catches on her helmet. "Yes?" she said. In her hands, the helmet came off her head like a shellfish that had lost its closing muscles.

"I think I have something new for the patent office. Maybe two somethings."

She grimaced. "That's nice. When do we get out of here?"

"Um . . . I don't know. I haven't thought that far ahead."

Indeed, his thoughts had lately extended no further than the workstation's assembly chamber. The work was *hard,* requiring every bit of his attention, and then some. Fortunately, Bowser's trouble kit had included a bottle marked SMART PILLS, and while David had never figured out just what the little blue capsules contained, he'd found that two of them could quicken and sharpen his mind and keep it roaring along smoothly for twelve hours or more. He was almost out of the pills, now, but they seemed to have done their work.

He'd recreated the MOCLU, or something very like it, in five days flat. But originally, MOCLU had not been designed to jam nanomachinery. It *did* this, of course, but now he could see how much time and energy it wasted, how ungainly and inelegant the whole process was. So he'd scrapped the whole thing and started fresh, whipping out a new chassis in a day and a half, wrapping the functional armature around it in an afternoon, and then . . . fussing with it. Now, at this very moment, he was willing to declare the project complete. Optimal. No one had ever built a sexier machine.

That was patent number one. He'd also modified the workstation's system software, adding a "path check" routine that kept it from trying to carry atoms through occupied spaces, which it kept trying to do, and he'd stripped a bunch of software lockouts so he could fiddle with the unit's configuration parameters. In the end he'd come up with what amounted to a new paradigm for laser nanoassembly: it involved juggling objects between the two laser triads, creating a number of "virtual" beam foci so that the machine could hold *four* molecules-to-be instead of just one. That let him use the workstation for assemblies never previously attempted, never previously *dreamed.* It let him pop the MOCLU apart, tinker with its insides and then pop it back together again, which was *worlds* ahead of the blind fumbling to which he would otherwise be limited.

Modesty aside, the new MOCLU particle was without question the most sophisticated molecular machine David had ever seen or heard of. And the workstation was now crafting them at the rate of one per second. Almost a hundred thousand a day. *And* he had several days' accumulation of the cruder designs, as well—more MOCLU than had ever before existed in one place.

"Well," Marian said, looking at him with a vague, tired relief. "I'm glad you're happy with it. For the record, I never doubted you."

"I know. Thanks."

"We can't just walk back to the university with a test tube in our hands. You know that, don't you?"

"Sure. It's late, though. Do we have to think about it right now?"

"No." She smiled thinly at him, waited for a moment to see if he had anything else to say, then slipped the VR helmet back over her head. The real world was only tolerable in small doses, it seemed.

"Say hi to the troll for me," he muttered, and heaved himself up out of his chair. *Damn* but gravity had gotten strong lately. The heater, an old steam radiator crouched beneath the window, hissed at him as he rose.

". . . we do what we must," the TV was saying, having thankfully given up on the commercials. "And we accept the burdens of what we do, in the knowledge that we do them not for spite but for love . . ."

He ambled over to the nook that was the apartment's kitchen. Opened the fridge, poured himself a glass of milk. His hand was shaking, his body weak with the strange fatigue that came from heavy intellectual labor. He felt in some ways as if he'd just woken up, just returned to an awareness of the world around him. But this wakefulness was not going to hang around much longer—he was going to sleep like the dead tonight.

Like the dead.

Jesus, he knew so many dead people these days. They came to him in his dreams, muddled and thick, telling him things he couldn't remember later on.

". . . because we were afraid to walk around our own neighborhoods at night . . ."

The voice drifted over from the TV set. A stern, paternal voice, one that sounded very familiar but which David could not immediately place. Milk glass in hand, he shuffled back into the living room where he could see what was on the screen.

Dark anger filled him at once, his brain going black and tarry with it. Colonel the Honorable John Harrison Quince was on the screen. The senator, the father figure, the graying chairman of the Gray Party. The killer, the man who had erased everything meaningful from David's life.

"Colonel, how do you *live* with yourself?" he demanded quietly.

A message scrolled by along the bottom of the screen, one of those flashing banners the local stations laid over the network feed, conveying local news without interrupting programming. Like when there was a weather alert or a fire somewhere or a big sale down at King of Prussia.

. . . *THE INDEPENDENCE MALL AT 9:45 A.M.*, the screen banner was saying. *REPEAT: SENATOR QUINCE WILL BE SPEAKING ON BEHALF OF CONGRESSIONAL CANDIDATE APRIL CUSACK TOMORROW AT THE INDEPENDENCE MALL AT 9:45 A.M.* REPEAT: SENATOR QUINCE WILL BE . . .

Jesus, the man was coming to Philadelphia? He orders three murders, maybe more, and two weeks later he's here making *speeches?*

God hairy damn it, Bowser would say at a time like this.

Shaking more violently than ever, David drained his glass. The milk ran down inside him, cool and slick against the lining of his throat.

The sky was colorless. The ground was colorless, the place generic, unreal, dreamlike. He stood on a medicine wheel, colored rocks laid out on the dirt in radial patterns, like a pie cut into wedges.

Bowser was here, standing in another wedge, grinning broadly. And Henry was here, and Otto. David's scalp and neck shivered with superstitious dread. Marian was here, as well. And Bitty. And Colonel the Honorable John Harrison Quince, dressed once more in his gray-and-white Uncle Sam outfit.

They all had rope in their hands, as did David, and the ropes all met in a fat knot at the center, drooping over a crisply dug cylindrical pit. In the pit were whirling gears, and whirling on those were smaller gears, and smaller ones, and smaller ones still, forming up into a spiky, fractal fog of mini-gears and micro-gears and nanogears. *What the hell kind of molecule are we supposed to be?* he thought, picturing complex schematics on his workstation screen. Whatever it was, he wasn't getting it.

Each pie wedge had its own color, marked by the stones surrounding it. And, he saw, by the stones inside it, stones that spelled out words in tall letters. His own sector was labeled PROGRESS. A cold wind blew over him, swirling out from the nowhere, nothing plains to caress him and then vanishing into nothingness once more.

"Hi, David," Bowser said cheerfully, giving his rope a sharp tug. Everyone was jerked slightly off-balance, until they pulled back on their own ropes and righted themselves. *Not a molecule, a tug-o'-war,* David realized, and suddenly the whole scene was clear in his mind:

This was the Wheel of Life, the Wheel of Fortune, the Wheel of Fate. The place where you found out who was right and who was wrong, or at least who was winning and losing. Everyone was looking at him expectantly.

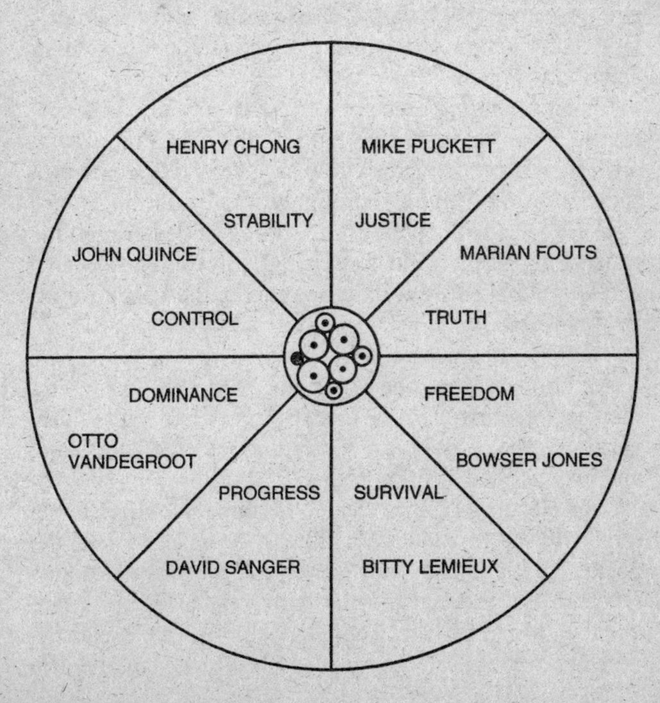

Marian! Why was Marian on the other side of the wheel from him? Why was Big Otto Vandegroot in the wedge right next to his? He was . . . closer to Quince than he was to Marian? How could that be? What could that mean?

"I'm sorry, David," Henry Chong said. He gave his rope a pull. David lost his balance, then regained it.

"Henry? Henry, what's happening? You sold me out. Didn't you? Why did you sell me out?"

Henry's wizened face looked pained. "You misunderstand, as always." He jerked his rope again.

This time, John Quince pulled back, hard, and Bowser flailed for a moment, then dug his heels in and heaved back. David took a step forward, and another, not quite able to regain his balance. Beside him, Bitty Lemieux jerked her own cable, flashing an apologetic grin in David's direction.

He took *another* step forward, and now this was getting *serious,* because if he fell into that whirling, fractal pit he'd be shredded instantly, atomized like paint in a spray gun, only more thoroughly, more literally *atomized.* He tried to drop the rope, but it was tied around his waist. Finally, his right foot found purchase in the dirt, and he put his entire weight on it and pulled back for all he was worth.

The rope was coarse in his hands.

All at once, everyone was pulling, grunting, scraping their feet against the dirt. David's rope tried, with wildly varying force, to drag him forward to the pit. He resisted, and even gained a little ground.

John Harrison Quince cleared his throat loudly. All eyes turned in his direction. Wordlessly, he reached into the pocket of his Uncle Sam jacket and withdrew a police revolver. He gestured broadly with it, as if lecturing to a class. In his fatherly voice, he spoke: "We are presented here with a classic example of chaotic dynamics. The equations are nonlinear and intractable, the outcome uncertain. However, the model can be simplified, as follows."

Quince was scientifically literate? That struck David as highly improbable, and suddenly it occurred to him that he was—

The gun went off much more quietly than it should, like a hammer striking a cement block. Like the banging of an old steam radiator. Big Otto Vandegroot crumpled nonetheless.

Quince raised his arm, turned and leveled it again, this time at Henry. Bang. Bang. Henry pitched forward. Quince turned toward Bowser, and the gun went off again.

"No!" David screamed, as Bowser's head came apart in a red spray.

Three ropes came loose from their owners. Above the pit, the heavy knot quivered. David's feet began to slide.

"As you can see," Quince lectured on, "the equations have been linearized, and the final result is clear even to the naked eye. The sum of the vectors is now sufficient to bring David Sanger to the center."

David could not find purchase in the soil beneath his feet. Across from him, Puckett and Marian continued to heave on their ropes, the efforts of Quince and Bitty Lemieux no longer sufficient to counter them. Whirling with complex mechanical fog, the pit loomed before him. His feet were mere centimeters from the edge. They were *at* the edge. They were over it.

"No!" he screamed, falling directly into the fog. He felt his body whipped apart, flying into pieces like snow in a tornado.

"No!" he screamed again, and sat up on the mattress.

Beside him, Marian stirred in the darkness.

"Jesus. Oh, Jesus. Oh, Jesus."

"David?"

"Just a dream," he said, though his hands clutched at the sides of his face. "I'm sorry."

"Are you OK?"

"Yes." His voice too tight, too quick. "Perfectly."

Marian reached over to pat his leg reassuringly, then curled away. Soon, her deep, slow breathing resumed.

David's heart took a long time to settle down, and by the time it did he could no longer quite remember what the dream had been about. Something very bad, he knew that much, and it didn't take a shrink to figure out where the dreams were coming from.

With no further interest in sleeping, he simply sat cross-legged on the bed, staring at the edges of the window shade. Eventually the sun would rise, and by the light of the new day he would once and for all put this matter to rest.

CHAPTER **TWENTY-TWO**

The sun was out today, not warm, but managing nonetheless to melt last night's slush into a city-wide puddle through which the traffic splashed. Everything seemed speckled with a fresh layer of grime, and even the air had a muddy dampness that chilled David through his jacket. The wig and baseball cap warmed his head nicely, though.

The Liberty Bell pavilion held some three or four hundred people, bundled and stamping against the chill, their breath puffing out in white clouds. The crowd seemed a perfect demographic reflection of the Gray Party itself: people with tiny empires to protect, against enemies real or imagined. Here were the "peaceful" racial separatists, all colors of them come together for this special occasion, and they stood shoulder to shoulder with immigrants, homosexuals, members of obscure and unpopular religions. Strange bedfellows indeed, people who distrusted one another only marginally less than they feared the wider world. Here also were the very tall and the very short, the unusually fat and thin, the healthy and the handicapped and the helpless. People from the edges of every bell curve, every straggler who'd ever felt exploited or threatened or picked on by the forces of mainstream society. And everywhere, of course, the elderly—at once frail and bitterly defiant.

The affluent freak show, the cartoonist IrRevere had once labeled this group. But that was years ago, before the Crackdown, before the party's explosive growth. Now the joke was *over 40 million served,* with the *4* ticking over to a *5* like an old rotary odometer. What society could possibly reject so many, excise such a large chunk of its own flesh? Where was the monolithic "they" against which these people struggled?

Ah. That, he sensed, was a crucial insight, a glimpse at the very wellspring of Gray power: the secret self. Who *wasn't* a freak, deep down inside? These people were busily exiling *themselves,* and recruiting judges and bureaucrats and industry captains to speed the process along. What they demanded was neither equality nor conformity, but instead a kind of Aristotelian speciation, a shocked electrolysis of the citizenry into identity groups as exclusive and clearly demarked as the gated suburbs in which they lived. And of course, a strong police force to guard it all, to guarantee an end not only to crime, but to *uncertainty.* As if the laws of chaos could be repealed with a stroke of the governor's pen: no "harmful talk," no weapons, no drugs, no flashy media violence or porn. No choices; to each his own little cell.

Or so it seemed to David on this bleak autumn morning. Maybe, in his own distress, he was judging too harshly. These people were not, after all, his enemies. They were just people, chasing whatever good they saw in the Gray Party rhetoric: sweet, bright promises that melted like cotton candy on the tongue, fulfilling nothing. The fault of external forces, the party would no doubt claim, but shit, Crackdown or no, the streets had never been more dangerous than they were today.

"Hello?" the amplified voice rang out, a feedback whine following closely behind it.

David turned his gaze back toward the pavilion's center, the people clustered on the stairs, between the Liberty Bell enclosure and a seething wall of cameras and microphones. April Cusack, that was the congressional candidate's name. She was at the podium, now, glaring out at the crowd with bright, angry eyes.

"Is this thing on?"

April Cusack turned to confer with her aide, a factory-issue politico with black wire coiling from an earphone down into his trench coat, beneath hair as neatly sculpted as a mannequin's. They spoke for a moment, and then Cusack was back at the microphone again.

"Good morning!"

Scattered applause from the crowd.

"Why are we here today? Why am I running for Congress? The simple answer is because I'm fed up with the system, and I want to see it changed. But of course, you people haven't come out here in the cold to hear the simple answer."

David tuned out the woman's droning and focused on the man standing to the left of her aide. *That* was his enemy. Colonel "the Killer" John Harrison Quince. Black wool topcoat, a fiery red necktie visible at the open collar. Apparently, he didn't much like waiting around while April Cusack spoke; his face was marred by a bored, spoiled expression, completely unlike the engagingly disapproving scowl he wore on the cover of his latest book, *A Three-Step Program for Saving the Nation.*

David had a hardcover copy of that book in his hands

right now. It was thick, and even heavier than it looked. He moved forward through the crowd.

If he had judged wrong, he could be arrested at any moment. But there were cops aplenty in this crowd, far more than normal security needs would warrant, and none of them had looked twice at David. Nor did they seem to be milling around with the kind of agitation a sniffer alarm would produce.

Market Street was all growl and wetness behind him as he moved, step by inexorable step, toward the pavilion's center.

Quince was silhouetted against the Liberty Bell itself, now, and behind him the State House and the original U.S. Congress and Supreme Court buildings were visible, all red brick and white trim, towers and steeples, whitewashed rail and clock faces. He thought of the men who had once walked these grounds, and wondered at the notion of social progress. What would Ben Franklin have to say about a man like Quince?

David had always pictured Franklin as a sort of philosopher-saint, first of the modern scientists, a lover of books and women and fine foods, and only very reluctantly turned to violence against his king's forces.

The tree of liberty must be refreshed from time to time with the blood of patriots and tyrants, quoted Bowser's voice in his mind.

David wasn't buying it.

No, Bowser insisted, *it's a real quote, from Thomas Jefferson. Buddy, don't you read?*

He sighed, shaking his head. The book he was carrying had been hollowed out, and inside it was Bowser's grandfather's handgun, dusted with David's entire supply of MOCLU. In theory, the MOCLU should diffuse through the air at least as well as any gunpowder residue, jamming any sniffers that were close enough to catch the scent. And so far, the theory had not failed him—he'd opened the dreaded coffee can over two hours ago and had yet to see any signs of trouble.

The Makarov was all plastic and ceramic, too, one of those early weapons that could pass through metal detectors without tripping the alarm. The first airport sniffers had been installed to counter this very threat.

John Quince was less than sixty feet away, now, and David could probably get a lot closer than that, his weapon invisible to Gray Party sensors. He could wave the book in the air, as if to demonstrate his approval, and then he could open the cover and whip out the gun, and punch holes through John Quince's body with hollow-tipped ceramic slugs, and . . .

And then what? Try to get away? Quince's death breaking the spell, the cops and the crowd suddenly awakening as if from a dream, and parting to let David, their savior, slip away into the city? Yeah, right.

Why else did you come? Bowser wondered.

David didn't have a clear answer for that. To test the MOCLU in a real-life situation, he might say, but it would be a lie. Really, he was just sniffing around, just slipping in for a close look at the enemy. Not even a scouting mission, more of a private symbolic gesture: *Look how close I can get to you, John Harrison Quince. Look what nasty toys I can bring with me.*

". . . and on that happy note," April Cusack was saying, up behind the podium on the steps ahead of him, "I'll conclude. I'll take questions in a few minutes, but Senator Quince has some things to discuss with you first, so I'll turn the microphone over to him."

Over enthusiastic applause, David watched the two of them trade places on the stairs. Loud whistles rose up from the audience as Quince approached the microphone.

"Thank—," Quince tried, and had to wait for the noise

to die down a bit. "Thank you, April, and thank *you* all for coming down here this morning. I guess we all know why we're here."

"Killer! Murderer!" David wanted to shout. But here he couldn't get away with even that. One false move would mark him, bring him into custody, destroy everything he and Marian had been working toward.

But *something* had to be done. John Harrison Quince had to be discredited, as David himself had been. Not martyred, no, and certainly not bargained with. Quince's guilt must be proclaimed, his crimes exposed, his name and his image vilified in some undeniable and irreversible way. But could David and Marian produce any credible evidence, without exposing themselves in the process?

Unfortunately, neither of them were specialists in the field of subtlety. For the thousandth time, he wished Bowser were still here, wily and unpredictable and fiercely unwilling to surrender. Of course, those were the very qualities that had gotten Bowser killed in the first place.

Idea fragments started clicking together in David's brain, and then suddenly comprehension dawned, like a new eye opening. *God,* he thought, *I've been an idiot.*

"Eventually we reach the point," John Quince was saying to the audience, "where we've simply had enough. Sorry, can't take it anymore. Eventually, we realize that change, radical change, is necessary. Ladies and gentlemen, April Cusack is a part of that change."

The sun cleared the top of the Supreme Court building, spilling cold light across Quince's shoulders, lighting him up from behind like a brilliant thermonuclear halo.

The subway took David as far as Kensington, from which he boarded a bus that cut back toward the

Delaware, toward Fishtown, toward home. He felt sick: hot and sweaty and stupid. His stomach churned as the buildings grew steadily shabbier, the parked cars along the street older, rarer, more decrepit. There was a sort of nineteenth-century charm about the place—if urban renewal ever found its way to Fishtown, it would uncover tile-floored basements, claw-footed bathtub/showers, fan windows of leaded glass that had weathered the decades like summer afternoons.

Of course, that same quaintness meant the walls were not built to hold power and telecom wires, nor water purifiers, nor domestic computing systems. These things had been retrofitted into the buildings like surgical implants in an ailing patient, and the scars had never really healed. David and Marian's apartment didn't even have a house computer, a fact which hadn't bothered them much until the first really cold night of the season. The radiator banged on and off all night, helpless with its primitive sensors and controls, unable to warm the place up with any consistency.

He pressed the SIGNAL DRIVER tape above his seat, got off at the appropriate stop.

The wind was sharper and colder here, and a trio of men in overcoats were huddled in the clear plastic bus-stop shelter, looking uncomfortable. Active jewelry twitched and flickered on them, ropes of memory plastic studded with conformal array video, hanging gaudily from their necks. Ugly, expensive stuff, but common enough here in Fishtown, symbols of a bogus prosperity, an ostentation purchased, as often as not, with the children's food money. Bright, cubistic images swarmed along the ropes as if seeking to escape. Good luck.

The men eyed him with vague hostility as he debarked. Sizing him up? Estimating his strengths and weaknesses, the worth of chasing him into an alley and robbing him? Well, maybe not—even in areas with the very highest crime rates, most of the citizens were honest. David had simply never learned to tell the difference.

The bus pulled away. Nervously, David hunched over and walked against the wind, keeping a tight grip on Quince's book. If he'd thought to wear the Hud Specs, he could keep an eye on the men now without turning around. As it was, his back itched with the need to know.

A glance over his shoulder revealed the worst: the three men were out of the shelter now, moving along unhurriedly in his wake. Clearly following. Fear made itself known to him. His skin, already sweaty beneath the coat, began to feel clammy. He had done a lot of fighting lately, and a lot of fleeing, but all of it sudden, fluid, too dynamic and immediate to respond to with anything but action.

Now, he had too many options. His brain was paralyzed with them. Whip the gun out and shoot them all, no questions asked? Whip the gun out and *menace* them? Stand his ground unarmed, bluffing them down?

Maybe they weren't following him at all.

He should say something to them. He turned around, opening his mouth to speak—

And found they had rushed him, were on him already, their hands around his shoulders, pushing him into the alley. *Street Defense,* he thought fleetingly. *This* he knew how to deal with.

One of the men was black, heavy, clothed in an overcoat and knitted cap, his hands ungloved. Shrugging off the hands that held him, David whipped *A Three-Step Program for Saving the Nation* around in a high arc that connected solidly with the big man's teeth. There was a yowl, the man falling back, his hands coming up to cover his face.

It was the only good blow David would land. The book

slipped from his fingers and fell, open and facedown, to the muddy pavement. The end of the Makarov's handgrip was just visible, peeking out from beneath the pages, and David was afraid they would see it, and while he was thus distracted one of the other men hit him in the face with something hard, a short length of pipe or something.

Stars exploded. He fell.

He had the idea that they had hit him a few times after that, or kicked him, maybe. Definitely they went through his pockets and, finding nothing there but a few dollar coins, hit or kicked him a few more times for spite's sake.

And then, after not very long at all, they were gone. David lay in the cold mud for a while, smelling muck and ice and pavement, slowly becoming aware of his pain. The pipe had connected with his forehead, and even without touching it he could feel a knot rising there. Other parts of him felt bruised, dislocated. He decided he would live, though, and eventually he opened his eyes and sat up.

The world was bright and swimmy. *A Three-Step Program For Saving the Nation* lay, open and facedown, on the wet alley pavement before him. He could still see the butt of the Makarov poking out from beneath the sodden pages. His head throbbed as he leaned forward and took up the book, scooping the Makarov back inside it, along with some runny street grime.

They had missed the one valuable thing he had. The one thing they probably wanted more than anything else.

He leaned back against a wall of cold bricks. His pants were wet, front and back. Wet and filthy and almost obscenely uncomfortable, but he needed a moment's rest.

Jesus, his head hurt.

When he finally emerged from the alley, a police cruiser was rolling slowly down the street, its windows down. The driver looked at David curiously, and the car pulled to a stop in front of him.

"What the hell were you doing back there?" the cop inquired. A collar of blue synthetic fur crowded up around his neck. His hat had an orange plastic cover on it.

David, feeling a little dizzy, just stood there.

"I said what were you doing?"

"Nothing."

"You've got a bump on your head," the cop said. "You're filthy. Been doing a little drinking?"

"No." It should have been "no, sir," David knew, but where the hell had these guys been five minutes ago?

"I don't want to catch you sleeping back there," the cop warned.

"Yeah, and there's no jacking off in public," his partner added from the passenger seat. Not really maliciously, David thought; it was just a bored attempt at self-amusement. A policeman's day is long.

"I was mugged," he said, deciding there was no harm just now in telling the truth. "Three men. They had a pipe."

"Really?" the driver exclaimed, feigning surprise. "In this neighborhood? Ah, I don't believe it."

"If there's paperwork involved I don't believe it," the partner said. "Let's let this guy off with a warning."

The driver put the car in gear, and David could hear the two of them laughing as they pulled away, kicking up slush, their red and blue bubble lights reflecting the pewter blankness of the sky.

The building was an old brownstone, drab and soot-stained, its front door faced with heavy steel bars. He opened the lock and passed through, strangely reminded just then of the entrance to the Molecular Sciences building back at U of Phil. He shuffled through the newspapers someone had spilled in the foyer and made his way up the stairs, which creaked tiredly under his weight.

His hands still shook, the fear and outrage of the mugging still bright in his mind, the pain still quavering at the edges of manageability. But his earlier thoughts were there as well, vying for his attention.

The apartment door was open when he got to it, Bitty's deep voice floating out from it like snatches of trombone music. He entered, closing the door behind him.

Bitty leaned against the windowsill on the far side of the room, with Marian sitting beside her on the couch, looking worried about something. Presently, she looked up.

"There you are! God damn it, David, where the hell have you been?" She eyed him with equal parts accusation and relief. But as she saw how he looked, the relief dropped away. "Are you all right? What happened?"

"Mugging."

He staggered to the couch, collapsed into it as Marian made room.

"Are you OK? What happened to your head?"

"They hit me with something. A pipe, I think. It, uh . . . I think I'll be OK. Can you get me some ice?"

Bitty slid off the windowsill, moved toward the kitchen.

Marian looked at the book in his hands, grimy and sodden. "You were at the Cusack rally in Center City," she said. It wasn't a question.

He cleared his throat. "I, uh . . . Yeah."

She looked away for a moment, drew a breath, looked back at him again with tight anger radiating from every pore. "That was pretty stupid, don't you think? Is that why you got hurt?"

"No. That was after. We live in a ghetto, remember?"

"Why didn't you talk to me about this? What did you think you were trying to do?"

"I really don't know. I saw him on TV last night, and . . . I don't know. It got me thinking, though, so that's a good thing."

"Uh-huh." She wasn't letting him off that easily. "You could have been seen. You realize that, don't you? Even here, you're afraid to walk the streets, but somehow it's OK for you to walk right up . . . They have neural cameras that can watch for certain faces. You *do* know that."

He spread his hands in surrender. "I'm sorry. It's done."

Bitty returned from the kitchen, handing him a bunch of ice cubes wrapped up in a dishtowel. Nodding gratefully, he put it against the bump on his head. The cooling there was blissful and swift.

"Oh. God, that's wonderful. I, uh, I know how we can get out of here."

"What?"

"It'll take a few weeks. I used up all the MOCLU today, and—"

"You *what?*"

He paused, moved the ice pack slightly. "I can explain. Let me ask you something first, though: how good are your press connections?"

"I'm not following this."

"Do you know anyone in national TV?"

"A couple of people, yeah. What's going on?"

"I'll explain in a minute. Bitty?"

"Uh-huh?" Bitty's voice was amused, mock-suspicious.

"Marian and I have some things to discuss in private, but later on I'm going to give you some gold coins. I need you to find me a cheap, media-capable computer, and some groceries. Do you know any place that stocks jalapeño peppers?"

She frowned crookedly. "Child, what *are* you talking about?"

He told them.

CHAPTER TWENTY-THREE

Sharps eyed David down the length of his sword, and up the length of David's, and David eyed him back with a steely resolve that no NEVERland VR rig could ever hope to convey. He was going to kill Sharps, put him right out of the game.

"Prepare to die," he said with his phoniest Errol Flynn grandeur, and lunged.

Sharps parried the blow, not surprisingly, for David had aimed it beneath the adept's armpit. Not trying for the kill right now, nor even for a wound, but simply to draw Sharps out, to get him excited, to remind him that his virtual life was indeed on the line here. This would be David's fourth live duel in NEVERland, and damn if he wasn't going to make it interesting this time.

Around them was a field of vividly green grass, and a handful of spectators, peasants and gaudily dressed players both, standing back at a respectful distance, and superimposed over this cartoon view was a shimmery, translucent red box of irregular shape that enclosed David and his opponent. Not a NEVERland enclosure of any sort but a real one—the walls and floor and ceiling of David and Marian's bedroom, projected here so that David would not crash into them or try to run his sword through the plaster while he was fighting.

The dueling rig, with position sensors on half the joints of his body, and on the heels and toes of his sneakers, and on the hilt and tip of his drop foil, allowed him to fight and move and dance away with perfectly natural movements, not the bizarre sitting-down, switch-clicking activities he would otherwise be forced to employ. It wasn't much good for walking around or doing magic or anything, but for the purposes of dueling, there was nothing better. Hence the name: dueling rig. Used, it had cost them nearly five hundred dollars.

But so far, David had gotten pretty good use out of it. Bitty had found him a couple of fencing books at the public library, and he had gone through them chapter by chapter, testing each move against stationary targets, and then against animated golems which, courtesy of Marian's sorcery, could wield a sword with fair competence.

And then, when he'd practiced enough that he could run the golems through on every attempt, he had gone out into the wider cartoon world, looking for fights. Monsters, yeah, but he was most interested in live opponents who, he'd thought, would have more tricks and surprises up their sleeves than any program sprite, and would therefore be more interesting and educational as opponents. Instead, he'd found they died almost instantly, their poor human minds thinking and plotting and projecting too much, where the golems would simply act and react with total conviction and attention until the encounter was over.

"All your hard work for naught, Sharps," David taunted. "Your game ends here, at the point of my sword."

His face drawing downward into a mask of anger, the adept Sharps lunged forward and slashed with the tip of his foil. Not a particularly effective move, but it *did* come as a surprise to David, who stepped back and raised his own weapon to parry. The swords clanged together with a heavy and altogether inappropriate ringing noise.

"You suck, Hapgood," Sharps called out.

Sharps had left his torso wide open, and though he was a good ten feet away David could have stolen in for the kill with a *flèche* or a *ballestra* or even a simple leap. Instead, he took a single shuffling step forward and stung Sharps on his outstretched knee.

"Hey!" the adept said, now looking alarmed. Looking as if he suddenly realized he was outmatched, that he was not, after all, very likely to win.

David moved in, throwing a series of quick blows. Surprisingly, Sharps parried them all, though he lost a good bit of ground in the process. He'd backed up almost through the shimmery-red bedroom wall, which only David could see, and past which David would not be able to strike unless he reset the dueling rig to a new coordinate set, which would mean dropping his guard and fumbling with the controls. He backed up instead, drawing Sharps in toward the center of the room once more. The adept was limping slightly on his damaged leg—the game throwing random movements and spasms in to simulate the effects of pain.

"Come on, kiddo," David teased. "I'm right here. Finish me if you can."

"You *suck,* Hapgood. It wasn't that big a deal. I'm *sorry,* OK?"

By way of reply, David launched another assault.

Again, though, he was not quite able to penetrate, until Sharps overbalanced and left his sword arm exposed. David stung it, but the blow was not a good one. Sharps would still have good use of the arm. Panting now, David gave a little ground, backing up a few steps to rest. This had turned out to be a good match after all. Sharps clearly didn't have any kind of self-defense training, but his instincts were keen, ditto his reflexes.

Which was good, because David had come to NEVERland to learn the art of dirty fighting. *You can't always get a finger lock,* he remembered his old Street Defense instructor telling him once. *You didn't hear this from me, okay? But in a fight with a stranger, you're better off taking the cheap shot. Elbow to the eyes, something like that.* Just words at the time, but David knew he'd come to a point in his life when those words needed to find a little practice.

"I didn't mean to disrupt your plans back there," the adept tried, a little more politely and formally. "I'll stay out of your way, OK? Maybe we can strike a deal or something; maybe I can help you. What do you think?"

Wordlessly, David moved in again, and this time got a clean strike through Sharps's upper arm. Yelping, the adept dropped his weapon and attempted to step back. He hit a foot switch wrong, though, or maybe his injured leg had refused to support him, because he collapsed to one knee, and belatedly began fumbling for the fallen sword with his left hand. He snatched it up just in time to parry another of David's blows.

"I yield!" he cried. "Hapgood, stop; I yield!"

"Not today," David said, and ran the drop foil through the center of Sharps's chest.

"Mortal," the adept said. "Oh, damn it."

And then he collapsed, and died.

The crowd of spectators applauded politely.

Now David reached for his controls, and gave the signal that meant he was ready to be transported back to Marian's castle. He was pretty sure Marian was busy in the real world at the moment, but her guards and wards would hear him, and do the right thing. Indeed, the scene around him went blue and flickery, and then faded, replaced by the cathedral grandeur of Marian's throne room.

His workout complete, David switched off the VR rig and removed his helmet, returning once more to the real world of the Fishtown bedroom, its floor cleared and swept for the day's encounters. He took a minute to shrug his way out of the dueling rig, wondering idly if he should be feeling guilty right now. Sharps had indeed inconvenienced him, bursting into the inn at the wrong time like that, and he hadn't been too sorry about it at the time. But really, the slight was a minor one, and now Sharps was dead, and the player, whoever that might be, would have to start all over again with zero everything, robbed of the time he'd invested in the character.

Was this wrong? Was this the act of a bully, striking out against the weak because the strong were too far out of reach? No, David simply couldn't find any sense of guilt over this. He didn't have to take a surrender if he didn't want to; there were no rules about that. And there'd been enough real-world violence in his life lately that he just couldn't get worked up about a cartoon. He *needed* to polish up his fighting skills, and Sharps was an object, a glorified program sprite that had served his needs and been used up in the process. No harm done, and even if there was, well . . .

In most of the world, David had learned, violence was simply the way things got done. Drop foils were getting cheaper and more common with each passing week, appearing more and more often in the hands of street ruffians. Increasingly, the characteristic deep, tiny puncture wounds were filling up the evening news and the city's trauma wards. The wise man would learn how to fence, especially if he lived in Fishtown. And if Sharps lived in a nice, safe, gated suburb somewhere, as seemed likely given his white-bread accent and the amount of time he seemed to have for the game, then God bless him anyway.

All the NEVERland practice these past few days had David's sore muscles aching worse than they had in years, but it felt good, too. Building up the surprise factor. His enemies, not the simple street thugs but the real bad guys of his world, must already regard him as dangerous—he'd toppled Big Otto, after all, and slipped away from the Goon Squad twice in a single evening. To surprise them again, he'd need to be really, seriously, over-the-top dangerous. So that was exactly what he intended to be.

When he entered the living room, he found Bitty sprawled on the sofa, and Marian seated at their tiny new desk, rattling furiously at the keys of their tiny new computer.

"How's it going?" he asked.

"Fine," she answered softly, pausing but not looking up. "Here, listen to this:

PRESS RELEASE: THREE DEAD IN
SNIFF-JAMMER INTRIGUE

Researchers at the University of Philadelphia, working under an Administration of Sciences grant, have developed a substance known as MOCLU, which is capable of jamming security sniffers. The substance can be dispersed as a gas, and is both colorless and odorless. Obviously, it also cannot be detected by the Vandegroot Molecular Sniffer, as

> even in small concentrations it is capable of *permanently disabling* any model of the device, whether commercial, industrial, police, or military.

"Uh, it isn't really a gas," David interrupted. "It's more of a suspension. And in concentration it's not colorless; it's white."

"Yeah, well, a journalist is allowed to play stupid if it helps the flow of the story. Here's the rest of it:

> "The discovery was an accident," says MOCLU inventor Dr. David H. Sanger. "We were looking for a special sort of lubricant, but this is what we ended up with. There was no intention to create this thing. Believe me, I wish to God all this trouble had never happened."
>
> Trouble indeed—Dr. Sanger is in hiding, following the murders of three people closely associated with the project. Early suspicion for these crimes fell on Dr. Sanger himself, although one of the victims, Sanger's attorney, was shot to death with a police revolver.
>
> The other two victims, one a chemistry professor at U of Phil, the other at Massachusetts Polytechnic Institute, died of stab wounds to the neck and head. Ironically, both men were known to have close ties to the Gray Party at the time of their deaths.
>
> "It's terrible," says Sanger. "This research has been plagued from the very beginning. At first there were lawsuits and other harassment of that sort. Then one of our laboratories was robbed and vandalized. And now I guess it's come to this."
>
> Sanger refuses to speculate on the killer's identity, saying only that it must be "somebody who is very dependent on the sniffer, and consequently very frightened of MOCLU's potential. I don't know

> who that might be, or why they have resorted to such an atrocity."
>
> A technical description of the substance, courtesy of Dr. Sanger, has been appended to this document in hypertext form.

"Huh," David said, when she'd paused long enough that he knew she was through. None of the quotes from him were things he'd actually said. And important details had been left out, such as the fact that one of the deceased was the Sniffer King himself, and the fact that she, Marian Fouts, the story's reporter, was also in hiding. These facts were not secret. Critics would swarm over the story, picking it apart detail by detail.

"I like it," he said. "I like it a lot. You make it sound so banal, like something you'd hear about on the radio."

"Well, that's kind of the point."

"You should also mention my rugged good looks," he suggested, striking a mock-heroic pose.

"Don't push your luck," she said. But she was smiling.

"Oh, by the way," he said, massaging his sword arm, "I killed Sharps just now. I thought you should know."

Marian's smile faded. "Sharps? David, he was an ally of mine."

"Yeah, I know; I'm sorry. He needed the fencing lesson even worse than I did, though. And maybe his next character will be . . . a little more careful whose toes he steps on."

"You're getting a reputation in there," she cautioned. "I think maybe you should cool it—people are starting to talk. The Grays know your middle name, right? Let's not give them two and two to put together. Now about this press release, I think if we email it, um . . ."

"Y'all ain't talkin' quiet enough," Bitty called out from across the room. "I can hear most every word. You know, you gonna get nailed mailing that press thing out over the wires. They after you, they gonna have a keyword program installed most every node in the city. Get a trace on you inside of five minutes. I was you, I'd put that sucker on a disk and send it street mail. I'd wear gloves, too."

"Um," Marian said, looking up, "it's really better if you don't get involved. For your protection as well as ours."

"I thought I *was* involved," Bitty mused, "but I'm not one to press the point, so I b'lieve I'll go take a nap. Y'all just carry on without me, all right?"

"Want to practice fencing with me?" David asked.

Groaning, Bitty heaved herself off the couch. "Yeah, right. God loves you, child; that's why he's gon' let you log back into NEVERland and practice there some more. Don't nobody get tired in NEVERland, that's what I hear."

•

The darkened office was dotted with glowing, wafer-sized targets, some in motion and some stationary. Bang. Bang. One by one, the targets winked out, David squeezing off shot after shot from his virtual pistol. The sound of it was muted thunder in his ears, a dull, unenthusiastic bark entirely unlike the crack of genuine gunfire. Well, that was fine with him—his ears had never quite recovered from the twelve-hertz pounding at his apartment and the Twilight Motel shootout the same night, and he suspected there would be some permanent hearing loss no matter what he did.

His scores were improving, which was good considering how little time he could actually spend here. These were the pirate NEVERs, the games that ran in Mexico and the Caribbean because their subject matter was illegal in the U.S. Technically, David wasn't breaking any laws, since the "bad" parts of the software were all at the remote end of the link, but the government despised these network sites, and if he hung around long enough, he feared they would somehow finger him on a media perversion charge and send the cops around.

Ten minutes at a time, that was all he allowed himself, and no more than three sessions in a day. Even that had begun to seem like too much. Maybe he should cut down, or even drop the practice entirely. Lord knew, he hoped never to fire a real gun.

He hit four out of ten this time, not bad at all. Maybe just one more set before he packed it in. He waved a hand, and the little bull's-eyes magically reappeared.

Plants in the corners, campaign posters on the walls, a lighted D.C. cityscape outside the window . . . this was a quick-and-dirty rendition of what David imagined J. H. Quince's office might look like. Targets hovered by the bookshelf, by the door, by the window, and one in the office chair, the glowing heart of a seated figure.

It only took David two shots to snuff it out.

When he took his helmet off, he saw the apartment had darkened, the sun having set on yet another day of exile. Murky gloom outside the windows, as if it might snow again. In the other room, he could hear Marian speaking sharply inside her own VR set.

In spare moments over the past few days, she'd been creating dummy personae and puppeting them around through the Kingdom of Llyr, bringing them all to the throne room in her palace and abandoning them there, to be inhabited by other players when the time came. And if things went well, that time would not be far away.

Meanwhile, somebody needed to cook dinner. He turned the lights on, moved out to the kitchen and set about the task. Red beans and rice again, the very cheapest of nutritious meals, and one that Bitty assured them could be left in a big pot on the stove for days at a time without going bad. His taste buds and digestive tract had finished rebelling against the insult, and now simply accepted their fate with quiet indignation. Really, there was nothing else he could feed them—Bowser's bank account had finally dried up. Five thousand dollars, almost exactly. They'd never known the account balance until it hit zero, but their paranoia about the ATM card had mounted steadily, and they were about to stop using it in any case.

So now, they really were broke. They really did belong in Fishtown, and in fact would be ejected from this apartment next month when the bills came due for rent, for electricity, for the truly enormous connect-time charges they'd racked up in NEVERland. But when that time came, David and Marian would be long gone, their plans finished one way or the other.

He was dishing the goopy, spicy-smelling mass of beans and rice into a pair of bowls when Marian came out of NEVERland, her red hair disheveled from the VR helmet.

"Hi," she offered, taking up a bowl and a spoon and beginning, without evident pleasure, to eat.

"Hello. How'd it go in there?"

"Fine."

"Are we ready?"

"Yes."

He frowned. Something was bothering her. "When?"

"Tomorrow morning. Nine-fifteen A.M."

"Ah. My dear, will you tell me what's the matter, or do I have to guess?"

She glared at him. "This whole thing is bothering me, this whole plan. I don't know how I let you talk me into this; it's the stupidest idea I've ever heard."

"If you have a better plan," he said sincerely, "I'm listening."

She set her bowl down, turned to face him with serious eyes. "Flee the country, go somewhere that'll never extradite us. We can't hide here forever, and we can't fight them, and that doesn't leave us many other options."

"We're not guilty of anything, Marian."

"Since when does that make a difference?" Her voice and posture were limp with defeat. Infectious defeat, she was clearly hoping, defeat that would worm its way into David's heart and mind and get him to call this whole thing off.

Well, he was having none of that. He rolled his shoulders back, slapped the knuckles of one hand into the palm of the other. "*Always* it makes a difference. If you just give up and let them have their way . . . Jesus. If we run away we may stay alive, but we *lose everything,* and there's no going back because running makes us look guilty as hell. If we try to hide, ditto: we lose everything. If they take us down in secret, like they did to Bowser, we lose everything."

"And if they take you down in public?" Tears were trembling at the corners of Marian's eyes. "You'll still be dead, probably both of us will be dead, and it won't be for a good cause because nobody's ever going to know the truth."

"Shh, honey, shh." He took her in his arms. "They won't hurt us; they *can't.* Put a spotlight on them and they'll freeze, like deer. People *will* know the truth."

She looked away, her eyes red, lips pursed tightly. But when she turned back toward him again, her expression was hard, resigned. "You're right. I'm sorry; I'm just . . . scared, venting some spleen."

"I know, honey. I'm scared, too. I've been scared so long I can't even . . . Tomorrow it'll be better; I promise."

"You *promise?"* she mocked, managing the ghost of a smirk. "That's a little far-fetched. Don't promise me the future, David. Just give me *now."*

The kitchen smelled of cumin and red pepper, of salt and rice and kidney beans, the pot on the stove ticking softly as it cooled.

He took the hand she offered, and it was soft and small and warm in his own, and he felt the tension go out of his muscles. For a while, at least, they could let everything be OK.

CHAPTER TWENTY-FOUR

"David!" From the living room, Marian's voice rose up in a shriek. "David, get in here!"

He rose so quickly his chair toppled behind him. His socks skidded on the worn carpeting as he threw himself across the bedroom and through the living room doorway, shouting, "What is it? What is it?"

Marian sat in her chair, VR helmet pushed up on her forehead, gloved hands trembling with rage.

"What happened?" he demanded.

"Woodruff happened. God *damn* it! He's put a force bubble over the guest bodies. I can't get to them! I can't touch them, can't move them, definitely can't log in through them. . . . *Damn* him, I'll wring his scrawny fucking neck. . . ."

David's blood went hot. This was no game; they had important business to conduct in Marian's throne room this morning. Their schedule was tight, their margin for error, zero. NEVERland was the perfect meeting place, the perfect hiding place, because Marian swore she could guarantee their privacy, and anyway, who would bother to bother them in a sim like the Kingdom of Llyr?

Other players, that's who. To them, it *was* a game, and Marian a distracted and therefore vulnerable player.

"Jesus," he said, angry and fearful. He suppressed the urge to find something to smash. "Woodruff is that other wizard, right? Can't you just kill him or something? Can *I?"*

She shook her head. "No, no way. He's much too powerful. He put a *force bubble* in my *throne room!* How the hell did he do that?"

"Can you *talk* to him?"

"To Woodruff?" She snorted. "He only wants one thing: my head on a plate. He's loving this, I'm sure. No matter what I do, he does his best to meddle. *Damn* it."

A light flicked on in David's head, and suddenly he knew what to do.

"Is my body still in your castle?" he asked.

"Yes, I've kept it safe."

He held up a thumb. "Great. If you can get Woodruff's attention for me, I'm going to log in and have a chat with him. I'll see you there in a couple minutes."

"But David, I—"

"It'll be all right," he assured her, rushing back into the bedroom where his own VR set lay. "But we have to hurry."

He got plugged in, pulled the gloves and helmet on, entered the screen he knew privately as "Menu Land." From there, it was a short hop into NEVERland, and thence to the Kingdom of Llyr.

He found himself, suddenly, standing in a tiny, low-ceilinged, stone-walled room, only three or four times the size of a bedroom closet. The door was open, and the cartoon body of Marian or, rather, of Queen Elishandra, stood in the doorway.

"What am I doing in here?" he asked her.

"Storage," she said, leading him out into the enormous throne room. Her boots clomped on the hand-sized tiles of the mosaic floor. "You weren't playing anymore, and I didn't need your uninhabited body cluttering up my throne room."

"Is Woodruff here?"

"Yes. So what's this great idea of yours?"

"Can't tell you," he said.

As promised, Woodruff was standing before Marian's throne, the ranks of seated guest bodies motionless behind him, and sealed in a shimmering dome like a soap bubble the size of a bus.

"Hapgood!" said the wizard with false delight. "How excellent it is to see you again. Any friend of the Queen's is a friend of mine, I say. You must tell me how I can be of help to you."

David favored the man (boy?) with a tight nod in the direction of Marian's guest bodies. "Is that your force bubble?"

Woodruff's plastic face snapped into a smile as if a switch had been thrown. "Ah. Of course. I noticed Elishandra was up to something here, and I thought I should put a stop to it until I understood better. Magic is a delicate balance, you know; you can't just throw it around without, um, *disrupting* people."

"Come with me," David said, beckoning, leading Woodruff back to the storage room he'd just left. "Mar, uh, Elishandra, you'd better wait here for a few minutes."

"And why is that?" Marian demanded, with a queen's icy authority. She followed them to the room's threshold, stood blocking the doorway after they'd entered.

"Just . . . trust me," David said, and closed the door.

He whirled on Woodruff, an accusing finger outstretched. "You listen to me, you little fucker; you're meddling in the affairs of the real world. People can get hurt, including you."

"My, my," Woodruff chuckled. "If that's the best you can do, I'm afraid this talk is over. You've gotten quite a reputation in your short time here, but I'm sure you know your sword is useless against me. As for the real world, well, I can't say I'm worried. You're not the first to threaten me like that."

David seethed. NEVERland was, by definition, anonymous. Connect charges were allocated by login site, not by account name or password. The game's administrators knew the billing addresses of every subscriber, but even they didn't know which characters belonged to which players. As Marian had explained, to have it otherwise would be to invite corruption of exactly the sort David was attempting.

"Why are you doing this?" he asked tightly.

Woodruff spread his arms, palms up, in an all-encompassing gesture. "Isn't it obvious? I intend to displace Elishandra as the ruler of Llyr. I am more powerful than her, so it is my right."

"OK," David sighed, mentally pulling out his trump card. "Fine. Can Elishandra hear us right now?"

"Certainly not."

"OK, then, listen: taking over the throne is obviously too hard for you right now, or you'd have done it already. You're just harassing Elishandra, trying to mess up her plans without even knowing what those plans might be. That's stupid."

"This conversation is over," Woodruff said, forming his hands into eldritch signs.

"Hold on!" David snapped. "I'm not finished. If you want Elishandra killed, I'll help you. But it has to be tomorrow. You have to wait that long."

Woodruff lowered his hands, his cartoon eyes narrowing comically. "You would betray her? You, her staunchest friend and ally?"

"Yes. What she's doing today is very important to me, and I won't let anyone stop it from happening."

"This is a trick," Woodruff said.

"No, in all honesty, I'll do whatever you want me to. But only if you *guarantee* you won't do anything until we're finished here today."

The wizard pondered that for a few seconds, and then an object, apparently an oversized gold coin, appeared in his hand with an electric flash of light.

"This," he said, "is the Talisman of Despair. It has two pieces." He demonstrated this by splitting the coin down a jagged middle line, like one of those two-piece necklaces lovers sometimes wore—half for him, half for her. "You will place one of the pieces under Elishandra's throne, right now. You will place the other piece there when you have completed your business today. If the second piece has not been placed by tomorrow morning, you will be killed. No! You will be imprisoned in my tower, forever."

"Fine," David said mildly. He held out a hand for the talisman.

Woodruff looked incredulous. "You will do this? You will betray her for me?"

"Sure."

"If this is a trick, you and Elishandra will both suffer."

"Just give me the fucking talisman! Jesus Christ."

Woodruff gave it to him.

"OK. Wait here until I come back."

David opened the door. Unsurprisingly, Marian still stood there on the other side.

"You'd better talk to him for a minute," he said. "I think he's starting to come around."

When she entered, David sprinted for the throne,

tossed one-half of the broken coin beneath it, and then sprinted back before his absence could be noticed. It seemed to him that Marian would find out about the talisman, that she would have some way of knowing these things, but right now that was Woodruff's problem.

The sorcerer was smiling broadly when David reentered the storage closet.

"It pleases me to please you, my queen. Your friend Hapgood here—" he nodded in David's direction, "is quite a bargainer. Keep him with you."

"You'll lift the force bubble, then?" Marian snarled unbelievingly.

"I have done so already, my queen," Woodruff said. He bowed deeply, and vanished in a flash of crackling blue.

David buzzed around delightedly, swooping down between the seated figures and then rising high up into the air again, the vaulted chamber spinning dizzyingly around him in stained-glass glory. Below, the puppet bodies had begun to stir, as souls arrived one by one to inhabit them.

"Claire," Marian had said, "will log in as 'Rachel the Wanderer.' Bernard will log in as 'Woundsmith.' Jennison will log in as . . ." The list had gone on, longer than David could remember.

Marian had become the first person in history ever to call a press conference in NEVERland, and the guests were now arriving. And David was, quite literally, a fly on the wall!

"Ladies and gentlemen," Marian called out, from the podium she had erected in front of her throne. "Is everyone here? Can I have a show of hands, please?"

All eight of the guest bodies raised their hands. Several began to speak, calling out fragmentary questions which Marian silenced with a look.

"Well then, I'd like to thank you all for coming, and I'd

also like to ask you to please hold your questions until I'm finished speaking. We don't have much time, and I have a lot to tell you, and also some favors to ask. Very briefly, I am Marian Fouts, reporter, editor, and co-owner of the *Philadelphia Bulletin,* and I am about to provide you the keys to unlock one of the greatest stories of your professional careers."

CHAPTER TWENTY-FIVE

This girding for battle was hard work, David decided, as Marian helped him get all his equipment ready. The bulletproof vest and skirt went on over his briefs and undershirt, and over that went a light, full-body nylon undergarment, to hold everything in place, and then black socks and a white Oxford dress shirt, over which he donned the so-called shoulder holster, actually a network of leather straps that snugged the Makarov under his left armpit. On his right arm went the drop-foil ejector and then, of course, the foil itself.

Sword and pistol, like the Froggy who went a-courtin'. *Miss Mousy, will you marry me?*

Next he pulled on his new trousers, made of some soft but rugged gray cloth that would be equally at home in swamps and jungles and corporate boardrooms. Then came the heavy, police-style leather belt, with further equipment dangling from it in custom holsters. Then a zippered necktie, cinched around his collar with break-away Velcro attachments. Then, over it all, a suit jacket that had no special properties so far as David knew, except that it covered his weapons without bulging, and matched the trousers reasonably well.

The motorcycle boots didn't quite go with his suit, but considering their steel-reinforced toes and heels, they didn't really have to. On his head went a sandy brown, short-haired wig, and over that a stylish businessman's cap lined with aircraft Kevlar. And then over his face, of course, the Hud Specs, loaded up with fresh batteries, internal clock and other instruments synched to local standard.

The bathroom sink dug into his back, not painful through all that clothing, but a source of pressure and discomfort nonetheless. He shifted position slightly.

"Hold still," Marian ordered, not for the first time.

She stood before him, tugging here and there at his clothing, eyeing his face with critical intensity. David had grown his beard out during their weeks in Fishtown, and now it was trimmed and dyed to match the photograph of "Wayne Schlagel" on Bowser's fake IDs. Evidently, though, he still looked too much like David Sanger for her tastes. Breaking out her cosmetics, she darkened his eyebrows with mascara, bringing them closer together in the center, and then brushed some light shading onto his cheekbones. Still not satisfied, she took a clip-on earring from the remains of Bowser's trouble kit, and attached it to David's left earlobe.

"Ouch," he said. "That pinches."

"Be quiet."

She stared at his face, then down at Wayne Schlagel's portrait in her hand, then back up at him again. She dabbed something under his eyes, just a light touch under each, then stood back. Nodding.

"OK, I think we're done. Your own mother wouldn't know you."

"Can I look?"

She nodded, turning him to face the mirror.

His heart skipped a beat. Jesus, he looked *completely different.* He didn't look like someone wearing a disguise; he looked like some perfectly ordinary Washington businessman or bureaucrat, maybe thirty-five years old, or a thin and healthy forty, the earring a feeble attempt to "stay in touch" with the world outside the capital. He looked like an older, slightly wiser version of the man on Bowser's ID cards, which was very strange indeed, because he didn't look even remotely like Bowser himself. He didn't look like anyone David Sanger would even know.

"My God, it's perfect."

Marian smiled humorlessly. "Do you feel any different?"

"Yeah." He did feel different: anonymous, untouchable, invulnerable. Invisible, even: he carried at most a few grams of metal, and every piece of his clothing and equipment had received a liberal dusting of MOCLU. He wouldn't be triggering any detectors today, that much was sure. He inhaled deeply through his nose, held it a moment, and then released it. He didn't even *smell* like himself.

He switched on the Hud Specs, turning the world into a very detailed drawing annotated in purple. R: 0.8M, it said of his image in the bathroom mirror. T: 37.1°C ID: HUMAN. Strike zones were illuminated here and there on the reflected David's body. This struck him as funny, and he had to suppress a giggle.

Without warning, Marian slapped him hard on the cheek.

"Ow!" He grabbed her wrist. What the hell? She struggled, tried to hit him again with her other hand. He grabbed that one, too.

"Ow!" she screamed. "David, let go!"

"What the hell was that?" Her ear was just below his mouth. He spoke softly, his voice trembling with surprise.

"Ow! Let *go!*"

He let her go. She glared, angry about something.

"What's going on?" he demanded quietly.

"You never saw that coming," she said. "You're too trusting."

"Of *you*, yeah."

She stepped forward, her arms outstretched. David flinched, back, but no, she was only hugging him this time. He let her do it.

"Buster," she said, "I'm the *only* one who's going to get that close to you today. Keep your guard up, and come back to me in one piece. Are you listening to me?"

"I'm listening," he said. Her sudden tears were wet and cool on his cheek.

"Kiss me," she said. He kissed her, and then kissed her some more, and then broke it off, pulling back, because it would be too easy to continue, to tumble back into bed with her and stay there all day.

He turned and hurried for the living room, and thence for the exit.

"David. Damn it, David, come back."

"It's time to go," he said, his voice edged with the sort of impatient fear that skydivers must feel before taking the big leap. It wasn't easy, he thought, to cast off common sense in that final moment, but at least it put an end to the waiting. The Hud Specs's chronometer announced in bold purple that the time was now 07:04:23. Time, indeed, to go. It amazed him that life should force such a choice upon them, but it had, and the choice was made, the ground already rushing up to meet them. "There's no point dragging it out. Keep your eye on the time, OK?"

"I'll keep my end up," she snapped.

"Hold that thought," he said, and left her there.

Bitty Lemieux was waiting for him at the base of the stairs. With a banshee yell of "SurrPRISE!" she hurled herself up from her hiding place, aiming clawed hands at his face in an attack that reminded him of jungle cats. Somehow, it didn't come as much of a surprise at all.

"I'm really much too busy for this," he said, ducking under her arms. He rushed for the front door, flung it open, stalked out with one hand raised behind him, palm out. *Stop. Do not follow me.*

The door swung closed behind him, and he could hear Bitty laughing on the other side of it, her breath howling out in belly-deep guffaws, as if his escape were the funniest thing she'd ever seen.

The weather was miserable, the snow drifting down in wet splatters, but even so the only moisture next to David's skin was his own perspiration—he was warm enough beneath his many layers of clothing. A topcoat might have made him a little less conspicuous in the crowds, but it would have heated him up still further, as well as inhibiting his movements. And weighing him down! Carrying all this gear, he was probably twenty pounds heavier than normal. Getting around was almost more like backpacking than taking a normal walk around the city.

Fortunately, he didn't have to walk very far.

For once, Fishtown had no power to intimidate him. He was not invisible here, and in fact he stood out like a beacon in his Washington Bureaucrat suit. However, armed and armored and electronically informed as he was, he carried himself like a soldier, or a cop, or a mafioso of some sort, and everyone seemed to be giving him a wide berth. Shabby people jumped smartly out of his way, and those who were neatly but cheaply dressed jumped even more quickly, sensing his up-to-no-good aura, and sensing also that his business was far away from here, and that things were best left that way.

He waited alone at his bus stop, and got a seat to himself when he finally boarded.

He took the bus to the train, and took the train downtown, and there he boarded a new train, bound southwest for Washington, D.C.

Alone in his thoughts, he passed through parts of the city he'd rarely seen, over the county line and into the western suburbs. Almost all of them were gated communities, further subdivided into wards and watches. There weren't many parks, but plenty of trees and plush lawns and, from what David could see of the dead earth beneath its deepening blanket of snow, large and elaborate gardens as well. They passed the airport and the Tinicum wetlands to the south, and then they were out of the Philadelphia Metropolitan Area and phasing into Wilmington, without ever leaving what David would call "the city." The state line was invisible when it came.

The scenery slid by for hours, the train parallelling I-95, and stopping frequently to exchange passengers with Delaware's cities, and then with Maryland's. The snow turned gradually to rain, which streaked back along the windows in jittery blobs. Finally, the train reached the Capital Beltway and stopped at the station there. New Carrollton Terminal, an exercise in whitewash and freshly scrubbed tile, contrasting starkly with the lived-in look of Philly's own rail stations. David was compelled to change trains, abandoning Amtrak for the D.C. Metrorail Orange Line. He bought a farecard from a machine, then followed the signs to the

Metrorail platform, strolling through the lively crowds past magazine stands and hot dog vendors.

The Orange Line train was smaller, tidier, possessed of fresher air and softer seats. It pulled out and rolled through suburbs for a time, then angled downward and dove into a tunnel, abandoning the gray skies of winter for subterranean darkness.

From there the stops were shorter but more frequent. Still, progress was steady, and soon the LCD display at the front of the car announced that the train was entering the District of Columbia. The tunnel walls and their clustered lights whizzed by at unguessable speed, the darkness between them penetrated in purple-white video negative by the Hud Specs. The stops now came only a few minutes apart. David found a nervous energy blossoming inside him, nudging him out of his cocoon of boredom and false apathy. Heart thumping a little more quickly, skin leaking a little more sweat in the heat beneath his armor and camouflage.

It was close, now, very close. He found himself looking again and again at his rearview "mirrors," for what, he did not know.

The tunnel widened, the train pulling to a stop once again, in a station called Eastern Market. His stop. He rose from the seat, stood up behind men and women dressed, like David himself, with soulless respectability. Silk scarves, synthetic fur collars, somber shades of brown and red and blue. And gray. The doors opened with a pneumatic whoosh, and he and the others exited in a blob, a projectile vomiting of humanity from this orifice and from all the others down the length of the train. A similar group of people out on the platform waited politely for a few moments, and then swarmed in against the flow, seeking the cars' interiors like hungry parasites.

The Hud Specs highlighted and explained the crowd's vulnerable points for him in cheerful purple.

The cavernous tube of the station was brightly lit, ludicrously clean, hung with commercial and political advertisements so tasteful they might almost be mistaken for art. David spotted a telephone booth up against a tiled pillar, and went over to it and got inside and shut the door behind him. The overhead light came on, a white diode array, making things even more unnecessarily bright.

He remembered the last time he was in a phone booth. What was it now, eight weeks ago? Shivering in his pajamas on a deserted street corner, calling Bowser out to his death.

Today he dialed a different number.

"Yeah," said Marian's voice before the first ring was finished. No video—as agreed, she had put a piece of black tape over the phone's tiny camera.

"It's me," he said. "I'm in D.C."

"Time?"

"Twelve-forty-six," he said, reading the purple number that hovered in the air before him.

"Is everything 'go'?"

"Yes." He paused. "Do you love me today?"

"Yes I do. Very much. That's why you're going to be very, very careful, right?"

"Believe me, I have no intention of not being careful."

"Well, just see to it. By the way, my NEVERland character seems to be dead. You wouldn't know anything about that, would you?"

"Not that I can think of, no. So Woodruff got your kingdom? I'm . . . sorry."

She paused. "It's just a game. I was getting a little tired of it, anyway."

"Well, it's still a shame." Indeed, it seemed a bad omen, a hint of betrayals yet to come. Events in that not-quite-imaginary world had shown a remarkable ability to spill over into the real one. His confidence faltered, his voice along with it. "Are . . . we go for conference at thirteen-oh-five?"

"Yes, we are."

He let out a breath. "This is it, then."

"Yes."

He paused again, waiting for her to say something. Finally, he asked her, "Aren't you going to say anything?"

"You know. Everything I want to say, you know. Just do it right, OK? I love you."

She cut the connection. Gone. Would that be the last time he heard her voice? No, Jesus, this was no time for that kind of thinking. But he stood there in the phone booth for a while, remembering the good times. Or trying to, at any rate; the memories were slippery as fish in his racing mind.

He finally opened the door and exited when a new train arrived to vomit its cargo onto the platform. He was swept up in the flow of their exiting, and he and they headed en masse for the escalators, were escalated by them and dumped politely beneath an awning on the street corner, from which they scattered like so many windblown seeds.

The rain had stopped but had left the city drenched and bedraggled, water dripping from every sill and corner to be whipped away by the chill wind. The sky, still featureless with overcast, refused to yield any hint of the future.

Of necessity, David had developed a guidebook familiarity with the city and its layout, but other than street signs and the jutting, phallic summit of the Washington Monument to the south, he could see no landmarks, no indication that the nation's leaders scurried about their business all around him, concentrated in perhaps a hundred buildings within a half-mile radius. Glibly deciding the fates of a quarter-billion people and more.

He was close, now; he was *so close.*

He walked two fragmentary blocks to a bus stop and boarded almost immediately a bus heading approximately north on Sixth Street. Every intersection was a mess, two or three or four streets coming together at bizarre angles, signs and traffic lights only marginally useful for informing drivers which directions they might go, and at what times.

You can recognize imperial capitals from space, Bowser said, his voice echoing up from some long-ago conversation. *The major streets all radiate from centers of influence, with no regard for terrain or compass direction. Plays hell with the traffic.*

The bus made several peculiar turns, ended up moving northeast on New York Avenue. David's stop approached. He struggled to remain invisible in the crowd, but surely anyone could see the fear and guilt and unsavory intentions written across his face. The simple folk of Fishtown had seen it—could the denizens of the capital be any less savvy? But no one glared at him, questioned him, seemed even to notice him at all. He rang the Signal Driver bell, waited for the bus to stop, debarked.

His nerves reached a new crescendo. His breathing shallow and rapid, heart beating so hard and fast he could hear it clicking wetly in his throat. Every muscle trembled with adrenaline, and sweat was pouring off him despite the damp chill of the breeze. He wiped his hands off on his pant legs, but in seconds they were clammy again.

I can still go back, he thought. *There's nothing that says I have to go through with this.* But even as he thought it, he continued walking toward his destination, drawn forward by its immense gravity. The distance that remained for him to cover was unmercifully short.

His nose caught the strong scent of sausage and onions frying somewhere nearby, but he was unable to locate the source.

CHAPTER TWENTY-SIX

The building was much smaller than he'd expected, an unassuming bit of mid-twentieth-century architecture, dolled up slightly with crenellations of cement and white plaster. Only five stories tall. He entered through a revolving door, passed through the goal posts of a metal detector and the covered arch of a Vandegroot molecular sniffer. No lights flashed for him; no buzzers sounded.

Inside was a lobby carpeted in soft green, with matching chairs and sofa arranged around a glass coffee table. Behind that was a guard station, two uniformed men sitting behind it, looking forward with polite vigilance. HUMAN, 36.8°C. HUMAN, 36.6°C. Their uniforms looked like something he'd seen around recently, though he couldn't immediately place them.

"Can I help you?" one guard asked politely as David approached the counter.

"Yes," he said, fighting hard against the nervous choking

in his throat, fighting harder still to remember the script he'd rehearsed so thoroughly. "Embassy courier. I have a delivery for Janet Stuhrman."

That was the name of the secretary, or rather the "administrative coordinator" to Colonel the Honorable John Harrison Quince. With distant, dreamy terror, David considered the lie, which would in all likelihood be believed. He considered, also, the strangeness of his circumstances, the deceptive innocence of his surroundings. Gray Party headquarters, the very belly of the beast.

Smiling, the guard reached for a clipboard. "Your name?"

"Wayne Schlagel."

The man frowned and squinted at his clipboard. "Huh, I don't have you down. You've spoken with her, I assume?"

David shrugged. "Not personally. Someone did, I guess."

"Here's a guest badge," the other guard said, slapping a thick white card down on the countertop. "Hang on while I call it in upstairs." His voice was low, at once nasal and hoarse, the sort of voice David associated with that rarest of beasts: the longtime habitual cigarette smoker. This particular raspy voice was oddly familiar, though in glancing at the man's face and name tag David saw nothing he recognized.

Except the uniform.

Except . . .

Leaning a little farther over the counter, he caught sight of a pair of white helmets bearing faded bronze shield decals, sitting side by side on a shelf with gloves and flashlights and other assorted equipment. D.C. SPECIAL POLICE, the decals said. There was no mistaking those helmets, and with that there was no mistaking the uniforms, nor the voice.

Where's the girl, this man had once asked David, brandishing a nightstick and gun in the darkness. Oh, Jesus. Had he been present at Bowser's murder as well? Had this man helped to kill Bowser Jones?

Something must have shown in David's face; the guards' expressions changed instantly. Mr. where's-the-girl, already reaching for a telephone (or something else!) beneath the counter, accelerated his movements considerably.

All at once, David's fear fell away. He had reached the critical juncture, hit the wall, as it were, and smashed right through. His enemies were alerted, his worst fears realized, and there was nothing he could do about it except ride the circumstances moment by moment, reacting to each event as it occurred. The time for plans and schemes and ethical judgments had passed, and the time of pure, cleansing vengeance had arrived.

With what felt like almost casual slowness, he reached for a spray canister on his belt, plucked it from its holster, aimed it at the two gards, disengaged the safety. They fumbled at their own belts, attempting to draw their service revolvers. David was just plain quicker than they were. He depressed the button atop his little canister, summoning a narrow cone of mist which enveloped the head and torso of one guard, and then of the other.

Both men screamed, toppling from their chairs, digging at their faces with clawed hands. Blinded, gasping for breath . . . David had hit them with a highly illegal blend of tranquilizers, rubbing alcohol, and red pepper capsicum.

As he had verified through a series of very painful and unpleasant tests, the mist was instantly and completely incapacitating, and unless these men had bottles of antidote close at hand, the worst effects would last for several hours at least. The edges of the cloud were reaching out for David, his eyes beginning to burn and sting, so he holstered the spray canister and withdrew from his pocket a handkerchief, stiff with a salve he had cooked up with a little household chemistry. He held this up to his face, so that it covered his mouth and nose and bunched up at the bottom and sides of the Hud Specs, partially protecting his eyes and also soothing them with rising vapors.

Quickly, he ran around behind the counter, pulling out a roll of surgical tape with which he quickly trussed the guards' hands and feet.

Again I am a criminal, he thought. *This is a criminal thing I'm doing right now.* But in a grander sense it was justice, a citizen's arrest of grander criminals, and it was also arguably an act of self-defense against overtly hostile forces. The guards looked bad, wheezing and kicking blindly on the floor. For the time being, they had lost even the ability to scream. David tried to comfort himself with the knowledge that they would do the same or worse to him if they could, and in fact *had* done worse on at least two occasions.

Ignoring their struggles, he picked up the guest badge they'd offered him and clipped it to his suit jacket, then began scanning the security panel. Finding the control he wanted, he buzzed the inner door, then opened it and raced through before the locks could reengage.

Behind the windowless portal was a corridor stretching in either direction, lined with closed falsewood doors, carpeted in that same soft, tasteful green. It looked almost like the inside of a hotel. Two women were standing in a doorway about thirty feet in, not looking in his direction, not paying any attention at all.

"And he actually was on time, for once," he could hear one of them saying, "but the microphones weren't set up yet and he had to stand around. You should have seen his face."

The other woman was nodding.

David brushed right past them like he had every right to be there, and as he verified in his rearview mirrors, they never even looked up. Continuing onward, he took a side corridor, found the elevator, and called it.

It didn't come right away. He stood in front of it, his nervousness creeping back, his hands fighting the urge to fidget. It was not quiet here; he could hear the racket of dot-matrix printers and other office equipment, hear the low rumble of heaters and the murmur of distant conversations. He sensed movement and other activity all around him, in offices behind the closed doors, and of course there must be hundreds of people in this building, coming and going as their jobs demanded. How long before one of them found the guards and hit a panic button?

The elevator opened for him with a soft chime, and a young, neatly dressed man emerged, brushing past David without a second look. David entered, let the door chime and close behind him. Quince's office, he knew, was on the top floor. He pressed 5, and waited. The floor indicator was holographic, green numerals hovering an inch or two in front of a gloss-black projector plate. The numbers were jarring in appearance, badly focused, just exactly like the ones he'd seen in Baltimore, lo these many weeks ago. He removed the Hud Specs and then replaced them, with no effect on the blur. Annoying. Who the hell was making these things, and who the hell was shelling out to buy them? Immature or inelegant technologies could so often prove worse than the more "primitive" items they replaced.

When the indicator said 5, the elevator came gently to a stop, chimed, and opened its door. He stepped out onto a floor that looked just like the one he'd left. Which way to Quince's office? There was no indication.

He couldn't tell anymore whether he was nervous or not. He was *hot,* certainly, the sweat pouring off him now in rivers, although his hands felt clammy and tingly-cold. He wiped them off once again on his trousers.

There were more people moving around up here than there had been on the first floor. With a politely inquiring look, he stopped a passerby, balding and bearded, a heavy man in his fifties or sixties wearing, of all things, a ponytail and a Hawaiian shirt. HUMAN, 36.9°C.

Are you on the wrong coast? David wanted to ask him. "Excuse me," he said instead, sticking out a hand. "Wayne Schlagel. I'm an embassy courier. Can, uh, you direct me to Janet Stuhrman's office? I seem to be lost."

"It's number five forty-one, that way," the man said, pointing. He seemed about to shake David's hand, but suddenly his eyes narrowed, mouth curling downward. It was a look more of concern than suspicion. "Are you all right?"

"A little warm," David said, waving the handkerchief he held in his other hand. "Thanks for the directions."

He broke contact, suddenly nervous again, trying to go off in the indicated direction without seeming to hurry.

"If you're sick, you shouldn't be spreading it around," the man called after him. "Have you had a flu shot?"

"Yup," David said without turning around. He allowed himself to sound a little irritated, which seemed reasonable under the circumstances. In his rearview, he watched the man shake his head in annoyance or disgust and turn away.

Sweat ran down David's face, into his eyes, into his mouth. He dabbed at it with the slimy, salve-heavy handkerchief.

These windowless hallways must get depressing, he thought. No light but the mercury-vapor fluorescents. He watched the numbers on passing doorways: 535, 537, 539. And then, yes, 541. The door stood open, propped, a brass sign on the inside of it announcing: J. STUHRMAN.

J. H. QUINCE. YOU DON'T HAVE TO GO GRAY TO VOTE GRAY. A little smiley face sticker punctuated this last remark.

David walked right inside, casual as you please.

It was a corner office, nice, well furnished. Hanging plants, standing plants, art prints on the walls. The Capitol and its attendant structures were visible through the huge, south-facing window. Quince's secretary, Janet Stuhrman, looked up with a professional smile and a tilt of the head as he entered.

HUMAN, 37.2°C.

"May I help you?" Her accent was southern. Auburn hair, green eyes, a rounded face with slightly chubby cheeks. She looked like somebody's mother.

"I'm here to see the colonel," David said, moving toward her. "No appointment."

Janet Stuhrman put on an apologetic look. "I'm so sorry; he's not to be disturbed right now. If you tell me what this is about, I can pass along the—"

She stopped. David had moved right up on her, standing over her desk like an angel of doom.

"Are you all right?" she asked, looking at him with genuine concern.

He felt the wind go out of his sails. He couldn't do it! The plan at this point was for him to take out his spray canister and disable the woman, truss her up and leave her gagging and weeping on the floor. That had sounded fine when she was just "John Quince's secretary," a name and a job description, a faceless enemy to be overcome.

"Shit," he said. The Hud Specs' chronometer showed 13:02:16. He was running out of time.

"I beg your pardon?"

He flared at her. "Get out of here. Get up and leave, right now. Go!"

"What?" She looked startled.

Not wanting to explain any further, he lowered and snapped his wrist, the drop foil popping down into his waiting hand. He pointed it at her, squeezed it, watched it deploy.

Her eyes widened, her mouth opening in horror. She rolled back in her chair a few inches, until a filing cabinet stopped her.

David pointed the sword at her eyes, the tip barely twelve inches away. He waved it in a small circle, for emphasis. "I don't want to hurt you. Please, just leave."

She didn't need to be told again. With a quiet scream, little more than a whimper, she shot up out of her chair and bolted for the exit. David followed her as far as the door, watched her flee down the hallway, her voice rising sharply.

Stupid, stupid. She would bring armies down upon him. Gritting his teeth, shaking his head with resigned amazement at what he had done, he quickly took out a tube of superglue gel and filled the door lock's keyhole with it, then kicked up the doorstop and let the door swing pneumatically shut. He locked the door from inside.

"Hey!"

A man's voice, behind him. David turned.

"What the hell do you think you're doing?" demanded John Harrison Quince, standing in the office's inner doorway.

R: 5.2m
T: 35.7°c
ID: HUMAN
WARNING: *HANDGUN*

Indeed, Quince clutched a gun in his bony fist, holding it low against his waist and pointing it more or less in David's direction. He saw the sword as David came around to face him, and the gun came up, its aim true.

David's hatred was like a blank, stain-resistant wall. Nothing could mark or change it. "Hello, Colonel," he said, utterly unsurprised.

"I just got a call there was an intruder in the building," Quince remarked, his voice falsely calm, almost casual. "I assume that's you?"

"Correct."

"What can I do for you?"

"My name is David Sanger."

Quince looked very startled to hear that. The gun barked.

Something hammered David in the chest, throwing him back against the door. In agony, he slumped. For a second, he couldn't even breathe.

WARNING: GUNFIRE
WARNING: GUNFIRE
WARNING: GUNFIRE

He gasped, gasped again, and then something caught in his chest and he was able to suck in a partial breath.

Across the room, Quince was studying him. A microbe under glass, a specimen in a box. The chairman of the Gray Party looked neither remorseful nor afraid, but simply surprised and curious, perhaps even slightly amused.

It was too much, too much to bear.

With a hoarse yell, David launched himself at Quince, leaping with his toes and running/falling forward on the balls of his feet, his center of gravity way out in front of him, sword arm extended horizontally. *Flèche*, the manuever was called.

Quince had clearly expected him to fall down. Startled, caught off guard, he fired the gun again and missed. Then, David was on him. Ignoring the high-lighted strike zones, he aimed the tip of the sword at Quince's right wrist. Off-balance and moving quickly, he missed, but the sword did enter flesh just above the crook of the elbow. Colonel the Honorable John Harrison Quince screamed, dropping the gun as David's weight slammed into him, crushing him up against the frame of the inner doorway. Slick with sweat, David's hand lost its grip on the drop foil's hilt. The sword fell clear, its tip bloodied.

David held Quince firmly with a forearm across the throat and, wincing in pain, reached into his own jacket to withdraw Bowser's Makarov. Quince's eyes widened, goggled. Now his detached, professional veneer had cracked. Now he was a real person, one who was in big trouble and knew it, and didn't know what to do about it.

David jammed the gun against Quince's temple. "Listen you mudering sack of shit, you've had it. This gun is *real,* it's *loaded,* and there isn't a sniffer in the world that can detect it. You hear what I'm saying?"

Quince nodded. Blood was drip, drip, dripping through the white fabric of his shirt, staining the carpet below.

"OK," David said. "I'm going to let go of you, and you're going to do what I tell you. Is that clear?"

Eyes blazing, Quince shot a look of hatred and disdain. *I didn't get where I am today by caving in to threats,* the look said. *I'm better than you, and don't forget it.*

Today you will cave in, David shot back with a look of his own. *My mistakes are all behind me and I have nothing left to lose. I am fully prepared to shoot you. I would actually enjoy it.*

With an expression of pure poison on his face, Quince nodded.

"Good."

David thrust the man into his office, closing and locking the door behind them. He urged Quince forward, toward the huge desk and the guest chairs arranged in front of it. This was a corner office, with huge windows looking south and east. Only five floors up, but even so the view was spectacular. Washington, D.C., sprawled almost literally at David's feet.

"Sit down," he commanded.

Quince sat. His blood was everywhere, soaking the whole right sleeve of his shirt, staining the chair and the carpet and David's own shirt and jacket. A trail of it, almost solid, led from the doorway to the chair.

David threw his handkerchief into Quince's lap. "Tie this around your arm. Stop that bleeding."

"Yes, sir!" Quince snapped, bitterly. "What are you supposed to be, some kind of terrorist?"

"No," David said, "I'm a scientist."

His chronometer kicked over to 13:05:00.

The telephone rang.

"Answer it," David said. "Turn it this way, so the camera can see the whole room, including both of us."

Quince did as he was told. The telephone screen came to life, a split-screen image with six boxed faces. One of them belonged to Marian Fouts. Two of the others David knew were TV news anchors; the others he didn't recognize.

"Hello?" said Marian from the telephone.

David nodded his head once, politely. "Ladies and gentlemen of the press. My name is David Sanger, and I'm a molecular fabrication researcher with the University of Philadelphia. As you can see, I'm standing in Washington, D.C., in the office of the Gray Party's chairman, John Harrison Quince, and am in fact holding Mr. Quince hostage, with this gun."

He turned and fired the gun into the bookshelf by the door, disintegrating a fat law volume bound in black-and-gold leather. The sound was shattering, painful. Wincing, he turned back to the camera, his eardrums ringing like tiny brass gongs.

"As you can see, the gun is loaded, and it works. However, a check of police records will confirm that no sniffer alarm has gone off in this building, or anywhere else in the immediate area. How did I get it in here? The answer is MOCLU."

He was sweating so much, now, he didn't think he *had* this much water in his body. His hands were so slick he felt the gun might pop right out of his grip like a bar of soap. His hands were trembling, as well, and his knees felt weak. Nervous, hell yes, he was *dizzy* with nervousness. He probably looked and sounded terrible, but even allowing for current events updates, the script was so clear in his mind, he didn't think he could stumble. He cleared his throat.

"As some of you may by know by this time, MOCLU is a substance developed accidentally at the U of Phil, a substance which can jam nanoscale machinery such as the Vandegroot Molecular Sniffer. Gray Party scions attempted to block publication of these results. The lawsuits against the university and against me in particular are a matter of public record.

"Also on the public record are the murders of Otto Vandegroot, the Sniffer King, and Henry Chong, chairman of the Molecular Sciences department at U of Phil. I personally witnessed a third murder, that of Philadelphia attorney T. Bowser Jones. This murder was carried out in cold blood, by District of Columbia Special Police, specifically those assigned to work security for Gray Party headquarters. These same men attempted, on two occasions, to murder me as well. It shouldn't be hard to find witnesses who can place them at the scenes of these crimes; I can name the dates, times, and locations. I can also identify at least one of the officers by sight."

He gestured at Quince with the gun.

"I have reason to believe that all of these murders were ordered by John Harrison Quince himself. The existence of MOCLU is a direct threat to the existence of the Gray Party, or so he believes. Do you have any comment, Colonel?"

Playing to the camera, Quince sat up straighter, turning to show off his bloodied arm. "This man is obviously deranged. I have no idea what he's talking about."

"You've never heard of MOCLU?" David asked.

"No."

David turned to the camera, smiling thinly. "That's a lie. The name John Harrison Quince appears on several court documents connected with the MOCLU lawsuit. Witness for the prosecution, never called. Also, I believe an investigation will show the prosecution was funded through Gray Party channels."

Outside in the hallway, he could hear shouting, the sounds of heavy equipment banging around. Someone tried the outer door.

He turned back to Quince. "Colonel, did you know any of the victims personally?"

Quince sat mutely, glaring at the telephone screen.

"Did you call Hyeon Chong on the evening of his death?"

Silence.

"Did you speak with Otto Vandegroot on the day that *he* died?"

"I'm not going to talk to you," Quince growled, with theatrical bravado.

The outer door burst with a thunderous crash. David could hear booted feet tromping into the outer office.

"Stay out!" he shouted. "I've got a gun!" He turned, attempting to show the camera a sheepish grin. He wiped at a rivulet of sweat. "Excuse me. Ladies and gentlemen of the press, this conference is nearly over. I hope the investigation of these murders will continue, with Gray Party motives in mind. If this does *not* occur, you people need to ask yourselves *why*. Special Agent Puckett, are you listening?

"I was in danger of disappearing quietly, without anyone ever knowing what happened to me. Now if I disappear, you will know exactly what happened. If the government declares a media blackout on these events, you will know exactly why. You've all been advised to record this conversation. If the police come around demanding those recordings, you will know why. Do the smart thing: make backup copies immediately.

"Please be aware that a twenty-page report, containing everything I know about the events surrounding these murders, is available on Usenet groups US. NEWS.CURRENT-EVENTS, US.NEWS.SCENCE, and the entire SCI.NANOTECH hierarchy. An encrypted version of the report has been safely archived offshore, along with a decryption key, and should be available for download from a number of URLs."

The inner door vibrated, whined with a mechanical, electrical sound. A drill bit punched through it in a spray of falsewood chips, then quickly withdrew.

At this point, the script called for him to hang up the phone, spray pepper juice into Quince's face, and quietly escape from the building. If he hadn't let the secretary go, he might have been able to do exactly that. Now, a different approach seemed called for.

"I apologize for any harm I've caused in bringing you this information," he said quickly into the telephone. "I am now surrendering. If anything happens to me, please tell the world."

The people on the other side of the door were sticking something through the hole, some kind of moving, flexible hose or cable, like a miniature elephant trunk. Fiber-optic periscope?

"I'm surrendering!" he shouted.

Quince flinched away at first as David tried to hand him the gun, but then he got the idea, and carefully accepted it in his left hand. Then, with the same hand, he reached over and hung up the phone. Its screen went dark. Quince then smashed the phone off the desktop with the end of the Makarov. He rose, grimacing, stepping forward into David's personal space.

David put his hands in the air.

Wham! The sound of a ram against the door. David didn't turn, didn't move. *Whack!* The ram struck again, and this time the door smashed open, slamming back hard against the bookcase. David cringed as the Hud Specs's rearview showed police swarming in behind him. He examined their negative, white-purple images, and confirmed his fears: D.C. Special Police in riot gear, smoked visors on decaled helmets hiding their faces.

"Hold your fire!" Quince shouted at them. "I've got him; hold your fire!"

Figures crowded around David. They threw him to the floor, knocking the wind out of him, bringing a new slam of pain to the place he'd been shot, the place his Kevlar vest had stopped Quince's bullet. They crushed him downward, face in the carpeting, their knees in his back. He offered no resistance as they cuffed his hands, his feet.

They shouted back and forth at one another, frisking him, removing his belt, emptying his pockets. They knelt on him for what seemed like a long time. Finally, the pain and pressure eased. He gasped in a breath of carpet as best he could.

Without warning, there was an excruciating *jerk* on his handcuffs, and he was hauled painfully to his feet. John Harrison Quince stood there before him, cradling the wounded arm.

"You know," Quince said, "you shouldn't resist arrest. People get choked doing that. People get shot."

"You wouldn't dare," David wheezed, as matter-of-factly as he could manage.

"Jesus H. Christ, boy. Do you *like* crime?" Quince blazed. "We're trying to suffocate it, all of it. Do you *like* seeing gangsters get rich kicking our country into the toilet? Is that why you're doing what you're doing?"

"Do you like killing innocent people?" David countered. "You even killed Big Otto, and he was one of yours."

One of the cops punched him hard in the shoulder for that one, and Quince literally turned his nose up, a gesture David wasn't sure he'd ever seen before. Then Quince drew back his left arm and struck David with the gun, *Bowser's* gun, hard across the temple.

Sharp pain. David's head rang and buzzed.

"Boy, I didn't kill Otto Vandegroot; the man was a friend of mine. Henry Chong did that."

"Henry?"

"Saving your skin, I believe," Quince said. Physical pain was written all over his face. One of the cops was trying to tend his arm, trying to keep him from moving around, but Quince kept shrugging him off. "Otto had orders to keep you down, and he was of a mind to do it permanently. Your . . . teacher persuaded him otherwise, and boy, has that caused us a mess."

"Henry?" David repeated. Henry Chong, shoving a sword through the back of Big Otto's skull in a hotel stairwell? He tried to picture it, and failed utterly.

Quince peered closely at David, almost squinting. "You know, in addition to being stupid, you're also very bad at this. What are you, sick? You don't look well."

David didn't feel well, either. Quince's left-handed blow still rang in his skull, but that was not the greatest source of his misery—his clothing was sodden with sweat, his skin clammy, and he was so *hot* inside. It couldn't be just the extra clothing; he must actually be running a low fever. That would account for his dizziness, as well. Was he getting sick?

MOCLU jams nanomachinery.

Oh God. What were the ribosomes in his cells, if not

nanomachinery? And the pores of every cell membrane, and the enzymes that replicated his DNA . . . Among his many crimes, had he somehow invented a deadly poison as well? He remembered he hadn't felt so good after Quince's Philadelphia rally, and today he'd dusted himself with at least twenty times as much MOCLU as he had then. If every ribosome in his body were to grind to a halt . . .

He coughed out a humorless chuckle.

Quince studied him, interested. "What's funny, little man? I don't personally see the humor in your situation."

"I just realized, you're going to be blamed for my death," David said, and promptly lost consciousness.

CHAPTER **TWENTY-SEVEN**

David knew right away that he was dreaming, because Bowser was there, standing up and smiling just like he was alive. He looked good: fit and calm and comfortably dressed. Death seemed to agree with him, but then, didn't everything?

Bowser was holding a pair of scissors in his hand, and he raised them as if showing them to David, the blades grinding and clicking closed, then open, then closed again.

"Pretty, huh?" Bowser said.

David simply stared, but Bowser smiled and nodded at him as though he had replied.

"See that point where the blades come together? The closer the blades get, the faster that little point moves. When the angle between the blades gets close to zero, the damn thing actually moves faster than light."

"Impossible," David said flatly, though he didn't know if he was responding to Bowser's statement, or merely his lively presence.

"Ah, you're not even thinking about it," Bowser said. "No fair. The crossing point isn't an object, OK? It has no mass; it has no physical properties at all. It's an abstract concept, and it can go as fast as it damn well pleases. Of course, all you really *see* is the light that touched it, a shadow of the actual event echoing down through time. A record, if you like."

The scissors opened and closed, opened and closed in Bowser's hand.

"It's a hell of a world," Bowser said, "where the fastest thing is an abstract concept. It's not much use, is it?"

David wanted to reach out to him, touch him, crush him in an embrace so tight he could never be lost again. But with that funny dream-certainty he knew he could not, knew that his arms would close on emptiness only. And then a thought occurred to him.

"Bowser, are *you* an abstract concept?"

The tanned face lit up with pleasure. "Right on the first try, my buddy. I am impressed."

"I've missed you," David said. "I need you here. Damn you, you can't be dead."

Bowser grew a little more serious at that. The scissors came together with a final *click*. "David, I think you've missed my point. Faster than light means backward in time. If you need me, more than a shadow of me, I mean, just look to your past. I'll always be there; I promise."

"I don't understand," David said, but really he did. Really, what he meant was, *that's not enough, that's not acceptable*. His eyes filled up with tears, warm and wet against the cool of his face, and it seemed a strange thing to have happen in a dream.

When he awoke, though, the wetness on his cheeks

was real enough, as real as the steel bars and cement walls of his cell. He'd been awakened by sounds at the door, and sitting up on his bunk, he saw there were people out there, a prison guard and another man, a man in gray jacket and slacks, white shirt, yellow tie.

That was Ron Zachs, the new lawyer David's parents had found to replace that damn public defender. The prison guard with him, rattling keys and banging levers into place, was opening the door to David's cell.

"Hi," Ron said, in the sort of vaguely condescending tone David associated with doctors' offices. "How are you feeling today?"

Oh brother. The guy probably thought he *was* a doctor, he'd come to visit David so many times in the prison's infirmary. Three days in intensive care, twelve more in a recuperation bed . . . The MOCLU poisoning had not proved fatal in the end, but it was a close thing, a fever-burned nightmare from which he could never quite awaken. Also, the man two beds over had had advanced tuberculosis that resisted all treatment, and had spent his days and nights coughing phlegm behind the bed curtains, growing weaker day by day as David grew stronger.

He'd actually been glad when they transferred him to a regular cell. Two bunks, here, but he had the place to himself. For the moment, presumption of innocence guaranteed him separation from the prison's general population.

"I'm not ill, if that's what you mean," David said in a neutral voice.

"Well, good." Zachs turned to the guard, thumped him on the shoulder. "Thanks, my friend; you can lock us in."

He stepped fully into the cell, and the guard closed and secured the door behind him, then moved on down the hallway, out of view.

"We're almost ready," Zachs told David, taking a seat at the little table he'd been provided. "Just a few formalities before the big event. Do you feel up to it?"

David shrugged. Ron Zachs was nice enough, and competent as far as David had been able to tell, but it was difficult to really trust him. David's life was literally in Zachs's hands, but the man was not what he expected, did not do the things David expected him to. The only other paid lawyer David had ever had was Bowser, and, well, Zachs was simply not a Bowser.

Nobody is, Bowser might have said. *Hell, that's not a crime. I'm not him, either.*

"I still need you to sign these documents," said Zachs. Then he squinted at David. "Are you all right?"

"I'm fine." David rose impatiently from the bed, scooted his chair across from Zachs. The chairs were small, uncomfortable. He didn't sit. "I'm not getting sick again, if that's what you mean."

Stretching to reach the shelf over his bed, David took his courtroom suit down and began putting it on. Gray flannel and yet humble somehow, the cheap blue shirt and paisley zipper tie proclaiming his innocence. *Learn to tie a knot, you ape,* Bowser had said to him once. Yeah, right, as if *he'd* ever worn a tie. Well, in court he had. And when they'd buried him. David had watched the ceremony on video, an echo three weeks delayed from the actual event, but real enough. Live or Memorex, it didn't seem to matter—the images looped endlessly through his mind.

"Didn't you sleep well?" Zachs asked him.

"No. Bad dreams." Then: " 'The distinction between past, present, and future is only a stubbornly persistent illusion.' Albert Einstein said that, on his deathbed. He was the last of the determinists, the last to believe the past and future were actual, solid things. Do you believe in ghosts, Mr. Zachs?"

Zachs blinked, the non sequitur catching him off guard. "Um, sure."

"No, I'm serious. I keep hearing the voice of my friend, the one that died, and I'm . . . wondering, I guess."

"I said yes, David." Zachs's face was serious, his eyes on David's own. He'd put down his pen, raised a hand to stroke the frame of his glasses. His face was . . . different than David had ever seen it. More awake. "We carry our loved ones with us in animate images. They never leave us, even for a moment."

David smiled mirthlessly, cinching the zipper tie shut. "Just memories, eh?"

"*Animate* memories. They talk, they think, they *dream* inside us. I call them ghosts."

"I see. You're a wise man, Ron Zachs." The comment sounded a little flip, David decided, but, in fact, he'd meant it quite sincerely. His eyes misted over again, and he suspected, suddenly, that the machinations of Ron Zachs's mind were somewhat stranger and more wonderful than appearances would indicate. He suspected he'd caught a glimpse of Zachs's secret self, that treasured identity hidden away in his mind with all the other ghosts.

He cleared his throat, smiled. "That's . . . a very nice thought; that cheers me up. Hey, we're going to have a victory today, right? Closing statements, closed case."

Zachs's normal expression snapped back into place. "It's too early to be asking that. We'll try to get across a persuasive argument, but jury trial is always kind of a crap shoot. We've discussed this already."

"That's not what I asked."

"No," Ron agreed, refusing to be pinned down. And in that moment, David realized that Ron and Bowser would have liked each other, and that thought put him suddenly at ease.

"Well," he said. "Let's do it. Let me borrow your pen."

He signed the documents, and together they hashed over their strategy until the guard returned to lead them into battle.

A tunnel connected the jail and courthouse, and as on previous days, three armed guards escorted David and Ron Zachs through it, and up a staircase to the courthouse's lower lobby. David's leg chains, connected to the cuffs that bound his wrists in front of him, allowed only a moderate, short-strided pace. They jingled as he walked, a remarkably pleasant sound, like the ringing of a dozen tiny bells. Everything was beautiful here, varnished wood paneling and marble floors that gleamed like black mirrors. The benches in the lower lobby were of red granite, at once aesthetic and securely immovable.

On one of the benches sat Marian Fouts.

"David," she called out, waving a hand as they emerged from the tunnel.

His heart leaped at the sound of her voice. She'd been the defense's first witness, on the stand for almost a full day, and had defended David's actions and character with a fierceness he could scarcely believe.

"You can't speak with the prisoner," one of the guards warned. "What are you doing down here?"

The world paused for a moment, and then Zachs put a hand on the guard's shoulder and spoke softly: "Officer, unless proven otherwise, this man is to be considered innocent. Let's be human beings here."

"Human beings, huh?" The guard drew a breath, released it, glanced side to side at his companions. "OK, miss, I suppose you can ride up in the elevator with us."

"Thank you," Marian said, touching the officer's arm and smiling warmly. In her formal blue dress with spidersilk cap and veil, she looked like some beautiful thing that had stepped out of a movie screen. "That's very kind."

"You look great," David said to her. "You come to see me off?"

Marian's smile turned to him, bathing him in warmth. "To the Big House? Not likely. I just wanted to make sure you were OK."

The guards summoned the elevator, and as a group they entered it and were enclosed.

"OK is a relative term," David allowed, trying not to let his voice sound grim. "I'm very anxious, and . . . well, I've been doing a lot of thinking. Marian, if things go badly today, I could be in prison for a very long time. I don't . . . expect you to wait. You deserve a lot better than the life I can offer you."

Marian sighed, her smile fading only a little. Her eyes were calm, moist. "I haven't stuck with you this long for nothing, Sanger. Get used to it: I love you."

"Yeah, well I don't know why. I think of somebody like Bowser, who gave his all for anyone who asked, and I know I could never be like that. I took everything Bowser had to give, and now he's dead. That seems to be what I do best: *take* things."

With some difficulty in the close quarters, Marian leaned across the barrel chest of a guard and gave David's shoulders a quick squeeze. "If that were true, I *would* leave you in here to rot. Bowser loved you. He would have died willingly to save you, and so would I. There are all kinds of taking, you know. There's the little kid who wants all the marbles, just so no one else can have them. Or the kid who likes the way they shine in the jar on his shelf, or the kid who wins them all because he just can't stand to lose. *You* want the marbles because you have a project in mind, something wonderful that you can give back to the world. That's not selfish; it's . . .

I don't know; maybe there isn't a word for it. But that's how things get done. It's one of the reasons I love you so much."

David didn't know what to say to that. His attraction to Marian had been simple and overwhelming from the very start, from the moment he'd first laid eyes on her in the U of Phil library, from the moment she'd first opened her mouth to speak. But *her* love had always been a kind of cipher, an inexplicable and therefore untrustworthy force that somehow bound her to him. But maybe it was a simple thing after all.

"Your, uh, taste is questionable," he finally said.

She snorted. "You need to learn to take a compliment. We'll work on it."

The elevator doors chimed and rolled open.

Butterflies exploded in David's stomach.

"Fifth floor, lingerie," the guard said, with gentle good humor. "I hate to break it up, lovebirds, but I'm afraid it's showtime."

"The defendant," said Ron Zachs to the jury of twelve, "has been charged with so many offenses, I can't even count them all. The prosecution—," and here he glared across at the appropriate group of seated figures, "—is hoping to keep him behind bars for about forty thousand years. Literally! And why is that? By their own admission, David Sanger hasn't killed anyone, hasn't inflicted any crippling injuries, and shows no inclination toward further criminal activity. Most of these charges are spurious, piled one upon the other to create an impression of guilt in the minds of you, the jury. Well, I feel you're smarter than that."

David watched him anxiously. This was it, this was where his future would be decided, and he hoped like hell it would go the right way. If he lost this case and it went to appeal, he'd be seeing a lot more of the insides of courtrooms and prison cells, and God knew he'd had his fill of that.

Still, his mood was improving with every word Zachs spoke. The prosecution's closing argument had painted a dark, damning portrait of David's life and his crimes, and he'd felt the sting of truth in much of what they'd said. *Callous disregard for his fellow man . . . working feverishly, day and night, on terrorist-style weapons and tactics . . . harming the innocent as well as his intended victims . . .* But Zachs's rebuttal was like a bright light switching on, illuminating the evidence, driving away the shadows, showing the dark corners to be empty. "It all hinges," he'd said, "on *intent.*"

That had been a recurring theme in the defense all along, but now it seemed to ring with special significance. An angry cloud had seemed to hover above the jury during the prosecution's final attacks, a wealth of emotion playing across their faces, making them shift and fidget and glare. But now it began to dissipate, giving way once more to impartiality and calm. The trial was almost over.

Marian was out in the audience, sitting with Bitty Lemieux alongside David's parents, and Bowser's. It was good of them all to make the trip. Mike Puckett was sitting out there as well. He'd testified as a witness the day before, but he was here today on his own time. The crowd was quite a thick one, actually, full of gawkers and politicians and no small number of molecular fabrication researchers. And the press, of course, with their microphones and pads of scribbled notes. Despite the no-cameras ruling, David's trial was all the rage in the media these days.

"The charge of resisting arrest," Zachs said, "is an example: the defendant surrendered peacefully, in front of witnesses. We've all seen it on video! I have run straight down the list, charge by charge, showing the same kinds of faults throughout the prosecution's case, and in my opinion this exercise has been an elaborate waste of the taxpayers' money."

"Objection," said the prosecutor. "Irrelevant."

"Sustained," said the judge, the Honorable Ethan McIntyre. He was a bald man, white, maybe sixty years old and very impatient with the attorneys, and had over the past few days listened to the evidence of David's case with great apparent interest, if little sympathy. "Confine your arguments to the matter at hand, counselor."

Zachs nodded his understanding. "My point is this: while we disagree sharply with the prosecution's *interpretation* of the events of November fourth, the sequence of events itself is only marginally in dispute. My client *admits* to breaking into Gray Party headquarters. He *admits* to the use of illegal weapons in the injury of three people and the menacing of a fourth.

"The prosecution has admitted, and the evidence has shown, that the defendant was under duress, having been unjustly accused of murder at the time of the assaults. The evidence also shows that several attempts had been made on the defendant's life by this point, and two of the injured parties are in fact *under indictment* for their involvement in these and other crimes."

"Objection, your honor," the prosecutor called out. "That evidence was stricken from the record."

"Objection sustained," the judge said. "Jury is instructed to disregard."

"My apologies, Your Honor," Zachs said, his eyes twinkling. "I forgot. My point is that the defendant was a desperate man, defending himself against forces that had conspired against him—"

"Objection!" the prosecutor shouted again.

"Sustained. Mr. Zachs, if you continue this line of defense, I'll be forced to find you in contempt, is that clear?"

"Yes, Your Honor." He turned to face the jury once more. "This is what happened: aggravated assault, three counts, extenuating circumstances, first offense." Zachs chopped one hand with the other repeatedly as he spoke. "My client has *already pled guilty* to these charges, but the prosecution has insisted on pressing for full conviction on twenty additional charges unrelated to the defendant's actual crimes. Once again, I feel you, the jury, are smarter than that.

"The fact is that my client, a young but widely respected scientist, has invented something revolutionary, something that will affect the future of this country, and indeed of the entire world."

"Objection. Irrelevant."

"Your Honor," Zachs protested, "I'm trying to make a point."

The judge pondered for a moment, then nodded. "Overruled. Make it quick, counselor."

"Thank you, Your Honor. Members of the jury, this trial is not about the events of November fourth at all. My client's research was well within the law, and remains so, but certain forces would like to see him punished for it nonetheless."

"Objection. Speculation."

"Sustained. Mr. Zachs, do you have anything *un*objectionable left to say?"

Zachs turned to face the judge. "Your Honor, I move for dismissal of all except the three assault charges."

"Motion denied," said the Honorable Ethan McIntyre. "Are you finished, counselor?"

"Not quite. Members of the jury, I appeal to your common sense, and to your sense of justice. I would like to ask you to convict Dr. Sanger on the three assault charges only, and to find him innocent of any other crimes. The eyes of history, and of God, are upon us. Thank you very much."

The Honorable Ethan McIntyre cleared his throat. "This concludes closing arguments. The bailiff will now escort the jury into seclusion, where they will make their determination."

"What do you think?" David asked quietly, as the jury members rose and shuffled from the room.

"I don't know," Zachs whispered back. "We'll see."

Humph. At least the MFE warehouse people hadn't pressed charges. Sympathetic to his plight, they'd said, though it certainly helped that he'd returned their workstation and paid restitution to the injured guard. *That* crime was the really unforgivable one, in David's opinion, and he didn't think a jury would be too understanding about it. The other stuff, well . . .

Nervous but expecting a long wait, he turned over his newspaper and started working on the crossword puzzle. Members of the audience, meekly quiet after repeated judicial threats, began cautiously to speak to one another in low tones. Minute by minute, their volume edged upward.

A six-letter word for dog—*canine.* An eleven-letter word for strong coffee—that one turned out to be *caffeinated,* which David thought was a little misleading. It went on like that for a hundred words, but to his surprise he'd only gotten to number ten, a wait of about five minutes, before the jury shuffled back in and resumed their seats.

The bailiff handed a clipboard up to the judge, and then went back to her own seat beside the jury box.

The Honorable Ethan McIntyre glared the audience to silence, and then began to speak. "The jury appears to have reached a determination, as follows: we find the defendant, David Hapgood Sanger, guilty on the charge of aggravated assault, three counts. We find the defendant innocent of all other charges, there being insufficient evidence to support them."

David's heart leaped. Twenty years, maximum, and that was for a repeat offender. No matter what happened next, he would not spend his *entire* life in jail.

Ron Zachs leaped to his feet. "Your Honor, my client has pled guilty to that charge. I therefore beg the court for leniency in his sentencing. Specifically, I move that the jail sentence be reduced to time already served." His voice was quick, with an air of rehearsal.

"Let's not get ahead of ourselves, counselor," McIntyre chided. "David Sanger, will you please rise?"

Obediently, David stood.

"Dr. Sanger," said McIntyre, "it's not my intention to strike fear into your heart, but I want you to know I'm a member of the Gray Party, and I'm frankly disgusted at the chaos your activities have caused. Three deaths, a crushing blow to the nation's ability to enforce its laws . . . This is not what you're on trial for, but I wish to determine whether you're aware of the gravity of your deeds."

"Your Honor," David said, with a sick, sinking feeling, "it was all a giant accident. If I had it to do over again, I wouldn't. It's as simple as that."

"That's a touching sentiment. Tell me, sir: having used your talents to spawn such mischief, do you now feel a compulsion to use them in the service of mankind?"

David stood straight. "Yes, Your Honor, I do."

"Very well, then. Being that you feel that way, and being that this is your first criminal offense of any sort, I find myself in sympathy with your circumstances. Having heard the evidence, and in consideration of your plea and the extenuating circumstances, I find I cannot, in good conscience, assign any further jail time. I therefore sentence you to a fine of not less than twenty thousand dollars, and to a period of community service not less than three thousand hours."

David's heart leaped again, and kept on leaping. He was getting out of jail! They were actually going to let him go! The audience exploded, attempts at conversation rising up over joyful cheers and shouts of angry protest.

Good going, buddy!

Ron Zachs grabbed David's hand and started pumping it vigorously. "Congratulations! Congratulations; this is wonderful!"

"Thank you," David said, with a gratitude deeper than any he'd ever previously felt. He was not going back to jail!

Already, though, his mind was working on the rest of it. Twenty thousand dollars? That was a lot of money, about twenty thousand more than he actually had. He'd have to borrow it somehow, and then somehow pay it back while working the community service time. Three thousand hours? That was full-time for a year and a half!

Oh, the hell with it. He'd work it out somehow, and gratefully, too.

Marian came racing toward him, her face beaming with surprise and delight beneath the navy blue cap and veil. His thoughts evaporated as she threw her arms around him, and he reciprocated, and then their lips met and they were kissing passionately, right there in the middle of the courtroom, with a dozen sketch artists roughing the scene for the evening news.

The courtroom stairs were so thick with reporters, David and Marian and their trail of attendants and relatives could barely squeeze through.

"Doctor Sanger!" one of them shouted, thrusting a microphone at him. "With MOCLU already in use as a privacy smoke screen, do you expect the crime rate to rise?"

David blinked, surprised by the question. "Not the *reported* crime rate, no."

There was scattered laughter at that remark.

"Do you expect MOCLU to be placed on the Recognized Hazardous Technology list?" another reporter asked.

This time, he nodded firmly. "Yes. About that, there is no doubt in my mind. But a lot of black market money is going to start changing hands over this. The genie is out of the bottle, and it's not going back."

"What are your plans, Dr. Sanger?"

"Plans? Jesus, give me a while to think about it. This morning I thought I was going to prison."

More laughter at that one. He was warming to the cameras, beginning to bask in the attention.

Another microphone thrust out at him. "Do you consider yourself a hero?"

David stopped. The sound of the crowd seemed to deaden slightly, to grow softer and more distant. Hero? The word had never occurred to him.

You've delivered fire into the hands of the common man, Dr. Prometheus, Bowser offered helpfully.

But how good a thing was that? In the years to come, how many more people would get hurt because of MOCLU? How many would be killed? Ugh, that wasn't something David wanted to think about, but the responsibility was definitely his.

"*I* consider him a hero," Marian said, jumping in to fill the silence. She threw her arms around him and kissed him firmly on the cheek, provoking delighted laughter all around.

The clip is a famous one, featured often in video collages. The day the sniffers died, the day the world changed. The Sangers at play on the eve of their marriage, at the dawning of the Molecular Age. The moment has even been captured in a well-known painting, *The Kiss,* which even now hangs in a position of honor, behind glass in the U of Phil's Molecular Sciences building. Who knows, maybe you've seen it.

ABOUT THE AUTHOR

An aerospace engineer for the Lockheed Martin Corporation, Wil McCarthy lives in Denver with his family. Since his debut in 1990, his short fiction has appeared in a variety of magazines and anthologies, and depending on your method of counting, this is either his third, fourth, or sixth novel. Complete bibliographic information can be found via World Wide Web at: http://www. sff.net/people/wmccarth